Zabel

a novel by

PEARL GRAY

CREDITS

Cover Photo by Richard Weatherall and technical assistance by Jason Gray

TRADEMARK AND COPYRIGHT NOTICE

Also by Pearl Gray

Salt Spring Island: A Place to Be

(with Ellie Thorburn)

Published by Heritage Press

For Rick

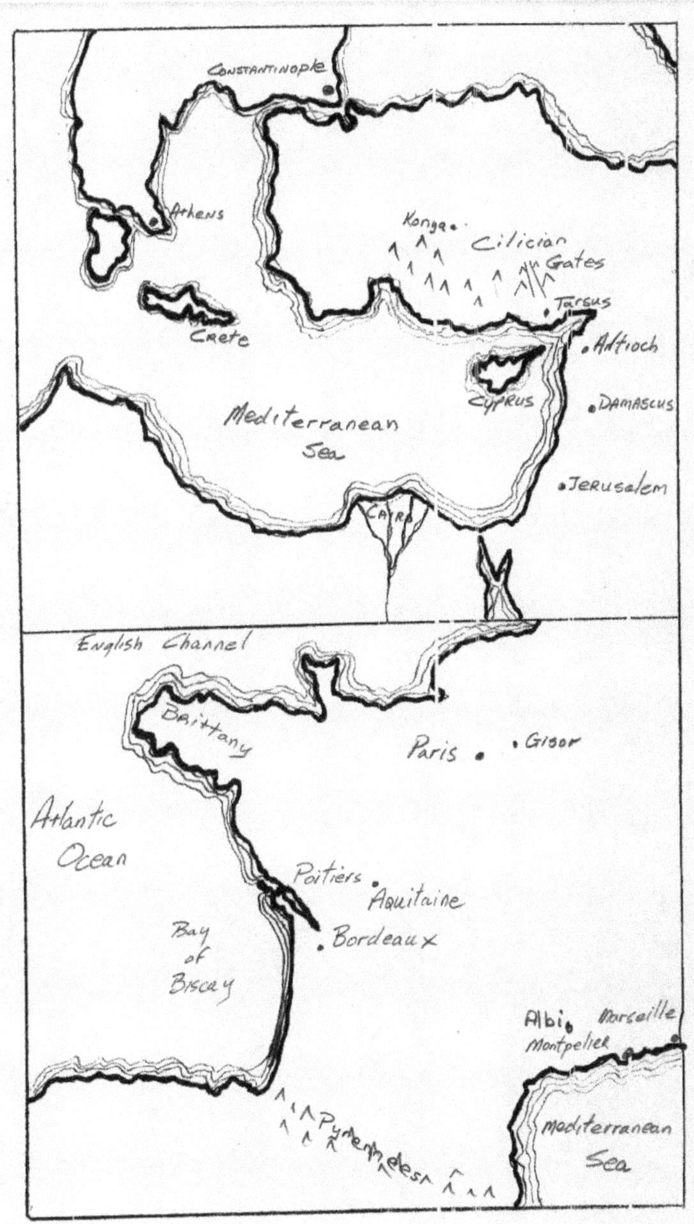

Constantinople
Athens
Konya
Cilician Gates
Tarsus
Antioch
Crete
Cyprus
Damascus
Mediterranean Sea
Cairo
Jerusalem
English Channel
Brittany
Paris
Gisor
Atlantic Ocean
Poitiers
Aquitaine
Bay of Biscay
Bordeaux
Albi
Marseille
Montpelier
Pyrenees
Mediterranean Sea

Book 1

Chapter 1

Lesser Armenia during the Crusades, c. 1150

The sky had turned a menacing grey. Queen Zabel took a deep breath to clear her head, relishing the humid, late afternoon air. She would need her wits about her for this first meeting with Bishop Scarfos and her councillors after her father's death. She leaned into the wind deciding to take a path that led past the stables.

"Make sure everything is well secured this night, Lucus. A storm is approaching."

"Yes, My Lady." He bowed slightly, turning from her, and continued conditioning a leather bridle.

Only a few years ago, as children, she and Lucas had played here, avidly grooming the horses whenever they were allowed. Now she was 'My Lady.' This change in the status of their relationship disappointed her. It had made no difference that he was the stable master's son; Lucas, being the elder, had often led their play even though she had always towered over him in height. But now that she was queen he treated her with deference.

Zabel ran her hand along the rump of her favorite horse, the black Arab she'd named Tambour, savoring the musky odor that always connected her to the earth. Tambour galloped like the drum he was named for, during the polo she played for military training. Her father, King Leo, had seen to it she could ride and shoot as well as any of the other young soldiers, but she was acutely aware he had neglected to give her the necessary skills to run the kingdom.

The wind had increased, a spiral about her feet, as she walked on towards the church. She pulled her cloak more tightly about her neck, letting the thick rabbit fur warm her. Great Mother, are you trying to warn me?

A footman pushed open the cedar doors to the vestry where a faint trace of incense floated in the still air. Intricately carved oil lamps cast flickering shapes on the bare walls that separated the faithful from the workings of their Church. As the door closed behind her the sudden gust made the flames jump and she caught the stale presence of the elders who made decisions here.

Three of her state counsellors rose from behind a long, wooden table and bowed to her. She pulled herself up to her full stature, looking down at them as each pair of eyes moved over her, judging, she felt, the unadorned silk gown she had chosen. Not only did its emerald green match her eyes, but also the contrast with her dark hair enhanced the image of power she hoped to achieve. These men were used to dealing with her father, not a young woman, even one as committed to royal duty as herself.

Bishop Scarfos stood beside his chair, his long black cassock gathered at the waist by a heavy chain from which hung a large iron cross. His back had been to the door, and when he turned he made no attempt to bow. She knew the cleric disliked her as much as she disdained him.

Counsellor Maurice motioned with a thick fleshy finger to the only chair on the opposite side of the table. "Your majesty, please take a seat." Once seated Zabel became aware of how the bishop's chair, at the head of the table, gave him authority in the room.

"I must begin by saying how deeply we regret the untimely passing of your father...rather, King Leo," the counselor continued. "Besides being an able ruler of Lesser Armenia, he was a great friend." He coughed delicately behind his hand. "But, we are confident you will successfully carry out your new duties. You are a gifted student of philosophy and have mastered three languages, so I understand."

Hearing the condescension in his voice, Zabel realized at once the mistake she had made. *I allowed them to summon me here as if I were a child.* Her pulse quickened, but she knew she had to make every attempt to sound self-assured. "My father is missed by all his people. But you are correct in assuming that he is especially missed by me." She looked at each man in turn. "What is it you wish to discuss?"

"I will get straight to the point, he said slowly. Regrettably, our strategic position has weakened."

Zabel wondered if her advisors had deliberately chosen Counsellor Maurice to speak hoping his lethargic manner would prevent her from reacting to whatever he said. If they did, they had made a mistake because his manner was irritating. "How is that?" she asked.

He touched a hand to his graying temple. "Tensions between the Christians, the Seljuks, and the Mamluks are increasing over who will have ultimate control of the spice trade. Saladin in Egypt has been flexing his muscle. A very large muscle, as you are undoubtedly aware. And we have heard reports of a new threat from the East. A savage group of warriors, the Mongols as they call themselves, are moving westward, conquering all before them. They will soon be a threat to us."

"Do you think our alliances are in jeopardy?"

"In the past, we have counted on the support of the Byzantines in Constantinople, but lately they have become less dependable." The counsellor shuffled his corpulent body, with obvious discomfort.

Zabel willed him to get to the point. "Do we not have other allies?" She wished she had asked her father to explain what these alliances meant and what to do if one broke down. Now it was too late.

"You are acquainted with the two Franks, Raymond and Guy de Gisor?"

Zabel brought to mind the polo practice she'd had that morning with the royal guards. The two knights were decent riders but they were unused to swinging mallets while atop small agile ponies. For their military campaigns they wore heavy armor and bred horses that could carry the extra weight. But, the Gisor brothers proved to be quick studies and had begun to handle the mallets with precision, acknowledging the effectiveness of using polo as military training. They were, however, unkempt. She was sure they never bathed.

"We've drilled together, yes."

"As you are aware, these knights were on their way to the Holy Land to liberate it from the Infidel."

"*Were* on their way to the Holy Land. Are they no longer going?"

Maurice shuffled again, straightening his caftan and looked to the other ministers for support. Zabel tensed. The storm clouds through the clerestory windows had turned steely grey and thunder rumbled in the distance.

"As Christians, we share their view that taking back the Holy Lands from the Mohammedans would be pleasing to God. But what you may not know is your father negotiated agreements with them shortly before his death that will greatly enhance our military might."

Zabel recalled her last conversation with her father. They'd been talking about the Franks when he'd fallen into unconsciousness, unable to finish his thoughts. "Do you mean we have made these Franks our allies?"

"We are about to."

"We are a peaceful people. Taking new allies could threaten the very people we want to reassure." Zabel gripped the arm of her chair, fear penetrating her body. She detested the idea of war. Now she was unsure if having alliances would keep her people safe from battles. More to the point, she was unsure whether her councillors would give her the best advice. Were they more loyal to the bishop?

The minister glanced at Bishop Scarfos before continuing. "It is the unfortunate fate of all small kingdoms to be vulnerable when surrounded by warlike states. Your father's concerns were always for the safety of Armenia. He concluded that the threats were real. We have, after all, been monitoring the situation for some time. As I said before, the loss of the Byzantines as our only Christian ally has necessitated this action. The Franks are willing to become entrenched in this part of the world."

"How entrenched?" Her voice sounded too loud, strained. She fought to gain control of herself but she was perspiring beneath her silk gown. She feared that all this skirting the issue meant she would dislike their plan.

"I must emphasize," Maurice said, "that we cannot possibly ward off any attack by ourselves. We lack the military strength."

Zabel raised her hand to interrupt, but the minister ignored her. "We have worked out an arrangement we believe will be most satisfactory to you, once you have had time to consider all the benefits." He held her gaze. "And, I should add, it was your father's idea."

"What is it?" She had no patience for this type of talk.

"Raymond de Gisor has agreed to your hand in marriage. With it, he will commit fifteen thousand troops to the ongoing defense of Armenia."

"Marriage! I've never intended to marry."

"It will secure his loyalty to our cause."

Bile rose in her at the thought of being forced into a marriage, any marriage, but especially one with the Frank. An image of Raymond de Gisor tossing bones on the carpets as he ate and wiping his greasy face with his sleeve came back to her. She shuddered to think of him as her husband. "No, I won't. If I married him, according to Armenian law, he would become king. My father would never want him to rule in my place. These Franks know nothing about us. No. I refuse!"

"Queen Zabel...."

"We control the pass through the Taurus Mountains which ensures trade flows smoothly between the empires. None of the states you mentioned would want an interruption in trade. The pass has always guaranteed our neutrality," she said. Her father had said as much.

"The balance of power your father worked to maintain is crumbling. He was concerned that any of our neighbors could simply take the pass from us."

She knew that its loss would be devastating. "So, you want me to marry a man we know nothing about, and hand over our state to him?"

Each face staring back at her was calm, implacable. She felt trapped.

"I will not marry this man."

"It would be most advantageous for you to get to know Raymond better." The counsellor's voice was now syrupy. "These knights are not barbarians. They simply have different ways. They are warriors, with a code of chivalry. And they're fond of their women folk. Many of the knights brought their wives with them on this holy campaign. In fact, King Louis of France has just passed through the Gates with his wife, Eleanor of Aquitaine. If you are worried about losing your powers as queen, let me assure you, they afford their wives great freedoms."

"Don't patronize me with ideas of petty freedoms. I am Queen Zabel, ruler of Lesser Armenia." She jumped from her seat, her eyes flashing. "I will take whatever freedoms I want and no one will tell me differently. Do not think your grey head gives you permission to force your will upon me? I will not do as you suggest."

The bishop who had been listening intently to the

conversation raised his hand, to speak. Zabel stared down at him, the vantage point calming her in spite of the fury visible in his close-set eyes.

"Do you honestly want to take the risk? If you are wrong, could you, a woman lead our armies to war?"

She kept her gaze fixed on him, ignoring the oath she had taken in accordance with her dead mother's wishes, she said, "I have trained with the army. My father saw to it that I ride and shoot like any man. I can hit a target with a bow and arrow from a moving horse with great accuracy."

Outside lightning flashed, followed instantly by thunder rumbling between the sky and the earth.

"Be that as it may, you are no match physically for a man. Woman's lack of strength is matched by a lack of will. Women must be looked after by men." A spray of spittle filled the air as he shouted his words at her. "I had hoped you would understand the necessity of this arrangement. Your father should have told you its importance for the continuing security of Lesser Armenia. But because you are behaving so foolishly, I remind you, it is by our good grace that we have brought this information to you so you can accept willingly."

Zabel faced the others. Their expressions retained the same unemotional calm. She felt dizzy. She relished the game of polo and enjoyed learning to shoot, but she had never contemplated leading her armies in war. It was unthinkable. And this man, Bishop Scarfos, who was supposed to minister to the souls of her countrymen, was a man dry and bereft of human sentiment. His belief in a sky god that advocated war to achieve power was not an ideal she shared.

"Bishop Scarfos is quite right, your majesty. If he chooses, he can simply have you removed."

"Removed...He can't do that."

"On the contrary, my dear," continued the bishop. "I crowned you. You rule by the sanction of the Holy Armenian Church. If you fail to comply with the will of God, that is, to be accountable to God for the Christians entrusted to you, we will make another woman queen. Understand...we will have this alliance with or without your co-operation." He fingered the iron cross that lay in his lap.

Zabel wondered if the gesture was to give the impression that he was silently praying for assistance. He looked at her and in that instant an image of her father, strong and sure, came into her mind. She willed his strength to become hers, and it did. She stared at the bishop, without saying a word.

Bishop Scarfos cleared his throat. "I see you are not yet ready to comply. Undoubtedly you're still suffering from the loss of your father." His face hardened into a sneer. "We will give you three weeks to come to your senses," he said, thrusting a bony finger at her. His eyes glistened from the joy of humiliating her.

The shock of the ultimatum chilled her. She had never felt so alone. "You men will be the destruction of our people," she declared and strode from the room.

Once outside, she headed to the palace. The sun was setting, fingers of lilac and turquoise escaped the thunderheads now the colour of old pewter.

In the library, a fire blazed in the tiled hearth. She picked up the king from the chessboard, stroking the fine-grained alabaster with her thumb, clenching it tightly. How many times had she played this game with her father? She ached with the loss of him.

She opened the shutter of the arched window as an

eagle dropped from the sky and heard the frightened shriek from its prey. We Armenians are like the eagle. We took this land by force. Now, as if the Spirits of peace are having their revenge, war threatens our borders. What she wanted at this moment was to be certain--certain she could rule this land, certain she could secure the trust of the people, certain she could keep her country out of war.

Chapter 2

Zabel called for mint tea and as the warm liquid began to relax her churning stomach she leaned into the cushions on the divan. Perhaps her father had intended she marry Raymond de Gisor.

She recalled a day, shortly before he died, when she'd been playing polo through a fierce, driving rain. Like today, lightning had filled the skies and the earth trembled as thunder rolled across the plain, agitating the horses. After the practice, she'd walked into this very room, the grills on the windows closed against the storm, and found her father talking to Bishop Scarfos. At the sound of her approach both men turned in her direction. The Bishop's penetrating eyes met hers, his thin lips pulled into a grimace. His cold demeanor chilled the room in spite of a blazing fire in the hearth.

Her father's shoulders were hunched in defeat, but he straightened suddenly as if he were reluctant to have her see him thus. His face brightened and he made an effort to look relaxed, but he was clearly uncomfortable about something the bishop and he had been discussing. "Zabel, did you finish the match?" he asked.

"I was teaching the two Frank knights, Guy and

Raymond, to play polo," she said, wrinkling her nose at the thought of them.

"You don't like them, Zabel?" the bishop asked. "They must surely find you fascinating. Their women do not participate in the military affairs of men." His sarcasm was unmistakable.

"They sit well on their horses, but they are barbarians," she said.

"It is your actions that are barbaric, my dear," the bishop said. "Your majesty, it is unbecoming your daughter should linger in the company of men, like a common harlot. If, one day, you want her to lead the Armenian people she must be respected." The bishop's face turned scarlet as he spoke. He glared at the king. Outside lightning flashed like arrows.

King Leo held his tongue and an awkward silence ensued.

"I am sure you must have things to discuss, so I will take my leave," Bishop Scarfos said. His statement had the quality of a command rather than a mere observation. He made a slight bow first to her father, then to Zabel and left.

"How could you let him speak about me like that? 'A common harlot?' Father..." Zabel's eyes flashed, their almond shape indicating some Persian in her bloodline. "He doesn't even feign politeness."

"You mustn't let him upset you, Zabel. He can be a difficult man, but he holds the well-being of the Armenian people as a sacred duty." The king pursed his lips. "Always remember that as God's representative on earth, he holds more power than you think."

Zabel ignored these comments, still smarting from the bishop's words. "In an educated man, such behavior is inexcusable. He's hardly a peasant."

"Come. Let's sit by the fire. You're shaking from the cold."

She knew that his lack of comment meant that her father wanted the subject dropped. She took a deep breath of incense rising from the bronze burners, willing it to calm her. Displeasing her father was something she was loath to do.

The storm continued. A great light flashed across the sky, the loud thunder shook the walls of the palace, and the air turned more oppressive.

"The lightning has brought much needed rain, Father."
"You are still shivering, Zabel. Would you like some spiced tea to warm you?" He leaned over and pressed her hand.
Her father's smile reassured her, as always. She began to relax.
"Tea would be just the thing."
King Leo nodded to the manservant who stood always at his side, and Zabel sank into a pile of richly embroidered pillows. The light from the gilded oil lamps turned the set of alabaster chess pieces translucent.

"Let's have a game," the king said, as he sat opposite her.

A serving girl placed an enameled cup of tea on the table beside Zabel. She savoured the aroma of cardamom and pepper before she took a sip.

"I'd rather play backgammon," Zabel said, returning to the debate she and her father had every time he suggested chess. She picked up the backgammon board and rubbed the smooth wood with her fingertips. She loved the intricate shell mosaic that set apart the points made of lapis lazuli from those of red limestone. "Chess is so slow. One must ponder every move." She took another sip of tea. "Backgammon is quick. You roll the die and meet your fate. With each new roll you adjust. It's like polo. You strike the ball with a mallet, and everyone stumbles over one another to get the upper hand without falling from their horse. That's how I like to live."

"Zabel, I live with risk every day."

She was startled by the brusqueness in his voice, so unlike the light banter they usually enjoyed. The king wiped his hands over his grey eyes and his shoulders sagged.

"I'm sure..." she began. But rather than commenting further she said, "We can play chess today."

"No, backgammon is fine." He sat silent for a few moments, his white head lowered in contemplation as she prepared the board.

He was keeping something from her. She could feel it.

When he spoke, his voice was a whisper, as if he had forgotten she was in the room. "I may have made a mistake. The Franks want more than an alliance."

"What do you mean? What kind of mistake? You told me to show them every courtesy. I've done that. I've answered all the questions they've had about our country."

Her father stood and began to pace the room, the light from the lamps flickering as he stirred the air.

"What do you think of these two young nobles, Zabel? Are they good warriors, good leaders of men?"

"I like them well enough, but there is cunning in the

character of Guy, that seems to be absent in Raymond." She felt uneasy.

Her father stopped pacing and again wiped his hands over his eyes in a gesture of profound fatigue. "Age brings despair, Zabel. One begins to realize that things will be left unfinished and I can see I have kept you out of these affairs too long. We must correct that."

Zabel noted he appeared shrunken, older. "Why did you permit these strangers to train among us?" Her voice had an unintended sharpness to it.

He stood perfectly still, as if she had shot him with an arrow.

She had never raised her voice in anger to him before. In all the years since her mother's death, he had taken care of everything. He seemed to know what she needed or wanted before she asked. There had never been a reason to criticize him.

But rather than returning her anger, he looked down at her and said, "We have one great asset, Zabel. We control the most important pass into Syria from Constantinople and 'The Cilician Gates' are our greatest source of income. It is something we must protect."

Zabel rubbed the die between her fingers, feeling the indentations. The bitterness in his tone was new. She rolled the die. As the cube of ivory hit the playing surface the thought occurred to her that until this moment her risks had been merely between one good and another. Now she saw life could be devastatingly altered from the vagaries of chance.

Chapter 3

After reflecting on the conversation with her father, Queen Zabel was still uncertain as to his intention. She placed the chess piece back on the board. He had come close to suggesting an alliance with the Franks. But was it to be cemented by this marriage? He could have been planning a grand military alliance with various concessions in land or a share in the proceeds from the customs duties at the Gates.

After they had completed their game of backgammon he had told her to prepare for dinner and that Guy and Raymond de Gisor were to be honored guests. If he had wanted to discuss the idea of an arranged marriage, surely it would have been better to have done so in the privacy of his study. She drained the last of the tea and tried to recall the details of that evening.

She remembered she had felt the need to walk, to absorb the energies of the earth so she'd left the palace enclosure and entered the surrounding woods that were budding with new leaves. A cat, hunting its prey, crossed her path, lifting its delicate feet to avoid the damp grass. *Killing is the nature of the world. Why can't I accept it? But the trouble is, cats rarely fight each other to the death as men do.*

She thought of the Armenian history she'd been

taught, of how throughout its long and turbulent history, her father and those ruling before him had cunningly preserved independence while existing amongst powerful neighbors.

The Armenians had learned the art of the goldsmith, decorative textile design, architectural styles, and the weaving of silks from the Persians, Greeks, and Byzantines. But they never forgot that in Greater Armenia, Mount Ararat stood where Noah's Ark came to rest at the end of the flood. They were the first race of men to appear in the world after the Deluge. They created their own alphabet, and welded together a religion, culture, and nationality that provided great material wealth.

Zabel had studied with the greatest scholars her father could assemble to educate his daughter in these things as well as to understand the greatest of Greek and Persian philosophies. But it was Jnana's lessons concerning the gifts of the Great Mother that intrigued her most.

It grew darker and a lone star appeared, dim and distant. War. Empire. I want no part of it. She'd hurled her anger into the night sky. Not finding the consolation she usually felt in the forest, she thought, I must find Jnana.

Zabel walked towards the palace kitchen. Abutting it was Jnana's small workroom with its low beams that hung with drying herbs. As she entered, the strong aroma of lavender and rose hips enveloped her. The essences evoked the reassuring nature of her guardian who was happiest here in the women's section of the palace where she was in command.

The older woman stood, her brow furrowed, behind the well-worn table. Lime-wood boxes for storing various dried roots and herbs, were strewn about. Jnana wore a green woolen tunic clasped at the neck by a wooden toggle carved with a symbol of a yoni, signifying she was about to act as midwife to one of the palace women.

"I can't seem to get this tincture to work properly, and a baby is due shortly." She was stirring a pungent smelling liquid. "The little ones don't wait for me to get things right. Now," she glanced at Zabel, "what's wrong with you?"

"There's no use trying to hide anything from you, is there?"

The soft light of the oil lamp inscribed lines on the face of the woman Zabel loved; the woman who was the only mother she had ever known. *She, too, is aging.*

"I've been talking with Father."

Jnana continued to stir her brew.

"He told me of new military threats."

Jnana picked up her mortar and pestle and ground some dried leaves, releasing the tart aroma of artemisia.

"He's looking frail."

Jnana paused in her grinding and looked up. "We all get older, Zabel."

"I know." Zabel's voice shook. "But he was talking of war. I will be queen when he dies."

Jnana released the pestle and took Zabel's hands. "Remember in the ancient times any female who owned land was called a queen. It is your birthright as a woman. You will do what you have to when the time comes."

Life emanates from Jnana; her hands strong and permanently warmed from the heat of birthing many babies, healing the sick, and preparing the dead for burial.

"You always told me my mother wanted me to avoid the ways of war."

"That's true."

"But if war becomes unavoidable..."Zabel stuck her finger in the tincture and licked it. It tasted better than she imagined. Jnana seemed intent on her measuring, seemingly ignoring her concerns. Annoyed, Zabel said, "If something happens to Father, I'd be in an impossible dilemma."

Jnana stopped her mixing. "I know what your mother wished. But, remember, she was young and inexperienced when she died." Jnana sighed and picked up the pestle. "I don't think your mother fully understood what would one day be asked of you." She looked at Zabel, her features intense. "Your father has taught you to think like a ruler. Perhaps more than you realize. But for now, I'm still in charge of you. Go to your quarters and bathe for dinner. Having the strength of a man on the inside doesn't mean you have to smell like one on the outside."

Zabel wanted to ask more but she could see Jnana was preoccupied. She made her way across the courtyard toward the palace, the fragrance from Jnana's herb garden permeating the night air. Rose bushes stood, strong and proud, wet from the rain. *Their scent and beauty are alluring but they have thorns that cut the flesh of those who do not respect the delicacy of the petals. Is this the kind of woman I am meant to be?*

As Zabel entered her chambers, she heard water running into the large marble tub. The scent of rose oil, as if Jnana's garden had been moved inside, wafted into the room as Marja poured the golden substance from a brass ewer.

Zabel took off her riding clothes and slipped on a robe, relishing the feel of the cool silk on her skin. As Marja brushed the knots from Zabel's tangled curls, she tried to make sense of her father's last comments. Had he, indeed, made a mistake by joining with the Franks in an alliance?

Zabel secured her hair on the top of her head with a gold pin before she slipped out of the gown and into the tub. Marja knelt and Zabel let the girl rub her back with perfumed soap. Then she lay back and let her mind drift as the hot water lapped against her body, her long taut thighs and firm, flat belly somehow reassuring. *But am I as strong as I need to be?*

She dressed in a silk gown, the color of cinnabar, gathered at the waist with a fine gold mesh girdle encrusted with small pearls, and made her way to the domed dining pavilion.

In a shaded corner Bishop Scarfos conversed with Guy de Gisor. She walked to her father's side across the thick camelhair carpet. He was standing with the elder brother, Raymond, and as she drew close she could see the Frank had not bothered to bathe or change his clothing. She backed away, but her father caught her elbow. King Leo then asked Raymond to sit between he and his daughter on the divan. He turned his back on Zabel and Raymond to speak to the bishop and Guy who sat to his other side. There was nothing for Zabel to do but to talk to the Frank.

"That was very dramatic lightning today. Do you have such storms in your country?" she asked.

Raymond said, "Yes, my home is a land of majestic trees watered by plentiful rains. I learned of lightning as a small child. I'd climb onto my straw bed for safety." He smiled; the glow of a fond memory warming his face.

Zabel was astonished. "You sleep on straw?"

"Yes, you are sheeted, of course, but it is the easiest thing to clean. When the straw becomes offensive and overrun with vermin, we have it burned. Servants replace it with clean straw covered with fresh woolen cloth newly-woven by our women."

The conversation was interrupted as the servants brought in platters of food. Raymond stabbed a piece of the succulent roasted pig with the blade of his knife and tore off great chunks with his teeth. He threw what he didn't want on the floor, smearing the carpet with grease. King Leo patted Zabel's arm to let her know he understood her revulsion, but his sharp look indicated it was important she endure this torture.

"What is it like in your homeland?" she enquired. "Do you miss it?"

"Very much. Our lands are in the north, near Paris. The hills are rolling and lush. We left during my favorite time of year when the ancient oak trees have turned to gold."

His rough wool tunic scratched Zabel's skin as he moved his arm to rub the fat dripping from his chin. But in spite of his uncouth manners and slovenly appearance, he had the soul of a poet rather than the bloodlust of a warrior.

"What made you leave? To travel all this way to Lesser Armenia?'

"The Pope called for all men trained in arms to free the Holy Land from the Infidel."

"It's very risky," she said. "The men who hold Jerusalem are fierce fighters."

"The Pope decreed those who pledge themselves to this cause will be forgiven their sins. I no longer fear eternal hellfire."

"You deeply believe in your Christian teachings, then."

"Yes, it is our faith." He tuned to her, with a puzzled expression on his face. "You Armenians share our beliefs, do you not?"

"In this part of the world, there are many different ways to honor the sacred. But, yes, Armenians are Christians." Zabel was unwilling to tell him of her relationship to the Great Mother.

"That may be true, but because our older brother will inherit our fiefdom, Guy and I are obliged to bring glory to our family name. It is our duty."

Zabel reached for a fig, thinking how averse she was to the idea that war, war for any reason, could bring glory.

When the meal ended, Raymond stood to take his leave but King Leo interrupted his departure. "Raymond, Bishop Scarfos and some of my counsellors will be meeting in the audience chamber. We would like you to join us."

"As you wish, Your Majesty."

"I would like to be there as well, Father," Zabel said.

"Not tonight, Zabel," the King said.

"But you said you would include me in the affairs of state. Why not begin now?"

Raymond looked uncomfortable.

The king said, "You may go ahead, Raymond. I'll be with you presently."

Zabel straightened her back and faced her father. "I want to be included."

"Not tonight! This is not a conversation for women.""

"But why? I don't understand. I'm heir to the throne, am I not?"

"I told you this afternoon I had made a mistake. I have actually made two. Warriors are killers, Zabel. I have let you learn to ride and shoot. It is only fitting that as future ruler you are able to display an ability to do these things, but you are not a hardened warrior. I never intended that for you. Tonight I will correct one of my mistakes. But not with you there. Now, do as I say."

Zabel was furious, but seeing the look of determination on her father's face, she turned on her heels. She would not permit him to see her rage.

Outside the cool night air calmed her. She reached out to touch the bark of an ancient walnut tree. *It is strong like Father. Not merely a thorny rose with soft petals. Maybe he's right. I love beautiful silks, fragrant baths, jewels, newborn lambs and horses. And I don't see the point of war, or men's desire to test themselves in useless slaughter.*

Chapter 4

The following morning Zabel received a message from her father. He planned a special dinner that evening for just the two of them. A group of Arab musicians would entertain. It was one way of apologizing for excluding her the night before, she thought. The king seldom had time for dinner alone with his daughter, so she looked forward to the evening with great anticipation.

Zabel spent the afternoon in the gardens amongst the blossoming almond trees, yellow narcissus and purple hyacinth indulging in Persian poetry.

When shadows began to lengthen she walked to the kitchen, which would be buzzing with its usual domestic chaos. When her father had announced dinner was for the two of them, he meant there would be no foreign guests. To the Armenian king, dining alone always included his closest retainers so the preparation of this small dinner was a large undertaking.

The aroma of lamb, slowly stewing with thyme, sweet marjoram and lemon, greeted her, as she entered the room. A large cauldron hung in the centre of the hearth over a brisk fire. Before her death, Zabel's mother had extracted a promise from Jnana to teach her daughter to cook. So in spite of her royal position, Zabel had learned to prepare food in the Armenian manner.

It was here, in the kitchen, that Jnana's instruction concerning the gifts from the Great Mother had their greatest impact on Zabel. The round cauldron was a visual reminder of the womb that nourished every unborn animal. Zabel leaned over the simmering stew, full of carrots, onions and lentils. Beside it, the pungent aroma of cumin, anise, and ginger, emanated from chickpeas simmering in a smaller iron pot. Before serving this dish, Jnana would add pine nuts and almonds. *It is beyond understanding how a seed planted in the warm earth becomes a fragrant green shoot to enhance our cookery.* Her mouth watered.

The friendly banter of the women brought Zabel out of her reverie. One of the serving girls was busily stuffing peppers with the chickpea mixture.

"What would you like me to do?" Zabel asked Jnana.

Jnana looked over at the worktables. "The trout has been cleaned. You can finish the bean paste. Just grind the garlic and spices together and add the lemon and onion."

Zabel picked up an onion, holding it reverently. *Your white flesh wrapped in parchment has grown full and rounded in the damp earth. It takes all my effort to cut into you.*

Jnana's voice prodded her. "Zabel, stop daydreaming and get busy." "When you're done there you can fill these containers with yoghurt and these others with the tabouleh. Jasine," she turned to a servant, "fill these bowls with fruit. And be sure to pile them high."

Jasine's hands moved quickly, placing figs and dates on the shiny brass bowls inlaid with silver and gold.

Finally everything was ready. The stew was left to simmer while the kitchen servants took their meal and a well-deserved rest. Zabel returned to her chamber to dress. From the time she was a young child, the luxurious silks in abundance at court had entranced her. The king had indulged her passion by allowing her to design her own extravagant wardrobe. Tonight she decided on an azure silk robe laboriously embroidered with gold thread. Two ebony combs held back her hair which the maid, Marja, wound with fresh rose buds.

Torches lit the gold on the coffered ceiling of the reception hall. Zabel settled herself beside her father on a cushioned divan, acknowledging, with a nod of her head, the court that were seated about the grand room.

"Tonight, you look exactly like your mother," her father began. "The way she was when I married her." His eyes sparkled, reflecting light from the oil lamps. He reached out and took her hand, folding it into his own large palm. "We will be well entertained. The Arab musicians who are visiting us have played for the caliph in Baghdad."

The meal was carried in while one of the musicians began to softly pluck the strings of his oud. In a sweet-throated voice he recited poetry, evoking in sweeping stanzas, a Persian prince's love for a lady.

"Only a people with a belief in the divine revelation of the Quar'an could have such enraptured sensitivity to every word they utter. Don't you agree, Father?"

"And to every word they write."

One of the palace cats jumped onto Zabel's lap. She began to stroke it with her long elegant fingers. "Yes, precisely."

The king cleared his throat and shifted to a more

upright position. "But I have decided we must no longer waste your intelligence on mere philosophy. Tomorrow I wish you to attend the morning council meeting where we will lay out our plan for your participation."

"Of course, Father. I will help any way you see fit." Zabel was thrilled. The prospect of exercising her power over the council was delicious.

He patted her hand and smiled. "I know I can count on your support."

The sound of a drum and a tambour joined that of the oud, their harmonies filling the room. The bard continued the ancient art of reciting poetry to music.

"When the moon's engulfed within the clouds

What will light the way if not the stars?"

The sounds of the music and poetry became more intense. Zabel and her father turned their attention to the Arab whose voice rose to a pleasing crescendo.

When he finished there was a pause in the music. King Leo turned to his daughter. "I want to talk with you more about the Franks, Zabel. I really must have you fully understand our position."

Zabel looked into his face and at the same instant she felt him slump against her.

"Father," she screamed. "Father, what is the matter?"

The king's attendants rushed to his side. King Leo was unconscious.

Aides carried him to his quarters while Zabel strode

alongside, holding her father's hand. His flesh was cold, as if the blood had stopped flowing. When they laid him on his bed, Zabel sat beside him, speechless.

Jnana rushed into the room, her chest heaving from the unaccustomed exertion.

"It's serious," Zabel said, looking into the old woman's face. "You must do something."

Jnana was about to answer when the door to the chamber opened, and the court doctor, an Arab from Aleppo, entered.

"You women must leave while I examine the king," he ordered.

Zabel was about to object when Bishop Scarfos walked in, looking arrogant and unruffled. She knew the bishop would allow only Greek medicine with its barbaric practice of blood letting, even though the Arab doctor could use herbs as Jnana did, or perform the surgery he was trained to do in Damascus.

Zabel rose to protest, but Jnana pulled her sleeve, signaling with her eyes for Zabel to remain silent.

Jnana whispered under her breath, "We have no choice but to leave. You have no authority over these men."

Zabel failed to comprehend what Jnana was saying; the shock of seeing her father lying unconscious was too great, and she allowed herself to be led from the room.

They waited in her father's study where a hearth fire burned cheerily, at odds with the fear the two women felt.

Chapter 5

Zabel paced the marble tiles of her father's chamber. "I don't ever remember Father being ill, Jnana. It feels strange. Silent. As if the palace were holding its breath."

"Your father is the centre of his kingdom. All activities radiate from him."

Zabel stopped and faced Jnana. "I will demand that the bishop let you treat Father."

"No. If he dies, you will be Queen. Making an enemy of the bishop would be very dangerous. He could make things very difficult for you."

"I don't care how dangerous it is. We can't just let Father die. Besides, when I'm queen, I will be the most powerful person in this country."

"If your father dies, the fate of Little Armenia will be in your hands. He trusts you will be able to cooperate with the leader of your church."

"You know I don't accept those teachings."

The door opened and Bishop Scarfos entered, followed by the Arab physician.

"I have done all I can for now," the doctor stated.

"We bled him to reduce the pressure on his heart. When he wakes we will give him the special elixir I have prepared for such cases."

"But what is the matter with him? Are you sure bleeding him was the best thing?" Zabel asked.

The bishop put his hand on the physician's arm to stop him from speaking, and looked from Jnana to Zabel.

"Your father's physician has done as I requested. You can return to your quarters. I will make sure an attendant is with King Leo. They will call you when he wakes."

"No, he is my father. I will stay with him tonight."

The bishop stood visibly grappling with this assertion. "Very well. I see no harm in it. But," and he turned to Jnana as he spoke, "you will not treat him with your pagan medicines. The attendant will inform me if my orders are disobeyed."

Zabel shook with rage as the two women entered the king's chamber. Jnana felt his pulse. It was weak. Dangerously weak.

"Jnana, do something."

She shook her head. "You should lie with him. Even in his unconscious state, he will feel your presence."

Zabel rested her head on the pillow beside her father's. She put her arm over him, willing him to wake. "He's barely breathing." Both women looked over at the attendant surveying them from across the room. There would be no chance to use Jnana's herbal remedies that were safer than the most often poisonous mineral elixirs the doctor administered. As the hours wore on, Zabel fell into a restless sleep.

"Father, wait. I can't keep up."

They were scrambling over a hillside made of golden rocks, heading for a sea, sparkling in the distance. A woman came forward to meet them, holding out her arms in a gesture of greeting.

"My father is sick. But he won't wait for me."

King Leo was running now, but the woman was quicker. She grabbed his arm and soon all three were tumbling in space, the earth and sea far below them.

"Where are we, what have you done, Father?"

Everything disappeared. Zabel and her father floated in a vast blue void. She held him there, engulfed in beautiful music. It was different from any music Zabel had ever heard. It flooded her with contentment.

The woman reappeared saying, "Health is a perfect condition of rhythm and tone. We understand the rhythms of nature, the vibrations of life. Your father is not vibrating properly. The music will heal him."

Zabel looked at the king. His face was stricken with panic. They were in the sea now. He shook loose from her hand and began swimming. She tried to catch him but he was too fast.

"Aren't you happy Father?"

"It's no good, Zabel, I have to leave."

Zabel woke, her heart pounding. "Jnana, I just had a dream. We can heal Father with music. We were floating in space. I heard it. I know it will work. Do you know about this? Can we play the music for him?"

"Calm down, Zabel. What are you talking about?"

"I don't know exactly. There was some special music. Wait. Let me try to remember. The sound has a particular vibration in harmony with the cosmos. It returns the circulation of the blood to its proper rhythm and speed. It will cure him, I'm sure of it. Do you know about such a way? You must. You know all the ancient remedies." Zabel grabbed Jnana's arm, feeling her nails dig into the flesh of the old woman. Jnana flinched, but Zabel continued to hold her. She had to make Jnana understand.

"There is a legend of vibrational rhythms once used by our people for this purpose...in the ancient times. But I'm sorry, Zabel, the knowledge has been lost. I know nothing about it."

"But you must try to remember. I know it will make him well."

"Perhaps in the future."

"I don't care about the future." Zabel stopped. "In the dream, he ran from me. He was terrified of the music. He wanted to die."

"Then we must grant his soul its wish."

Zabel stared at Jnana. Her expression paled, as the truth sank in. She crumpled onto her guardian. "No, Jnana, no." But Jnana was right. The king had made up his mind.

The surgeon continued to bleed the king for three days, and on the fourth morning, as harsh daylight entered the chamber, King Leo did not awake.

Chapter 6

I've ceased to wind fresh roses in my hair. I can no longer ride on horseback unencumbered by the responsibilities of state. My innocence is gone.

She stood in the great hall. Coronation robes bordered with white ermine obtained from her powerful Muscovy neighbour to the north, draped around her. Bishop Scarfos was talking, but she wasn't listening. The room contained the stony-faced councillors and the two Franks. Guy with his steely gaze, observed everyone with keen interest; Raymond looked as if he would rather be anywhere else.

The bishop cleared his throat and Zabel turned to him. "As the representative of God," he said, "Do you swear to impose justice, defend the weak, insure the prosperity of the land?"

"I do."

"By the power vested in me by the Holy Armenian Church, I declare thee, Queen Zabel." It was done. The jewel-encrusted crown that had so recently belonged to her father was placed on her head.

She rode through the streets ahead of her soldiers

who carried the royal ensigns aloft; a tradition to assure the people the coronation was accepted fully by the army. Cheers rose from her subjects as she passed. She was thankful the crown forced her to sit upright, concealing the overwhelming grief she felt.

When she returned to the palace she indicated she was to be left undisturbed for the remainder of the evening. Tomorrow was her father's funeral. Tonight, the only person she wanted was Jnana.

They sat in her father's study, her study now, Zabel staring at the white queen on the chessboard…the most powerful piece that stood ready for a game on the table beside them.

Zabel sobbed, racked by sadness and loss, clinging to Jnana who held her as if she were still a child. When the tears were spent at last, her emotion changed to anger remembering her father was to be buried in the royal tomb the following day.

"Father's body must be left for the carrion birds to pick clean before his bones are buried. You've always told me it is the way of the Great Mother."

"You know it's impossible."

"I am Queen Zabel now. Why can't I have my way?"

"Stop this. Your father was a Christian. The Armenian people, his subjects- -your Christian subjects- - expect he will be buried according to Christian beliefs."

"It's your fault. By teaching me about the Great Mother, you've split my soul in two. It's impossible for me to honor the religion of my father and the ancient ways of my mother." It felt good to turn her anger on the older woman. "I'm going to the chapel. Alone."

Jnana said nothing as Zabel hurried down the

corridor.

He lay in the coffin beneath the rustic cloth of a pilgrim to join his God as church tradition dictated. The king's face was as waxen as the tall candles that lit the chamber. Zabel whispered to him, "Death's appetite was stronger than my will to keep you here." Her fingers traced every line of his face. "I have so many questions, but you won't answer me." A tear fell and she wiped it away. "This is the last tear I will shed for you. I know you want me to be strong."

The door opened. It was Jnana. "Come with me. We'll go to the ancient burial ground and have our own ceremony to return the spirit of your father to the Earth. Bring his wedding ring."

Jnana led Zabel to the stables where their horses had been saddled. They rode out the palace gates and followed a path across the plain, the moonlight a silver river leading up into the hills.

A fine Arabian is a magnificent horse. Nothing is as sublime as riding such a steed, the full moon hanging overhead, nothing following me but the wind. The mystery of creation is honored by night. Darkness in all its depth; where illusion becomes reality. The familiar reduced to its simplest elements, shapes emphasized, the clutter of daytime hides. I'm riding with your soul, Father.

They tied the horses to a tree that had been struck by lightning, the broken and empty limbs silhouetted against the night sky. It marked a trail that led to the mouth of a cave. Jnana passed the metal bucket of hot coals she had brought with her to Zabel and she carried the unlit torches.

"Legend has it that Zeus destroyed this tree of life sacred to our people," Jnana said, "taking its power for himself. It is since that time that men have insisted on power over women."

As they walked, Zabel could hear the tinkle of a goat's bell. The distant herd would be settled for the night now after having grazed on the pungent herbs that grew in this desolate place.

"Even though I am a queen, Jnana, I feel despair because of the power the Church has over me as a woman. I always believed that my father was strong enough to do anything, but the reality is that he could or would do nothing to change things, either."

"Your father accepted that his power as king came through his God. And he was a man, after all. Men don't understand what it is to be a woman. The idea we are weaker seems natural to them."

"You know how much I loved my father, but I am puzzled by his blindness. I so wanted him to understand true power comes from revering Nature."

Jnana removed some coals from the bucket and lit a torch that cast an amber light on the faces of the two women.

They entered a vast silent chamber; all the sounds of the wind in the trees, the tinkling goat's bells, and the snorting of the horses had disappeared. Niches carved into the rock walls were filled with bones bleached from days in the sun, once the vultures and ravens had eaten the flesh.

Zabel moved her fingers along the spirals carved into a stone altar that stood in the middle of the cave. The design symbolized the breath of the Great Mother moving matter in the eternal motion of birth, death, and regeneration.

Zabel felt the power of the Earth surge into her body, but then in her mind she could hear the voice of the bishop admonishing the women from his pulpit. "The priests say that Eve brought Death into the world by her disobedience.

Did I kill my father?"

"You don't believe that," Jnana chided her. "Have you forgotten everything I've taught you? The Great Mother gives and destroys life. It is the way. Nothing remains forever. The seasons follow each other in a never-ending cycle. Everything exists in a deep web of meaning that Her life force animates. We're born from Her and return to Her in death."

"Why is the church so intent on denying this truth?"

"As I've said, the ancient Greeks were the first to usurp the Great Mother's power. By demonizing the female, the Greek warriors dominated their women. You've read the Greek tragedies where they call women weak and evil. But the writing doesn't make it true. Still many women abdicate their power. They believe they're sinners and then they turn their power against each other accepting how men treat them."

Jnana pulled a knife from her girdle and handed it to Zabel. Two intertwined snakes were incised on the silver handle and the obsidian blade glowed, as if the volcanic forces from which it was made, energized it. It felt powerful in her hands.

"With this stone blade," Jnana said, "I cut the umbilical cord when you were born. It belonged to your mother. She wanted you to have it...at the right time."

"Why are you giving it to me now? I'm not a mother."

"To call the Spirits to us."

Is this energy I feel coming from my mother or the Great Mother? Perhaps both.

"Guard it well," Jnana said, "and remember, it's vital

that Bishop Scarfos never sees it. He knows its meaning and will take it from you.”

“Of course…I’ll guard it with my life.”

Zabel pointed the knife to the north and said, “In the name of the Great Mother let the circle that I invoke protect us from all harm. Enter, Healing Spirits.” She lifted her arms and energy hummed throughout her body.

She turned to the east, pulling the knife through the air as she moved. “Great Mother, by the spirit of the air, wind and rain that nourish the land, fill our rivers and quench the thirst of all living things. Come.”

She faced south and an image of the bright noonday sun came into her mind. “Mother of the Great Fire who is the spark that regenerates all living things. Come.”

She moved the knife to the west. “Come Mother who provides the abundance that feeds all your creatures.”

Finally Zabel turned back to the north where she had begun. “The sacred circle is now complete. Come Spirit of the Air, Earth, Fire and Water.”

Jnana placed the king’s ring on the altar, and she said, “Come to claim King Leo back into your womb of regeneration. Let all that was good and great in him return to the earth to bless your creations.”

It felt to Zabel every creature born that instant would have something of her father in it.

Jnana and Zabel joined hands over the altar and began to move around it, stamping their feet on the hard ground celebrating their connection to Her.

The torches began guttering. “We must leave,” Jnana said.

Zabel reversed the circle and released the spirits.

Jnana and Zabel emerged into the light of the moon and rode slowly home, each woman thinking of the future and what it would entail.

Chapter 7

The storm that seemed likely during her meeting with the bishop and her councillors had dissipated, the sky now dark and filled with stars. Queen Zabel sat pondering all her memories of the events before her father's death, still uncertain if her father had made an alliance with the Franks and pledged her hand in marriage. *The future is now.* She called for more tea and sent for Jnana.

"You have brought me from my evening meal. I'm an old woman in need of what comforts I can get," Jnana said as she entered the room.

Zabel ignored Jnana's attempt at levity, relating instead the details of her encounter with the bishop. "Father would never have wanted me to turn my power over to the Franks. He couldn't have."

"But, Zabel, you told me your father had a private conference with the two young men which he refused to let you attend. Could it be that a marriage between you and Raymond de Gisor was what they discussed?"

Zabel's eyes blazed. "Father would never have done such a thing without consulting me. He never forced me do anything. You know that."

The maid brought the tea, the aroma of mint mingling with the jasmine incense from the brass braziers.

Jnana answered Zabel in slow measured tones, as she always did when she wanted to quell the younger woman's anger. "I know. But you said he was distressed...that he thought he'd made some mistakes and planned to correct them."

Zabel rose and paced the tiled floor. "It's just..."she collapsed onto the divan. "I don't want to marry Raymond in twenty days as Bishop Scarfos demands. I want to rule Armenia alone. I want to make decisions, encourage people in the ancient ways when women owned their own land and chose who would father their children. When women didn't have to marry."

"It may be that people in power have fewer rights than you think."

Zabel glared at Jnana wondering if she had lost her only ally.

"Perhaps your father *did* think marriage was the best solution and died before he could tell you. Perhaps he had that meeting without you because he wanted to secure an agreement before he told you."

"Perhaps, perhaps, is that all you can say? I will not marry him." Zabel stood and paced the room again. "I have to think of a scheme to stop this lunacy. But, my mind is a blank. Jnana, you always know what to do. Suggest something."

The old woman sat staring at the fire, her brow furrowed, tracing the rim of her cup with her index finger. "There is someone who may see an alternative."

"Who?"

"Before the Church outlawed such activity, the ancient leaders would seek advice from a prophet, a seer."

"If they're outlawed, I would surely be unable to find one."

"Just because the Church outlaws something doesn't mean the people comply. What destiny holds is still of interest to many people."

"Do you know of someone?"

"There is a woman...her name is Mazora. She lives near the market, in the old town.   There are things she knows. She sees. Perhaps..."

Zabel stopped pacing. "I must see her. Can you arrange it?"

Waiting for the messenger to return was unbearable for Zabel. But she forced herself to sit staring at the fire in silence, a silence broken only by the continuous cooing of mourning doves. She reminded herself it was Jnana, always Jnana who was there for her. She recalled the night she had awoken, breathless, from the most important dream she had ever had. Jnana had rushed to her side.

"They killed our sacred deer," Zabel screamed.

"Zabel, I'm here."

Zabel blinked, rousing herself as Jnana's warm touch penetrated her dream state.

"What were you dreaming about?" Jnana asked.

"I was wearing a green suit of clothes. Carrying a long bow. I lived in an oak forest...happy among the animals. It was fall. The leaves had turned, the forces of

Nature called the buck to reproduce his kind and he entered the sacred grove to rut with the female. She was coy. It excited him. She ran, tail in the air, the buck in hot pursuit."

Zabel gasped for air; the words had been coming at a frenzied pace.

"Take a breath, Zabel. Calm down. What happened next?"

"I was in the sacred grove with the deer. It was filled with fig trees, all the leaves in the shape of the yoni. But someone had entered the grove and slaughtered the sacred animals. There was blood everywhere, soaking into the forest floor. Some of the deer were trying to stand but they were too injured. Their calls were horrifying.

I screamed at the Great Mother, "How could you let your beautiful creatures die?"

I hugged one of the injured to my chest. The deep brown eyes looked at me in disbelief. I wept uncontrollably. I shouted again, "We have tried to keep this grove a sanctuary. How could you let murderous strangers in here?"

"I felt alone, alone against the cruel forces in the world." I cried out again, "You, Great Mother, are silent. I cannot hear you speaking. For all that is Holy, tell me. Why is this happening? But always you are silent."

I hugged Jnana, sobbing. "What does it mean, what does it mean?"

Jnana rocked Zabel for a while in silence, her presence working its magic. "You have had a very portentous dream, Zabel. Sleep now and I promise I will explain it to you tomorrow."

Zabel remembered the dream had been *the* turning point in her life. Afterwards, she had made irrevocable decisions, had learned more about her family, become certain of her path. Until now.

Jnana appeared in the doorway. She joined Zabel on the divan and accepted the mint tea offered by the maid. "Mazora will see you tomorrow. She lives on the far side of the suq. A veil will be enough to conceal your identity as you walk past the shops. No one will expect the Queen to be alone and on foot."

Zabel barely slept, anxious to hear what Mazora would say. In the morning she dressed in a plain tunic and woolen wrap and covered her head with a heavy cotton veil, before she hurried from the palace.

On the main street she passed children flying a kite painted like a hawk. The wind tossed their hair as it whipped the colorful silk in wild circles above them. Zabel envied their joyful shrieks, longing for a return to the certainty of childhood when nothing was frightening as long as she had her father and Jnana. She would have been satisfied with a home, like the earthen hovels she passed. Zabel nodded to a small, rotund woman who was working a mixture of mud and straw with her feet to replace the clay that had fallen off the walls of the family's house. *None of these people fully understand that living a peaceful life depends on me.*

She crossed a road, near the entrance to the suq, the cities market. Sounds of braying camels announced their presence in the caravanserai courtyard as she passed. It was filled with the laughter of men unloading their goods; precious spices and fabrics from far-off lands. *The inn protects the travelers who bring these luxuries that fill the soul with joy. What hardship these men and their animals must endure on the silk routes so we can season our dinners, and caress our skin with delicate silks.*

Two women wearing brightly coloured shawls brushed past Zabel, their voices matching the tinkling of the silver bracelets on their wrists and ankles. Beads of every hue dangled from their necks. Zabel knew that these women were there to satisfy the lust of the caravan drivers who took their sexual pleasures as it pleased them. She pulled her wool wrap more closely around her shoulders and hurried along.

She came to the high brick walls that protected the suq, looking up to the storks that nested in rows over the arched entrance. *The superstitious among us believe these storks indicate one will receive a message. I hope to.*

She quickened her pace along the labyrinthine alleys crowded with women buying the purple eggplant, onions, and peas they carried home in wicker baskets. Oregano, mint, and basil mingled with the pungent scent of freshly ground spices as she passed each stall. She concentrated on Jnana's directions until she stood, at last, in front of a door displaying the carving of a moon held between the horns of a bull.

She took a deep breath and knocked. A woman with large round eyes and a full, sensuous mouth opened the door. She was not the wizened old woman Zabel had imagined a prophetess to be. Mazora was opulently dressed in a robe the color of the midnight sky. She bowed gracefully, and then moved aside, asking Zabel to enter.

"I have had word of your visit, Your Majesty. Welcome. I am Mazora. Come. We will have tea."

Zabel entered a room in which massive cedar beams supported a vaulted ceiling. Whitewashed walls were hung with richly colored tapestries, the gold threads reflecting light from many small oil lamps. The scent of jasmine filled the air as Zabel moved across the carpets.

"Please, sit," Mazora said. "It will take me a while to prepare the tea as I am not used to kitchen duties. I dismissed my maid as I was sure you would want privacy."

"Take your time. I'm in no hurry."

When Mazora left the room, Zabel was drawn to a large alabaster carving that filled a corner of the room. Each sign of the zodiac was placed in a circle around a central moon.

Mazora reappeared, setting a delicate cloth on the low table in front of a divan. "It's beautiful, isn't it?" she said. "It has been in my family for generations. According to the ancients, the zodiac was the Moon's grove. She passed through it each night."

Zabel gently ran her fingers over the smooth stone. "Oh," she said. Between Scorpio and Sagittarius was a carving of a woman holding her hands above her head and in each hand she held a writhing snake, "the thirteenth sign."

"I see you know of the sign now missing from the Zodiac."

"Yes, I do," Zabel admitted.

"That sign was present when all peoples lived in peace. It was a time of pleasure, of great fecundity. People honored the Great Mother. These stars disappeared from the zodiac when men decided military force and the laws they created were mightier than She. I await the time when they will see the error of their ways and cease senseless warfare."

"That is what I want also. It's why I've come." Zabel took her place on the divan.

"I'll get the tea."

Zabel leaned into the cushions and closed her eyes, letting the mystical ambience in the room permeate her being.

She remembered when she had first learned about the snake goddess. It was the morning after the dream where the sacred deer were slaughtered.

Jnana had wakened her before dawn.

"Get dressed, Zabel. And don't light any lamps. We don't want to wake anyone. Dress warmly, we will be on horseback."

Zabel had stumbled about in the dark, the last night of a waning moon. They passed through the kitchen and Jnana wrapped goat cheese and a loaf of bread in a cloth and stowed them in her saddlebag.

Outside, the Earth was cool. The perfume of spring hyacinth lingered in the air as they hurried along the stone path, the splash of the fountains in the garden concealing their footsteps. A night heron flew silently overhead, its long legs trailing.

"That's a good omen," Jnana said. They watched the bird disappear into the darkness. "The heron is a messenger from the spirit world," she continued. "You will be shown your path, which has been woven for you inside the whole of creation." Jnana turned into the stables. "That is, if you choose to find out."

Zabel was still shaken from the suffering of the deer in her dream. *I should tell her that I'm not ready to know my spirit's path. But here she is waking Lucas, the stable boy, to help us saddle the horses, instructing him to give the king the message that I've gone to help her with a birth and that we could possibly be away for three nights. I'll have to go.*

They left the city and headed north toward the distant hills, now visible in the dawn. After a couple of hours, Jnana pulled up her mount in a glade formed by birch trees in bud, unfolding with new life. Shafts of gauzy light warmed the still air. She indicated to Zabel to dismount, and they let the horses graze on the succulent new spring shoots. The two women sat on a fallen tree where tiny beetles silently turned the log to earth, the decaying wood pungent. Zabel took off her boots and pushed her toes into the damp, fecund soil.

Jnana unwrapped the bread and cheese, broke off a portion of each and made an offering to the Spirits of the Earth.

Zabel was tired. "Why did you have to wake me before dawn? I had a terrible sleep."

"I made a promise to your mother that when the time was right I would reveal things about her to you."

"Why have you not told me before? You know I want you to share every memory, every thought you have about her."

"Because your father does not want it."

A knot formed in Zabel's stomach.

"I must have your word that you will reveal to no one what I am about to tell you. Especially your father."

Zabel chewed a piece of bread slowly. "It is not my habit to conceal things from Father. We share everything."

Jnana made no attempt to persuade her, allowing Zabel time to decide.

"But, I will risk upsetting him in order to know more about my mother. I give you my word," Zabel said.

Jnana was silent for a few moments, gathering her thoughts. "Your mother was not Armenian."

Zabel frowned. "Then where was she from?"

"Her people are a local clan who have cultivated this land for eons...before the Armenians wrested it from us."

"'Us'?"

"Yes, I'm of the same tribe as your mother. I came to the palace with her not only as her maid, but also to be her friend."

"What are you saying? Am I not of royal blood?"

"Oh, that's not in question. Your father's blood makes you a royal Armenian. But while the Armenians are interlopers here, you are of the blood of this land."

"Why are you telling me this now?"

"Because of your dream. You dreamt of the sacred grove of the Great Mother. You see, your mother named you Zabel for a special reason. It means 'messenger of the Goddess' in our ancient tongue. She hoped your spirit would be called to be initiated in the ancient ways as she and I were." Jnana finished her bread and brushed the crumbs from her lap waiting for Zabel to speak.

"You have taught me the ways of the Great Mother all my life. I'm awed by Nature. I *am* a messenger of the Goddess. Why all this secrecy?"

"There's more you need to learn, to experience. But there are dangers. You must be sure it's what you want as we are surrounded by people who despise our ways."

"I read the Christian bible as father asked."

"Bishop Scarfos..." Jnana began.

Zabel's face colored and her eyes narrowed at the mention of the bishop's name. "I do not understand why Father tolerates that horrible man."

Jnana wrapped the remaining bread and cheese and put it back into the saddlebag. "There is much you have to learn. Suffice to say, if the bishop discovers you have accepted the Ancient Ways, he would make things difficult for your father."

"But the king is the most powerful man in Lesser Armenia."

Jnana stood and paced up and down, thinking. "I can see you will not be satisfied until you know the whole story." She returned to Zabel's side. "Bishop Scarfos wanted your father to marry a high-ranking Armenian woman to keep the blood pure. But the truth was it would have united the land and wealth of the two most powerful Armenian families. Your father agrees with this logic. It was how he was raised."

Zabel threw the remainder of her breakfast into the woods, her tongue too dry to chew. "Why did he not marry the other woman?"

"He met your mother. No one could resist her. She was a rare and elegant jewel. Your father was willing to risk everything to make her his wife. They were deeply in love."

"So that's why the bishop dislikes me so much."

"Your father understood that even though he defied the wishes of Bishop Scarfos, he had to serve Armenia. He made your mother promise to reject the ancient ways and accept the Christian faith. After he put you in my care, he made me promise, that I would not let you participate in our rites."

"But you broke your word. We've taught me the

Earth is holy."

"Zabel, we followers of the Great Mother have had this continuous dilemma throughout our long history. Like countless women before her, your mother agreed to join the religion of the ruling elite knowing her sacred oath could never be undone. We continued the rites in private. It was the only secret she kept from her husband."

"You have done your job well, Jnana. To me, everything *is* the body of the Goddess. What more do I need to know?"

"You need to be initiated. The Goddess has called you."

"How dangerous do you think this would be?"

"Christians believe that keeping the laws of the church guarantees them immortality, but never forget due to their fear of eternal damnation they will stop at nothing to protect their church and their beliefs."

"They were the ones in my dream who entered the sacred grove," Zabel said. "They killed the deer."

"Yes. They have forgotten the debt they owe to the Great Mother. They take it for granted they can kill an animal or plant to feed themselves, while forgetting they're eating a divine being. But most of all, they've abolished the understanding of the circle of birth, death and rebirth, and rejected it for a belief in an eternal life that is only attainable through their priests."

"But your herbal remedies and your midwifery. Why has Bishop Scarfos not forbidden these things?"

"As long as we attend his church, he lets us keep some of our traditions-- the rites of the seasons, the herbs we give to our sick. He believes the prattling of old women can do no harm.”

“Then he will not worry about me.”

“That’s where you’re wrong. One day you will be queen. You will be expected to lead the people by following the dictates of the priests. With Bishop Scarfos as their head, these priests use the fear of death to control people, and to fortify the state. Never underestimate the power he wields.”

“Then...I am two people.”

Jnana waited.

Zabel said, “To hear the voices of the wind and to see the Spirits in stone. These mean more to me than the scriptures I learned in church. A church that has little room for women, as you have pointed out. We should resist. Fight them.”

“We are not war-like people, Zabel. We deem it better to live our lives quietly, in the shadow of power and wealth. It makes no sense to force our insight onto others. We must wait until people are ready to see.”

Jnana looked uneasy.

“There is something else you’re not telling me.” Zabel said.

Jnana said nothing for a moment, needing time to control her emotions. “I wasn’t your mother’s maid, or her friend, Zabel.”

The grove grew silent. Waiting.

“I was her mother,” Jnana whispered.

The Earth released a sigh and the sounds of the woodland refilled the grove. The profound way Jnana cared for her now made sense. "You're my grandmother. That's why you want me to do this."

"Yes, you are my granddaughter," Jnana said, her voice cracking. "It has been my greatest joy to pass down our knowledge to you, a woman in my direct line of descent."

"Is there an initiation site?"

"Yes, but it's a full day's ride. If you want to go, you must decide quickly."

Zabel felt calm. Certain. She stood to tighten the cinch on the saddles. "We'll depart now."

They mounted and rode swiftly toward the mountains. When they drew closer, Jnana pointed out a feature Zabel had never noticed before.

"There. Do you see the peak with the cleft resembling the horns of the great auroch bulls that used to roam freely here on the plains of Anatolia? On the morning of the winter solstice, the sun rises, sending a shaft of light through that orb. The bull fertilizing the Great Mother's womb. All our initiations are held just below in a sacred cave. That's our destination."

Chapter 8

When the land began to rise from the river valley, the women branched off onto a narrow trail. Tall grasses made it harder to follow, but indicated it was seldom used. They climbed steadily, pausing at vantage points to see the valley now far below.

The woods grew thicker and the trail more precipitous. The horses, stumbled occasionally on loose rocks, sweating under their task. The women dismounted, deciding to lead the horses for the remainder of the journey. Zabel wiped her brow as she trudged upward, marveling at Jnana's stamina. By the position of the sun, she estimated they had been climbing for three hours.

Eventually the trail reached a plateau and they followed a stream flowing gently over granite rocks and red jasper pebbles smoothed by time. They stopped to give the horses a rest and a long drink. Zabel knelt and immersed her hands and wrists in the coolness. She wrung out a cloth for herself and one for Jnana to cool their necks as they resumed their climb.

They were rising to another world. The trees were smaller and more widely spaced, allowing the heat of the sun its full impact. The trail now turned from the stream and steepened again. Zabel stopped to catch her breath. She heard water moving over the rock bed in the distance. The horses whinnied, restless to drink again, but the two women pushed on.

After another hour they stopped and Jnana gave a sharp whistle. The thick brush in front of them parted. Two women nodded a welcome and guided them through. They returned the vegetation to its original position, covering any signs of the new trail that now parted the forest.

Presently they came to a clearing directly below the cleft in the mountain peak. Women in colorful robes moved about purposefully. A sprightly young girl dressed all in green took the horses, leading them to water and food.

"We were beginning to think you wouldn't arrive in time. The sun is about to set," said a woman with thick wavy hair who approached. Her broad smile lit her face in welcome.

Zabel remembered her as someone from the palace who always cheerfully performed her duties. "You're one of our kitchen maids." Her thick waist and ample bosom gave Zabel the feeling she would be smothered were the woman to embrace her.

"We are equals here," the woman said.

Zabel felt the prick of her reprimand.

The woman quickly added, "Ah, but you are new to us. You will learn our ways."

The clearing was a level area roughly the size of the cathedral rotunda at the palace, but instead of solid brick walls, pines that were heated by the sun, giving off a pungent scent, enclosed the space. It was a courtyard leading to the mouth of a cave, a triangular opening in the rock face. A spring gave forth its waters from a crevice adjacent to the opening. The rock face shimmered bright terra cotta in the setting sun, matching a campfire that crackled in the centre of the clearing.

Zabel was offered a white robe that slipped over her clothes. Jnana told Zabel to remove her boots. "In the sacred grove we allow the energy from the Great Mother to enter us from Her body." Then she tied a red sash about Zabel's waist, and donned her own robe, a deep purple, encircled with a silver girdle. "The colors indicate the levels of initiation. You will learn what they mean later," Jnana said.

How does she always know the question I am about to ask?

Zabel looked about the group of strangers and noted a few of the others were dressed as she was. She was handed an earthen jug filled with wine, the sacred intoxicant. She took a deep draught and passed it to the next in the circle that formed around the flames escaping from the fire pit, and lighting the faces.

A frame drum sounded. Then a sistrum, strung with metal discs, began sending its silvery overtones skyward. Zabel turned toward the last fingers of the setting sun where a figure resplendent in flowing, iridescent white now stood; a pure gold girdle that reflected the sun's rays like a molten mirror, held her bared breasts. From the girdle hung small brass discs that tinkled as she moved. The drum intensified, beating the rhythmic energy of life, its mystic sound the heartbeat of the Great Mother maintaining the order of the universe.

The priestess's rich dark hair was piled high on her head, covered with a cap on which rested a carved serpent's head. The hem of her skirt was embroidered with silver threads depicting the moon and stars. As she moved toward the circle the drumming increased in intensity.

"Move now, Zabel. Keep time to the rhythm of the drum," Jnana whispered.

Zabel watched as the drummer struck the taut skin with her bare hand. Some of the sounds were open, and deep, some high pitched, others soft, like the brushing of the wind at dusk.

In a clear strong voice the priestess said, "We are here, Oh Sacred One, to honor desire and union, the rhythm in all life that instigates creation, with the pounding of our feet, with the beat of the drum, we honor the rhythms that cause the womb of the female to contract, bringing forth life, here into your web of life."

Soon another drum sounded, then another, sending a force through Zabel's body, so powerful it filled her with elation. She moved and swayed as her feet beat the smooth earthen floor of the clearing, smooth from the countless number of women who had danced here together.

The great bonfire was reduced to intensely burning coals. The priestess raised her arms above her head in an evocative gesture to the night sky. In the darkness of the new moon, Zabel saw countless stars above the silhouette of the horned peak. The silken sleeves of the priestess' gown slid back revealing two silver amulets in the shape of a snake with gems for shimmering eyes, high on each arm. "Goddess, in the ancient days, when the darkness reached its zenith at the winter solstice, you appeared in the sky each year, holding a sacred serpent in each hand to mark the ascending and descending phases of the moon."

As she spoke two handmaidens brought forth a basket. From within it, the priestess pulled out a live snake, its silver skin glistening in the firelight. She held it aloft.

"Thou, Great Mother, fiery serpent, breathing fire and light upon your primordial waters. Thou are the long tail of mist moving and writhing to incubate cosmic matter." She gyrated as she wove her dance.

"Thou disappeared from the sky when the warriors came and triumphed with their sky gods. We long for your return. We wait for the society of violent men, for those greedy and lusting after power, to once again honor all of your creation. Use your healing fire to burn away the anger and fear that drives all hatred."

Zabel danced, moving and swaying, round and round the fire, at one with the energy. But, she wondered if the others realized that one day it would be she herself who would face the anger of violent men who wanted this land? Zabel pounded her feet harder, adding all her strength to the rhythm, a rhythm she hoped would keep her world in order.

Zabel felt Jnana take her hand and join it to that of another woman. Those in white robes with red sashes were being formed into a line. Still moving to the beat of the drum, they were led by the priestess to the cave entrance.

Once inside, they moved down a short passageway and formed a circle that became a spiral, descending into a pit. The leader held a torch aloft to light their way.

"We are entering through the yoni, into the womb of the Mother," she said. "We will arrive at the Source. The Sacred Spring. The Womb of Creation."

But as Zabel's turn came to enter the Earth, an enormous fear gripped her. *Run. Run, before all is lost. I won't make it out alive. I'm crazy for doing this. I am the princess of the royal household. I am powerful. I will be queen one day and will rule my country. This is blasphemous. I will burn in hell forever for being here with these people. They're trying to destroy me. I must run."*

She shook, stumbling but the hand holding hers

pulled her along. *Jnana has already taught me to love and revere the Great Mother. I don't need to be initiated.* Tears streamed down her cheeks.

She could hear others crying as they coiled their way to the bottom of the pit. *I must get out of here.*

Zabel turned, heading the way she'd come, pushing past those behind her.

It was then she heard a terrible thud. The light from the fire disappeared as a large boulder covered the entrance of the pit.

She could no longer hear the sound of the drums, just the intense beating of her own heart and her ragged breathing.

I am afraid, afraid of never seeing the light again, afraid of being alone. Forever. Dead. I'm trapped.

Zabel looked back. The group had stopped by the Sacred Spring and the torch was guttering. Soon it would be extinguished.

Fear coursed through her. She turned and hurried along the path taking her place with the others. The Earth was wet. Mud squished between her toes.

At least I'm not alone.

When the light from the torch died, the darkness was like nothing Zabel had ever experienced. It was so utterly black she had to touch her eyes to determine if the lids were open or closed.

The voice of the priestess, echoed off the walls, "You come from the Sacred Womb and to It you will one day return. You are here to be born again with this knowledge. Lie on Her Body. Breathe in the love of the Great Mother.

Breathe out your fear. Breathe. Breathe. Breathe.”

Zabel became aware of the stillness of the air. *The cosmic stillness, before the rhythm of life began.* With each deep breath she became calmer, matching the eternal calm. She let herself sink onto the moist Earth.

At last her mind became still. She could feel each grain of clay, each tiny stone beneath her body. *Her living body.* A different voice, echoed what she felt,

“This is my body. I am alive. I am the Great Mother.”

Mystic vapors rose from the Sacred Spring melding with the tears of joy now flowing down Zabel’s cheeks. *Safe. I feel safe. Loved.* She felt her body merge with that of the Force of Creation.

Jnana had always told her that knowing must be awakened, not taught. Now, she understood.

Zabel’s memory was interrupted by the sound of Mazora who returned with a tray containing two pear-shaped glass cups and a large brass pot with a long curving spout. “I’m sorry that took so long.”

“Please don’t worry,” Zabel said. “It gave me time to think about my first encounter with the snake goddess.”

Mazora lifted the pot and poured the steaming liquid. The pungent scent of fresh mint quickly filled the room. She handed Zabel a cup. “As you know, different peoples have their own name for the Great Mother. My people referred to her as Isis. But it makes no difference what we call Her. She allows me to see the destiny of people who come to me with reverence for Her. It is the only stipulation."

"I hope Isis will find me worthy, Mazora. You see, I am certain that if I do not take appropriate measures, my power to rule will be usurped."

Mazora was silent for a moment. "We shall begin. Do you have an object? Something that comes from the earth, something that you wear all the time that I can hold?"

Zabel pulled the obsidian knife from the folds of her girdle and handed it to Mazora. "I have not had it long, but I keep it with me always. It was my mother's."

Mazora closely examined the intertwined snakes on the handle. "It's beautiful." With the blade held firmly between her fingers, she closed her eyes and breathed deeply. "First I must tell you, the joy your mother experienced because you were born a woman, was boundless. She was certain, that through you, her line of women would continue the ways of the Earth. She died happy in this knowledge."

"But she knew nothing of how difficult it would be for me," Zabel cried. I'm in the middle, between my mother's way of being and the demands of my country. The threat of war is upon us and I can't reconcile how to lead my country and stay true to the ancient teachings."

"Destiny rarely leads us in a straight line," Mazora said. "We humans often think we see a path that is not ours. You must be patient. Your true path will reveal itself."

"I don't have time to be patient," Zabel blurted, instantly regretting her tone of voice.

But Mazora paid it no mind. "What I do see, is that you will make a journey to the town of Konya."

"That's in Rum, is it not? Do you know why?"

"There you must speak to the local Maulana who is of the Mohammedan faith. He is very wise and will reveal great truths...truths you will have trouble accepting." Mazora stared at Zabel as if she were making sure her message was being comprehended.

"You have discovered my nature, Mazora. I rarely accept advice."

"Remember, it is not I who sees these things, but Isis," Mazora said.

Zabel was grateful for Mazora's easy laugh.

"But," Mazora continued, "Something of great significance will happen on the journey. You must go. It is your destiny."

Zabel sat back, the cup warming her hands. *The dice have been rolled once again. Konya is many days from here along the caravan route. How can I keep such a journey from the bishop? He would surely object.* She closed her eyes and invited the power of the Goddess to enter her body. Then all was clear. She remembered the women at the caravanserai. *I will disguise myself as a camp follower, dress like the women I saw. Jnana will undoubtedly have an herb that will sedate any caravan driver who tries to share my bed.*

Chapter 9

In the grayness before dawn, Jnana helped Zabel dress. Layers of brightly colored cotton skirts, tinkling beads around her neck and silver bracelets on both ankles and wrists transformed Zabel before their eyes. Jnana painted dark kohl lines above and below her eyelashes.

"As you walk the sunlight will be reflected."

Finally she wrapped her granddaughter in a multicolored shawl with long tassels.

"No one will recognize you," she said. "It is a marvelous disguise, but still I worry. So much could happen. I'm not convinced you should go. The men you will be travelling with are like none like you have ever known."

"Perhaps, but the women I saw entering the caravanserai looked happy to be offering their bodies in exchange for food for themselves and their children if they have any." Zabel caught her grandmother's eye and raised her eyebrows, wanting to make her laugh. But the truth was she had no idea what the men would be like. The adventure was fraught with risk.

Jnana smiled briefly and again became serious.

“What do you suppose happens to those young women when they’re no longer sexually desired?” Jnana asked. “Remember this is not the ancient times when women chose the men who would father their children. Now children carry the father’s name. To rob us of our power, the Church has convinced us that to enjoy coupling with men is sinful. We can’t even own land.”

Zabel had listened to her grandmother complain bitterly about these issues many times. She was right, of course.

“And remember, Zabel, even though half of the Christian population are women, overall, they have accepted rule by men.” Jnana sighed heavily and brushed the hair from her forehead. “Perhaps after one has children, it is the easiest road.”

“But, I *do* have land and resources. Perhaps I should begin to change our society for the better. If one of the men in the caravan pleases me, I won’t use the potion you stayed up all night concocting. Perhaps I should just allow myself the pleasure I’ve overheard the kitchen maids talking about,” Zabel said, examining the dark liquid in the tiny bottle. A teasing smile twisted her lips as she tried once more to lighten her grandmother’s mood.

“You may jest, but I doubt that any of those men will satisfy the likes of you, Zabel, when you refuse to wed a knight.”

The day now cast a pink glow on the mud walls of the caravanserai as Zabel hurried through the large cedar doors. Inside, the scene was one of intense activity. Camels kneeling in the large courtyard bellowed as carpets to be traded in Konya were piled on their backs.

The excitement of creating the deception, coupled with her fear of being discovered, had made Zabel hungry. She leaned against a pillar, opened her string bag, and began to eat the dates Jnana had packed. She licked her fingers absentmindedly as she watched the herdsmen, turbaned and loosely gowned, barter kilims and knotted rugs for cooking oils and other items their families would need in the coming months. Zabel knew that any extra money these men garnered would be converted to jewelry that would be worn by their women. It was a convenient way to store the family's wealth as they followed their herds.

Everything these people need to weave carpets is available from the land: yarn from the sheep, camel hair for fine embroidery, streams to soak the fleece, plants for the dying and timber to make the frames for weaving. I envy them their ability to live so directly from the gifts of the Great Mother.

The bartering continued. Carpets were opened for inspection before being loaded onto the camels. Zabel noted one with bold, diamond-shaped medallions woven in bands. The natural gold color of camel hair marked the borders. Spiders, rams horns, all with sacred significance, filled the inner portion. Zabel imagined the weaver sitting on the Earth with a loom, working intricate designs, learned from a mother or grandmother. Each design was an expression of gratitude for the mystery that is life.

As Zabel finished the last piece of fruit, a commanding figure emerged from a doorway. As he moved she could see the body beneath his flowing robes was lean but muscular. He strode boldly, paying close attention to all the activities. Zabel breathed in sharply. *He must be the leader.*

The man gazed about the caravanserai, then satisfied that the trading was complete, he gave an order and the camels were brought to a standing position on legs that looked too slender to carry their burdens. Bells hanging from cords about their necks tinkled, adding to the cacophony of calls and whistles. The camels linked by ropes in twos and threes, were led through the massive double doors. The leader mounted a black Arabian whose nostrils flared as the horse and rider moved among the train urging the stragglers.

Outside the walls of the caravanserai, the rising sun created intricately shaped lilac shadows from the loaded camels and walkers as the caravan moved along. Zabel filed in behind a group of camp followers, careful not to talk to anyone.

One of the women pointed to a wiry-looking man with dark eyes and a sharp nose like a falcon's beak. "See that one leading the large bay camel? He wants to lie with me again tonight."

"But, I have heard the sword between his legs is but the size of a mouse," rejoined another. The women jabbed each other playfully.

"Hardly. He pays as well as he is endowed," said the first, clutching a large bag of coins that she removed from her robe.

Zabel knew nothing of their world, but the ribald nature of their conversation amused her as they wound their way out of the city and into the hills beyond.

After an hour Zabel was already weary. *What was I thinking? I can ride a horse for hours while playing polo, chase a stag in the forest, but I'm not used to walking. Every muscle begs me to stop.*

But she had to get to Konya. She struggled on, one

foot after the other over the dusty road. Presently, the sound of a tambourine, beating rhythmically, spread over the caravan. Soon her mind stilled, the fatigue forgotten. Glancing sideways, Zabel noted that the faces of the other girls had become serene, entranced. The entire caravan, even the animals, had become quiet as the road rose toward the mountains. *The drum of the Goddess is protecting those who tread on Her.*

When they stopped for the evening at a distant caravanserai, the moon stood alone in the darkening sky. After the camels were unloaded and couched in their pens, dinner was prepared and then the women and men paired up amidst sounds of music and laughter. *It seems that no one has noticed the chill upon the mountain air.* Zabel was mystified there was energy left for lustful pleasure, but concluded they were far more used to the journey than she. Her feet were burning, her leg muscles exhausted; she was weary to the bone and Konya was still seven days away.

She stole unobserved into the darkest corner of the camels' pens and nestled amongst the straw with her back warmed by one of the animals. She ignored the mucus adhering to its nostrils and rubbed the animal behind its ears like she did the palace cats. It closed its eyes, luxuriating in this unexpected attention, and Zabel could see the double row of lashes that protected its eyes during sandstorms.

She laid her head on the camel's neck and gazed into the night sky. An astonishing number of stars had burst forth to accompany the moon on her journey. She tried to see her fate written there, but could decipher nothing. Finally, overtaken by fatigue, she slept, enclosed by the night, her hand resting on the obsidian knife at her waist.

Something woke her.

Stillness had settled over the compound. Her hand tightened over the hilt of her knife.

She became aware of a presence.

A sure voice said, "What are you doing here? Are you so inept at pleasing men, that they've all rejected you?"

It was the caravan leader.

Zabel stared, unable to emit any sound.

He bent closer, shoving a small lantern at her face. Zabel instinctively covered her eyes with her hand, but still uttered no sound.

"Were you treated poorly?" he said, his voice softening. "I do not allow women to be beaten in my caravan. Speak, what are you doing here?"

His demeanor forbade concealment or deceit. Zabel decided he would catch her out in a lie. She had to tell him some version of the truth. She took a deep breath and looked directly into his eyes.

"I'm not who you think. My family has sent me on an important mission. If I'm found out, we will be ruined. Please let me continue to travel with you. I beg you, my family is depending on me."

Black eyes studied her intently. The leader of a caravan must be able to quickly judge character, she surmised, as a mistake could cost him his life. He straightened.

"How far are you going?"

Zabel relaxed. *He's accepted my explanation, even though he can have no idea that my family is an entire nation.*

"To Konya."

"And how long will you need to be in Konya?" he

asked, his voice taking on an amused tone.

Zabel was annoyed he found her plight frivolous, but she forced her anger down and answered him civilly. "Just one day."

He became serious. "We will be returning to Cilicia at that time so be sure to rejoin this caravan. Not all leaders are as respectful of lone women travelers as I am. I will watch over you, but see you do nothing unwise to make this difficult for me."

He left as abruptly as he came. Zabel fell asleep, relieved to be guarded by this decent and virile man.

A fresh morning breeze rose on the last day of the journey as the caravan descended from a low pass onto the fertile Konya plain. New lambs grazed on the fresh spring grass. They proceeded through a string of small villages until twin volcanoes appeared in the distance through the hazy light at sunset. Jnana had told her they were called the breasts of the Great Mother. Zabel had the uncanny feeling that she had been here before. But it was not possible. Then she recalled her recurring dream in which she lived near such mountains.

Did the volcanoes have something to do with her fate? She touched the knife at her waist wrought from their lava flow. In her dream the people traded such tools for black chunks of bitumen that were mined in far-off Jericho and for salt from the Dead Sea. On this plain the scythe-horned auroch bulls had roamed.

The dream always ended the same. Bands of warriors invaded her village to steal their sheep. Her mother lay dying at her feet, bleeding into the warm earth. Zabel would wake up screaming. It was the reason she hated war.

They arrived at the outskirts of the town with its minaret piercing the sky. She took a guest chamber inside the caravanserai. Now that the leader accepted her mission, it

 was unnecessary to continue her charade. She hurried to the public baths, needing to remove the dust of the journey before she took her evening meal.

Chapter 10

In the stillness of dawn, Zabel lay in the blissful state between waking and sleeping. A voice, spread over the city calling the faithful to prayer. Its longing stirred her soul, as if it were the very voice of Allah.

Mazora said there was a message here for me, a message I would have trouble accepting. Zabel pushed back the covers, planting her feet on the tiles, icy in the spring morning, speculating if the message had something to do with the Mohammedan faith.

Because the Maulana was the spiritual guide in the community as well as the councilor for the local sheik, she dressed in a simple cotton gown, covering her head with a matching scarf.

Jnana had arranged for a guide to lead her to the mosque. As Zabel entered the street, a young man who had been standing in the shade of a plane tree, approached her.

"I am Hussein. Are you the lady from Tarsus?"

They set off down the winding alleys as the carpet dealers and small embroidery shops were opening their doors to begin the business of the day. They turned into the spice market where barrels filled with red, orange, and ochre spices accosted her nose with their pungent aroma. Then they passed a kiosk emitting the perfume of the rose oil she liked to pour in her bath.

Although this market reminded her of Tarsus, the faces were not like those at home. They stared at her as if they knew she was an imposter, not a veiled slave girl who was bargaining for the daily needs of her household. She hurried to keep up with the blue-gowned Hussein.

She felt relieved as they emerged from the bustle of the market and stood before a mosque. Its shimmering green tiles reflected the morning light. Zabel looked up at the minaret that pointed to the heaven from which Mohammedans believed Allah ordered all life. It was from its crenellated balcony the booming voice had called the faithful to prayer.

They entered the adjoining courtyard. Walnut trees and mulberry bushes shaded tombs placed tightly together as if all were seeking holy ground. Her guide directed her to wash her hands and feet before entering the sacred space of his faith.

"In other mosques, you would not be able to sit in the main area," he stated. "They are reserved for men, but here, the dervishes welcome women."

Zabel adjusted her veil and entered a vast room lit from openings in the high walls that were adorned with multi-colored tiles. People sat on intricately woven carpets listening to a voice that filled the air with the clarity and assurance of a mountain stream.

Zabel moved further into the room and saw the speaker sat in a tiled niche, nestled against large cushions. He wore a scholar's turban above the coarse cotton robes of a peasant, his flowing beard moving with the passion of his verse. Light shone from his eyes reflecting a vision from another world.

His poetry spoke of life and love, the heart connecting all existence. At the end of a poem the holy man answered each questioner with the utmost respect. His answers always came in the form of another poem. As he spoke, men, in the centre of the room where the carpets had been removed, whirled in circles, pivoting around their right foot as if it were attached to the floor.

"They're Dervishes," explained Hussein. "While twirling they attain union with the Divine."

Zabel was transfixed by the supernatural aura that engulfed the great mosque, by the ecstasy on the faces of the men lost in a mystic trance, and seemingly lost to time.

"Shall I tell the Maulana you are ready for your audience?"

His voice startled her. *Ready. How does one become ready to meet a man such as this?*

Hussein approached the Maulana, bowed his head, and whispered into his ear. There was a nod of recognition and presently Zabel was led into an adjoining room. The walls and ceiling were covered with an exquisite script praising Allah. The design led upward to a dome inlaid with turquoise and white tiles forming a star pattern. She could find no beginning, no end to the pattern. *Infinity in physical form.* The apex of the dome had an opening that allowed the stars to reflect in a small pool directly below. *I have spent the entire day listening to the Maulana. His poetry speaks of the unutterable. But time and space are somehow visible in this pond.*

A slight breeze from the opening of the door interrupted her reverie. The Maulana stood before her.

"Are you here, Queen Zabel, for political advice, or is this a spiritual matter? I do advise the Sultan in both areas, as you undoubtedly know." She saw nothing but compassion in his eyes.

"Political advice, as I am not of the Mohammedan faith."

"It is my belief that God is unconcerned about our form of worship. But, be that as it may, what is the difficulty that has brought you to Konya?"

Not sure where to begin, Zabel paused for a moment before blurting out, "My kingdom of Lesser Armenia is a relatively new state, formed during some times of trouble when my people moved from south of the Caucasus Mountains."

"I know of your history. And it is widely accepted that your father, King Leo, was a great and wise ruler."

"He was," she said, startled that the Maulana knew of her father's death. The king had never mentioned the Maulana. "But," she continued, "Concerns he had for the fate of our kingdom were more than his heart could bear. I must deal with these problems now."

The Maulana seated himself on a cushioned divan and motioned for Zabel to sit across from him.

"Please continue."

"The Franks, many of whom pass through my lands on their way to the Holy War, are looking rather covetously at our position. Partly, because we are also Christians."

"I am aware of your problem. It seems that Emperor Alexis of Byzantium wrote to Pope Urban in Rome, asking for aid for the ongoing threats to his empire. Urban is from a noble French family. The Franks are experiencing an unusual time of peace both with their neighbors and inside the Frankish realm. Unfortunately, an entire generation of young warriors has no wars to fight at home and was fomenting trouble. Pope Urban cleverly determined that by sending these young knights to help Alexis, he can maintain peace at home and perhaps, if Byzantium becomes dependent on Western arms, the unity of Christendom will be restored."

"How do you know all this? You know more than my councilors."

"As I said, my position here is, political as well as spiritual." He smiled. "I have informers who tell me a reunited Christendom might well become a threat to the Sultanate here in Rum."

"Then, perhaps you are aware I am being forced into a marriage with a Frankish knight. My kingdom would become, in effect, a Crusader state." Zabel could no longer sit still, but began to pace the room.

The Maulana watched her silently for a few moments before he responded. "I have noticed these Franks are enamored with our civilized way of life. Many have adopted our dress, eat our local dishes, and they have discovered that Arab physicians are superior to those they've brought with them. Many knights have married Syrian women."

"Aren't these liaisons the very thing that give your sultan cause for alarm? We would have a much larger army if I were to marry a Frank."

"Your crusader states may find that they will maintain their lands not by going to war with additional armies, but by the disunity of your enemies."

"What do you mean?"

"Almost since the very inception of Islam we have divided ourselves into sects. We fight each other over who should be our rightful caliph and how we should worship

Allah. So, to many, Christians are not the most obnoxious enemies. Any Muslim leader strong enough to threaten the Christians is seen as an even greater threat to his Islamic neighbors." He sighed, straightening the cord of his caftan. "So we continue to fight among ourselves."

"If I could convince my counselors we faced no threat, I could avoid marrying the Frank."

"What is your objection to marrying him?"

"He is not one of us."

"He is a Christian."

"You don't understand." She stopped to consider how much she would reveal. "As you know, when our people were unable to stay in our homeland, we moved to Cilicia. There was a war and the Cilicians became our subjects. What you may not know is that my father married one of the Cilician women. My mother's ancestors inhabited that land from a time before the written word. They revere the Great Mother. The blood of both my parent's ancestors runs in my veins. But, this Frank knows nothing of the Ancient Ways. I will not risk his ignorance and endanger my mother's people."

"You could rule at his side. Advise him, as do our sultan's wives."

"I don't want to give advice." Her voice rose, matching the color on her cheeks. "I want to rule alone. It is what I was raised to do. Besides, he is a knight. He loves war. I abhor the idea of killing. I would rather surrender to your sultan than fight." Zabel sank back onto the Divan, sure she had said too much.

The Maulana sat for some moments as Zabel's breathing slowed. "Wait patiently and see what God has ordained for you. Your pearl," he said, "is you. For if it were merely a possession, it would be other than you."

"It is not my destiny to wait patiently. I have been given three weeks to wed the Frank or I will have my title revoked." Zabel jumped up. She glared at the seated Maulana. "He is a brute, a boor. I refuse to marry him."

"It seems to me you are idolizing your crown."

Anger surged through her.

"That is not the purpose of life," he continued. "We must work to obliterate such idolatry, to discipline ourselves, to achieve self-effacement in God. When we meet with God, our journey will be at an end."

"That may be true for the vast majority of people, but I was given a sacred trust. The crown of Little Armenia was placed on my head. I have a duty. My father wanted me to rule."

"You are talking about the human order of things. Are you sure it is what God wants? We reach God when we are in a thicket of calamity, a prison of catastrophe, and laugh lightheartedly. You see, there are some things too immense for one person to change. To be free of your burden, all that you need do is shift your consciousness. You can fight them, these dukes, and the bishop of your church, but they will likely throw you in prison to live out your days, or if you are lucky, kill you."

"Anger still rippled through her. That the Maulana remained calm infuriated her further. "Yes, yes. I have considered that possibility, but, as I have already stated, I don't want my people to suffer the ravages of war. It was my mother's wish that I never resort to the use of weapons. This is my dilemma."

"It is the history of this region, Queen Zabel, that when new rulers take over a land, the people continue on with their lives. It is only the ruling classes that are affected."

She pondered his statement for a moment, and decided to ignore it. Zabel was shouting now. "But, I am being made to do something against my will."

"You are a queen. Used to getting your way, but who are you under your title? Perhaps your anger is an attempt to cover your fear."

Zabel fumed. *This is not what I came to hear. Why am I listening to this man, holy or not?*   "I   am   not afraid."

"It is my job to advise the sultan, but my message is always a spiritual one. I cannot tell you how to be a queen. I can lead you to purify and sanctify your soul. For me, the all-consuming problem of human existence comes from the painful experience of imperfection and non-fulfillment that is caused by our alienation from God. What we are seeking can never be found through logic or reason, but by experiencing Him. How much pride do you have in being queen? Is your pride leading you from humility? Will your pride help or hinder your people in their search for answers to the problem of existence? True Life is the ecstasy that comes from experiencing the wonders of creation. From planting and harvesting."

"That is what my mother's people believe."

"In essence, none of our religious differences are important. Yours, mine, or that of the Franks. We are one soul emanating from God."

A knock came at the door and a turbaned clerk entered. The Maulana nodded as the clerk spoke quietly into his ear.

"I have been summoned by the sultan. I, too, have

my duties. Our discussion has come to an end." He stood,
bowing slightly to Zabel, turned, and left the room.

Chapter 11

The sound of muffled laughter floated across the courtyard as Zabel entered the caravanserai. The light from the moon, just one day from being full, flooded her room through an open window set high on the wall. She sat cross-legged on the straw mattress, pulled a rough wool blanket around her shoulders and closed her eyes. The moon's energy, the energy of the Great Mother, flowed into her, soothing her nerves. *I prefer the night. With the edges blurred, complex things seem simple.*

But the conversation with the Maulana haunted her. She wrestled with his words, trying to determine what had made her so angry, so defensive. She thought of the poems he had recited. *He is a mystic, unlike our bishop, but they are both men of the Book. They offer salvation, an ongoing life in their heaven, not the eternal cycle of the Great Mother. Why should I take his advice? Why is it such a bad thing to want to be queen? To want to protect my mother's people...to have a life unhindered by such men.* Zabel threw the blanket from her and paced up and down the small room. *The Maulana gave me no reason to avoid marrying Raymond. In fact, he seemed to approve of it.* She sat once more on the bed. *Mazora was right. I'm having a hard time accepting his advice.*

A soft knock at the door startled her.

"Who is it?" Zabel had been quite sure no one had seen her return, but she might still have to keep a lustful man at bay. She fumbled for the sedative Jnana had prepared for her.

"It is Siraj."

The caravan leader. She recognized his voice, so she slid the wooden bolt aside and pulled the door open.

"Wandering the streets at night can set a chill in the bones. Perhaps you would care for some tea to warm you before sleep. I have just put another log on the fire in the dining hall."

In the bright moonlight she could see a small scar running across his left eyebrow. *No doubt he has been in confrontations. The Silk Road is notorious for thieves and cutthroats.*

"I would enjoy that," Zabel replied, realizing she hadn't eaten all day.

She wrapped herself in her woolen cloak and followed Siraj. *I am alone with a man who believes I'm an ordinary woman, albeit on a secret mission. I must enjoy every moment. It may be the last time I ever taste such freedom.*

At the end of the covered passage, Siraj pushed open the plain wooden door to the dining hall. Two men playing backgammon in the far corner were arguing heatedly, one accusing the other of an illegal move. *They must spend many such hours during the countless nights they roam the earth, transporting their goods. They would be shocked to know this simple tunic conceals the finest silken undergarments they likely carried to my court.*

The argument abated and one of the men threw the dice. The clicking of the ivory pieces gave her the strange sensation that tonight her fate was being decided.

Siraj pulled two stout cedar chairs, their cushions discolored and worn, close to the blazing fire and invited her to sit.

"I am Persian," Siraj began. "Have you been to my country?"

"No, I have never been to the East. Your name, it means 'luminous light,' does it not?" Zabel asked, regretting this example of her learning that might lead to difficult questions.

"Yes, you are correct. But how is it that you speak my language if you have not traveled? Why do you need to know other tongues?"

"My father," Zabel hesitated for a moment, "gave me the education he would have given a son. I learned that in ancient times we Armenians paid tribute in horses to your Persian kings." *I need to change the subject.* "Ah..." she continued, "it must be very interesting to travel to different lands. Tell me about the places you've seen...what's it like leading a large caravan?"

"My journeys have taken me east, to Cathay and south to the far ends of Arabia, where I have traded with merchants sailing on great dhows from India, Java, and the Sudan. I've carried rare and expensive incense, frankincense and myrrh, used, as I'm sure you know, since ancient times to heal the body and perhaps, more importantly in sacred ceremonies so men can communicate with their gods."

A serving girl entered the room and Siraj ordered spiced tea and fruit.

"It is very dangerous," he continued. "The trade routes are rife with thieves. But it is extremely profitable. So profitable legend has it that the largest portion of King

Solomon's yearly income came from his spice merchants."

Listening to him, Zabel realized how confined her life had been. Coming to Konya was the only journey she had ever made. "Where will you take this caravan next?"

"On one of the most ancient routes. East through Tashkent then across the Pamir steppes where the pastures are so lush you can fatten a lamb in ten days. Then we will move steadily upward to mountains covered by glaciers."

Siraj paused, his eyes gazing into the distance. Zabel remained silent, unwilling to break the spell he had created.

"Then we reach a lake between two mountains from which a river flows where we can drink at last." His face became increasingly animated. "At that place, there are wild sheep with horns six palms in length. The air is so pure it will cure any malady. But then, the sand dunes of the great Gobi Desert begin." He looked at her and reddened slightly, seemingly aware that he had been talking for some time, lost in his memories.

"Heat, cold, thirst. It sounds like a life only the strongest could endure," Zabel said.

"The greater the privation, the greater the value of the goods. It's an odd quirk in people, don't you think?"

He has developed his philosophy from a close observation of people, not through books, as I have done. She felt herself drawn to him.

"You have seen all the great cities, too."

"Ah, yes. Damascus, fed by the snow waters of the great mountains; Aleppo, magnificent Aleppo, with its citadel rising from the dusty plain on sheer cliff walls, and many more. But it is the people and their ways that interest me most. Peasants who have tilled land that has been in their families for generations; these are the people I most respect. They have not forgotten to revere the land and all that lives from it. You see, in my travels, I have come to see it is Nature that provides."

Does this man share my understanding? "Really? Doesn't God provide?"

"I have had much time to contemplate man and his gods. Building empires by means of war is a way for men who shun humble trades to take what others have produced."

Zabel was suddenly uncomfortable. Her father had done exactly that. Normally she would object to such an accusation, but she decided to hold her tongue.

"I am ashamed to say the silk and spices I transport add to the decadence of empires. But, I did not invite you here to lecture you on the follies of the rich. I have seen the most beautiful mountains, waterfalls, silent deserts and forested valleys, but I have not seen a woman as lovely as you. You are more lovely than the fat tail of a sheep."

His good-humoured laugh, as rich as a Persian tapestry, rang throughout the room. She knew his comment was a sincere compliment from a man who knew the advantage of a strong and healthy animal. Zabel blushed but nodded her acceptance of his praise.

"You may think I am attempting to woo you with such flattery, but as leader of this caravan, I have no need of such foolishness. If I want you for the evening, you are obliged to be mine."

Zabel stared at him, wide-eyed. She had not expected their conversation to take this turn. *But, would it be such a terrible thing?*

"I can see I have startled you," he said.

Zabel was grateful he saw only her surprise. Before she could respond, Siraj said, "However, you are not a true camp follower, but a woman performing a heroic deed for her family. The camp rules do not apply in your case." His eyes twinkled in merriment as he mocked her. "Did you succeed in your mission?"

Zabel tried to decide whether to be angry or not, but managed to say, "I'm not sure yet."

They were interrupted by the serving girl, who set before them a tray with a pot of tea, a plate of fruit, and sweets. Zabel attempted to eat slowly but she was ravenous.

"Why would a father send his daughter on such a mission? Would it not have been better to send a son? A woman should be kept at home and protected."

"I do not have a brother, so the task has fallen to me. Besides, women are as capable as men. My country is led by Queen Zabel who rides and hunts as well as any man. She was trained to be a ruler."

"Such a woman is a fool."

Zabel flushed from the criticism but remained calm. "Why would you say such a thing?"

"If she wears a crown, men will want it. They will overpower her. As a woman she has no defense."

"She must have an army, trusted protectors."

"Protectors can be eliminated or they, too, may covet her power. It is not the way of the world. Women are delicate. Beautiful. They need the protection of strong men. They are not meant for war. I have been in battles. It is nothing for a woman to see, let alone participate in."

It always comes to this. To the same dilemma. I

don't want to go to war but I don't want to be protected either, or have my power usurped. "There must be something women are good for besides being ornamental." Zabel fingered a fig, finally feeling satiated. To her embarrassment, she had eaten nearly all the fruit.

"Women use the drum and flute to call their gods to protect men in battle. This is proper."

Zabel flushed with anger. "Sacred music is not to be abused as a tool of war."

"But, you must realize, men have taken over the spirit of music for the purposes of war. Christian soldiers have told me that when they come up against the Saracens in battle, the sound of their trumpets, drums, cymbals and pipes are more frightening than the Saracen's famous swords."

"Surely the Franks wouldn't be frightened by the mere sound of musical instruments. They are fierce warriors." Zabel remembered the stories Raymond and Guy had told about some of their battles. *But perhaps they did not tell me the complete tale.*

"The Crusaders are aware that musical instruments are used to excite the fighting spirit and increase courage. The more violent the clamour; the more bold the men. But I agree with you. It is a terrible sacrilege to turn a sound intended to inspire awe into an agency of death, rape and pillage. We must honour women and their connection to Nature. The battlefield is no place for them."

At first Zabel was elated that Siraj held ideas similar to her own, but became depressed as the validity of his observations became clearer; the idea of war frightened her even more. She had never defended herself against aggression, wondering under what circumstances it would be necessary. "There must be times when women have to defend themselves, are there not?"

"It is a sad state of affairs that women try, but usually fail. Men are brutes. They like to wield a fearsome lance and feel a sword penetrate an enemy's body, cut out a tongue with a sharpened knife or hold it at the throat of a woman while they rape her and turn anyone left standing after a battle into a slave. You must understand; the sharp edge of a blade erases any sense of impotence in men. Look at me. I have escaped death many times, like a cat with nine lives. I have seen brutality and have been brutal in turn. To witness such things, let alone perform them...you could not do it."

Zabel felt a chill go through her. She rose with her back to the fire. No doubt, a man of his strength could defend himself. His very presence charged the room with energy. She felt it. He gave her the same message that the Maulana had given her, but in much more graphic detail. Her palms were sweating.

Siraj picked up his glass of tea and sipped. *He seems calm. Has he noticed the effect his words have had? Perhaps he upset me on purpose.* Zabel stared at his hands. His fingers were strong but lean. *How many men has he killed with those hands? But I wonder what it would feel like to have them caressing my body.* She trembled, shocked at the lustful nature of her thoughts. *Undoubtedly he has lain with many women who have been stirred by the animal nature he evokes. But a man such as this is likely so sure of himself he can focus on the woman beneath him, take the necessary time to give her slow and intimate pleasure.*

Zabel inhaled deeply to calm herself. *Could it be the talk of war that aroused me?* She now had doubts about everything she believed, as well as about herself. The dream in which her mother was killed came back to her; its horror always caused her to awaken screaming. But if Siraj's description of war had aroused her, had she just had a glimpse of the pleasure that war brings?

She was disgusted by her thoughts, so she forced herself to visualize her dead mother lying on the ground in a pool of blood. The idea of achieving pleasure from violence was evil. She took another steadying breath. *Your revulsion must point to an answer, the one you have come all this way to realize. Be calm, Zabel. A solution is right here.*

Then, in the stillness of her mind, as if she had walked through a cleansing fire, the fog had burned away. It was stunningly clear. She would marry the Frank as Bishop Scarfos insisted. If there was to be a war, Raymond could lead their troops. Yes, she would marry him, but she would choose the father of the royal heir as the women of the Ancient Ways had. There were many days while the caravan returned home for Siraj to sire her child.

Zabel's confidence rose, and her voice, from deep in her chest, sounded soft and sultry. "I must go now."

Siraj slowly placed his glass on the table, keeping his eyes on her face. "I will take you."

He pulled open the heavy door and waited while Zabel walked into the cool night.

Men may use brute force to get their way, but woman have a force more subtle and at least as powerful.

They walked without talking past peach trees in bud, anticipating the fruit of autumn. *It's a good omen.*

When they reached her room Siraj stood blocking the door. The night wind whispered its encouragement as his eyes sought her permission. His kiss was both hunger and control as she had imagined. Siraj pushed the door and pulled her after him.

Chapter 12

Zabel woke to orange light filtering through the early morning mist. Siraj had crept silently out of her room before dawn. She had heard him, but happy within her own thoughts, she pretended to sleep. Lying naked with him, discovering his body and above all, allowing him to give her pleasure that she had never before experienced, had been completely natural, joyous.

She was hungry but preferred not to join the camp to break her fast. She remembered there was a hard-boiled egg in her string bag, and found it lying beneath the gown Siraj had removed only hours before.

Zabel cracked the egg, peeled it, and extracted the yolk intact. She placed it on her tongue, rolling it about her mouth until it began to dissolve into a thick paste. Her body still tingled from the night's pleasure.

"Your skin is as smooth as the silk you are wearing," Siraj had said as his hands moved over her naked body and awakened a delicious tingling sensation both relaxing and exciting.

She dressed hurriedly. There would be just enough time for her to indulge in the public baths before the caravan left, if she wasted no more time.

She was not looking forward to the day's long walk but she took her place with the other women.   As the caravan proceeded back over the Konya plain, she imagined the massive Auroch bulls, the lusty consorts of the Great Mother, as legend had it. Zabel worried a single night of lovemaking with Siraj, though a man as virile as those great beasts, would not ensure she was with child. Would he want her again?

"So our leader has picked you as his woman for this journey," a voice said as a thin brown arm encircled her waist. The other women giggled behind their veils.

Zabel was unable to think of an excuse for Siraj's presence in her room. "I, ah," she stuttered. *How do they know? No one had seemed awake.*

Ignoring Zabel's embarrassment the woman continued, "When you've worked at this trade as long as some of us, you know the walls have ears. Nothing is secret."

Zabel blushed, thankful for her veil. But had they discovered her identity? She must keep that secret until she returned to the palace.

"Siraj will come to give you a camel to ride. It is his custom. Those who lie with him are always far too relaxed to walk." They were making sport of her; their laughter meant she'd been accepted as one of them.

At that moment Siraj rode up, a film of dust filling the air with tiny motes of light that danced in the morning sun.

Muffled giggles erupted behind the veils. "You see. He's here to get you."

Without saying a word Siraj bent down from his

horse and swept Zabel up in his powerful arms.

"Your camel, the one you slept with on the journey here, has been missing you," Siraj said. Effortlessly he held her to him and set her neatly on the back of the camel that snorted its welcome.

Zabel looked over her shoulder at the women. They waved and giggled, clicking their tongues. *I've made some friends. They're not jealous. I guess they take life as it comes. And with a sense of humour.*

From her new vantage point, Zabel observed Siraj at his work. He was masterful with the animals. Camels could be obstinate, but a word or a touch from Siraj had them moving as he wished. Her own body had reacted in much the same way. She recalled his hands and his mouth on her, his warm breath on her neck.

As day ended, the caravan stopped in the open countryside and set up camp. The camel drivers unloaded the animals, massaging each hump by noisily flapping a blanket on its hair, and led them to graze on the new spring grass before securing them for the night.

Copper pots were affixed above the flames of cooking fires. Zabel's new friends were helping with the food preparation so she moved among them and was given the task of cutting garlic. Soon the savory aroma of whitefish and mushrooms purchased in the last market town filled the air.

Dusk descended into darkness. The sound of easy laughter and quiet conversation permeated the warm night air as tin plates were heaped with food. The poignant sound of a reed flute, played sensuously, melded with the soft braying of camels. As the coupling began, Zabel sat against her camel, welcoming its warmth against the cool night breeze. She had lost sight of Siraj who made his way about the caravan ensuring all was well for the night.

She felt uneasy, uncertain about waiting to be chosen. Her life of privilege ensured her needs were always met. Waiting was new. Her irritation rose, but added to it was a sexually charged hunger, heightening her senses.

Zabel picked up a smooth stone and pressed its coolness to her hot cheeks. The caravan rested where the mountain flattened into an alpine meadow. As the darkness deepened, she forced herself to concentrate on the canopy of luminous stars. In his long journeys through the desert, Siraj would use these constellations to set his course in the trackless sands.

She thought back to the night of her initiation, the night that confirmed her relationship to the Great Mother and to the cosmos that swirled above Her. *Siraj has achieved the same reverence in his own way, wandering, surrounded by the Earth's abundance under the same night sky.* This thought brought her peace.

Zabel sat up, wrapping herself in her coarse blanket. The camel lifted its head, so she rubbed behind his ears, reassuring the beast she would stay. But her anxiety returned along with the anger she had stifled earlier. She must conceive a child. Then her thoughts turned to the idea of original sin she'd learned in the cathedral in Tarsus, kneeling with the congregation as the voice of Bishop Scarfos broke over their bowed heads. He admonished his flock about Eve's guilt, about the shame of human coupling. But last night had confirmed for Zabel these teachings were false.

Footsteps disturbed her contemplation. Siraj's intense eyes gazed at her from under his headdress. "Are you cold? You're a long way from the fire. I humbly apologize for my neglect," he said in his formal way.

She was surprised all vestiges of irritation

disappeared the moment she heard his voice. "The beast is warm and I have been absorbed in my thoughts. You have much to do." She admonished herself for this show of understanding for a man who took any woman he pleased. That thought aroused a feeling of jealousy in her, anger she wished to hide. She forced herself to feign indifference.

"My days are often long," Siraj said. "But my work brings me here, out of the city." He waved his arm to encompass the firmament. "Inside walls, I am like a caged tiger. Here beneath the night sky I am at peace."

"Tomorrow we traverse the limestone ridges on the slope of this great mountain on our way to the Cilician Pass, the Gates, as they are called. The people who control this pass dominate trade between Asia and the West. Ah, but why am I telling you this? You are Armenian."

Fear of discovery gripped Zabel again. Her mind raced to find an alternate subject on which to converse. "These mountains, the Taurus Mountains are the second sign of the Zodiac. Are you familiar with astrology?'

"Yes, of course. The bull. The Zodiac is my companion, moving with the seasons with each succeeding year."

Zabel surrendered, unable to remain offended. His sensibility to the natural world cancelled any feelings she had of punishing him for making her wait.

Siraj continued, "The great Greek god, Zeus, assumed the form of a bull to abduct Hera." He paused for a moment to be sure he had her attention. "Legend has it that it was on this mountain that Zeus was abandoned as a small child."

"I have heard that also."

"I always make my quarters in one of these caves." He looked intently at her. "You would do me the greatest honor to lie with me there tonight. I have made a room fit for a princess. Come, you will see.”

The word 'princess' made her body tighten with apprehension. Had he guessed her identity?

She had no time to object. Siraj had taken her hand and was leading her through the small scrubby underbrush, away from the camp and up a gently sloping embankment.

A vein of red jasper marked the opening to the cave he had chosen. Overhead, the waxing moon had risen. *It is at such a time that Jnana plants the seeds in her garden.* Zabel's heart beat faster with desire and the thought of his seed impregnating her.

He led her into a large cavernous space filled with flickering oil lights scented with sweet jasmine. Excitement rose within her. He had prepared a mystical place in the womb of the Great Mother. Still holding her hand, Siraj led her to a straw mattress covered with silken sheets.

The Oracle said I would discover my destiny on this journey. I know now it is to be a line of women begun by Siraj and me who both revere Mother Earth. This bloodline will rule Little Armenia.

Siraj swept her into his arms and laid her on the bed. “You are like a graceful gazelle,” he said, as he softly covered her mouth with his own.

His appetite for her was unbounded. Zabel responded with equal passion, savoring this time with Siraj who would soon disappear forever like a mirage in the desert.

The oil lamps had long since burned out. Siraj and Zabel lay in the dark, their passion satiated yet savoring the intimacy that seemed to stretch to the far corners of the universe. She wanted to be fully known by him so she said, "I am Queen Zabel."

"I know."

She was shocked. "How?"

"Your grandmother came to see me before you joined the caravan."

Zabel was silent.

"You don't' think she would have let you embark on such a dangerous journey without making sure I could be entrusted to protect you, do you?"

Part of her was angry that Jnana would do such a thing without confiding in her, but she wasn't entirely surprised. Then the thought came into her mind that Siraj had known her identity when he first lay with her. She felt her anger flare, feeling betrayed by his dishonesty. Then another thought followed. *He knew and he still risked intimacy with me. As Queen Zabel I can have him arrested as soon as we re-enter Armenia. He knows that, too.* Obviously, he wanted her regardless of the risk, and that thought thrilled her. He must have felt assured their passion was mutual, and she would do him no harm.

She slept in a contentment she had never known, listening to his breathing as she pressed herself against the warmth of his skin.

She awoke to the light of a single lamp. Siraj was gone. Zabel dressed and moved towards the mouth of the cave. The pink of a new dawn appeared on the horizon lighting the camp below. Siraj sat meditating in the meadow adrift with alpine flowers in bloom. A host of yellow butterflies hovered about him.

Chapter 13

As they approached the mountain pass, piles of jagged granite jutted above the tree line. Zabel had been too preoccupied on the forward journey to notice the majesty of the place. But now her senses were alive as never before. Jnana told her that all women knew intuitively when the womb had been quickened. Light breezes whispered confirmation of her thoughts as birds flitted from branch to branch intent on their own mating. Zabel studied Siraj tend the caravan, wanting to absorb all she could of him before he was gone from her life.

"Tell me about this Buddhism you believe in," she said as he rejoined her.
"It is not a belief," he began in his deliberate way, "but a way of being."
"What do you mean?"

"It's about being at peace." He paused. "I have seen war and its aftermath. Any god that sanctions war is not worth following."

"Peace. A worthy ambition, but surely even in the isolated mountain villages of Cathay there are men of violence."

He was silent. When at last he spoke his voice as still and pure as the remote peaks that surrounded them. "You are right to question me. All I can tell you is what I have witnessed. It seems to me Buddhists are above day-to-day emotion. Even if violence does occur, their first reaction to an enemy is compassion."

"That is impossible. No man would behave that way."

"I have seen it. Because of years of meditation practice, it is natural for their minds to become still. It is like walking for years in the desert vastness." He looked at her to ensure she was following his train of thought before he continued. "The dunes shift, the road is never the same, but the way...it is how the Orientals refer to being in rhythm with nature, when one is aware of it, it is...the way. When the mind is still, the emotions are stilled. Then there is peace."

Zabel thought about the political reality of her life. Each step her camel took brought her closer to the possibility of a battle to be waged for control of this very pass. The Turks, the Arabs, the Byzantines, none practiced Buddhism. They would fight her people to the death if they were ordered to. The soldiers in her armies would fight to protect their land. "Have you never had thieves who threatened your caravan, stole your goods, injured your friends? Would not any compassion you felt for the attackers quickly turn to hate?"

Siraj laughed his warm, full laugh. "You are determined to find my human weakness. But you are right. My instincts are like those of any man. I have been pushed to defend what I consider mine. But, what I learned from the Buddhists is not to fight from anger or fear. If I first discard personal emotion, then whatever happens will not bring me misery."

"I don't fully understand what you mean. I want my possessions. After all, I have a right to them."

"To the Buddhist, your attitude is one of ignorance."

Zabel sat indignantly on her camel. "Ignorance. I am a well-educated woman, Siraj. My father made sure that I was taught in astronomy, mathematics, music and philosophy. I speak many languages. I hardly think I could be accused of being ignorant."

"Do not be upset, little one. I am not talking about knowledge. I have no doubt you are wise in the ways of civilization, but you are ignorant of your relationship with the universe.

"In the East, it is understood that an unknowable force, what we call God, made the cosmos by dividing itself in two, and from these two, begat all things. Therefore, everything is part of God. In your tradition, God created heaven and earth from nothing. You are not one with your God, but, instead, are always looking for ways to get back to His presence. To the Buddhist, everything *is* God: the mountains, the sea and all things that live and grow. The task is not to forget this. You see, when you remember, it makes no difference who possesses what."

Zabel was about to tell him she was not a Christian as he assumed, when he continued, "But we can not speak further. We are nearing the customs gate. You must walk now."

She relinquished the camel and stood silently as the caravan proceeded past her. When the cook and his helpers walked by she stepped in amongst them. She removed her shoes and dropped them by the side of the trail in case she should be searched. Soft leather shoes would raise a suspicion with the guards who may be looking for her if Bishop Scarfos had discovered her absence. When she married Raymond, she wanted no one to question the child she bore was other than her husband's, suspicion that might arise if it were learned she had left the country. With a gasp, she realized Siraj would never know she carried his child;

never know his child would be the next ruler of Lesser Armenia.

The pace slowed as the guards inspected the loaded camels, which snorted and hissed at this interruption that produced no food or drink. When it was her turn, Zabel humbly averted her eyes to the ground in front of her. She knew these young men were on duty for weeks at a time. A warm woman to nestle with in the guard's tent would be a welcome respite. She was poked and prodded, and then waved forward.

She passed Siraj, this solitary man, as he sat observing the guards, ever vigilant. She had never asked him if he had a wife and children somewhere or perhaps several children sprinkled along the Spice Road like precious jewels. *Fugitive, fleeting, transient. Siraj, you're like the clouds forming overhead, and then, gone.*

As the caravan made its descent from the high pass, they walked beside an increasing number of trees all now budding with new life. He feet squished into the trail made muddy from a spring shower that had passed earlier in the day. They followed a swiftly moving stream as it rushed down the mountain. Zabel felt these same forces pushing her to her life below in Armenia.

At twilight they neared Tarsus, a shiny quartz moon lighting the way. Siraj would leave her here and continue his journey east. Should she say good-bye or just leave?

In the shadow of the suq walls she felt a strong arm circle her waist and lift her. "Here we must part, little one." She saw the muscles in Siraj's jaw work, holding back emotion. "Know that if you were not queen, if you had not the responsibility for your people on your shoulders, I would take you with me." He shifted and straightened himself, before continuing, "You are a splendid woman, Zabel."

It was the first time he had used her name. She loved the way it sounded on his tongue, deep and wrought with meaning.

"Each night when I lie in camp and Venus comes into the night sky, I will think of you, remember holding you," he said. And with that Siraj let her slip back to the earth. The caravan entered the medina and Zabel made her way to the palace.

Chapter 14

Zabel summoned Bishop Scarfos. She remembered the mistake she had made after her father's death, the humiliation of defending herself in his office. This time she sat on the carved wooden throne with the jeweled crown on her head when he entered. A deep crimson robe, lined with ermine fur to ward off the cool spring air and gold rings shining from her fingers left no doubt she was queen.

"Welcome, Bishop."

"My Lady," the Bishop said as he bowed to her. "You sent for me, I presume, to inform me of your decision regarding the Frank."

Zabel enjoyed gazing down on him from the raised dais. There was no need to rush. He could await her pleasure.

He shuffled his weight from one foot to the other. Then his voice rose with annoyance. "If it pleases my Lady, I should like to know your decision."

She remained silent, fingering the ruby that hung on a heavy gold chain about her neck, and then spoke. "I have considered the risks my country faces. Many nations covet the revenue we acquire from the Cilician Gates. You have advised me, for that reason alone, we face imminent attack. I, as sovereign, have a duty to protect my people. I have decided, therefore, it would greatly enhance the military power of our country, if we made an alliance with the Christian Franks.”

“I know, my lady. That is our proposal,” the bishop began.

“You know nothing of how I arrived at my decision. You will speak no more of a proposal *you* made.”

The Bishop bowed to her, and remained silent.

“I order you to arrange a marriage between the Frank, Raymond de Gisor, and myself. For my hand in marriage, he will pledge fifteen thousand knights and fighting men to the army of Armenia. He must reply by this time tomorrow. If he declines, he and his army must leave Armenia at once. If he accepts, the wedding, including the crowning of Raymond as king, will be three days hence.”

Bishop Scarfos passed his tongue over dry lips before he spoke. “As you wish. And if it pleases your Highness, I think you’ve made a very wise decision.”

She dismissed him with a wave of her hand. “Don’t waste my time with flattery, bishop.”

As the door closed behind him, Zabel breathed a sigh of relief. She had maintained control of the interview. No doubt she would need to do so again in the future.

She found her grandmother sitting in front of a hearty fire, lost in contemplation. Zabel asked the maid to pour tea from the samovar that steamed on a side table, then sat across from Jnana, the wooden table holding the chessboard between them. “Jnana, what troubles you?”

"I was thinking of the father of your child."

"Yes."

Jnana put her tea on the table and looked up at Zabel. "Was it the wisest of choices?"

Zabel had learned strategy, playing chess with her father, and was certain her decision had been sound. Her eyes were alight with agitation. "You taught me that women in the ancient times chose the men who would father their children. I'm old enough and powerful enough to make such a choice. Besides, you've met Siraj. How could you question me on this?" A look of smug satisfaction spread across Zabel's face.

"I'll admit to his manliness, but our society is not as it used to be when women owned the land and there was no need for marriage. We must hope the Frank will follow through with the alliance."

With an irritated wave of her hand, Zabel said, "Bishop Scarfos is arranging that. Our concern is to insure everyone believes I am a virgin."

"I'm confident we can achieve that. But something else is troubling me. A war may come and Raymond will fight it, but after the battles are but a memory, can you lie with him for the rest of your life? If he is abhorrent to you, each night will seem an eternity."

"Siraj was like a dream," Zabel began. "He is a philosopher, a poet, a man of high spiritual attainment. He awakened a passion I never expect Raymond to fill. But...I have a duty to Armenia. I believe Raymond to be a sensitive man. We will teach him to bathe and to eat his food politely. It will never be like it was with Siraj but I will learn to love this man." She paused. "This man who will be my king. Only you and I know the child I carry was chosen in the way of the ancient queens. It is enough."

Jnana took a sip of tea. "The old women believe a child born from an unstoppable passion, will be a most vigorous person. A girl, I hope. To carry on our line."

Zabel reached over and pressed Jnana's hand. "We have much to teach this child. This time we'll do it together as it should have been with you and my mother."

Chapter 15

Zabel sat at the window, in the darkness before dawn. She pulled open the wooden shutter and the scent of apple blossoms filled her chamber. According to the Church, darkness was chaos, the nothingness before creation, but not to her. She felt oneness with the Great Mother, the omphalos from which Her creations were birthed and to which they returned at the cycle's end. As the sky lightened, it was as if she were watching the mountains in the distance being created, as they became visible objects.

"Wake up, Jnana. I must get ready."

The old woman brushed the sleep from her eyes. Zabel's hair had fallen loose from its braid, large curls caressing her shoulders. Jnana took Zabel's hands in hers and pressed them to her cheeks, feeling their warmth. "Your wedding day. I have told the maid to leave us. I want you to myself. The last morning before you belong to another."

"I will always belong to you. How can you say such a thing?"

"I know you have chosen Raymond for reasons of state, but I also know *you*. You said you will learn to love this man, but I believe you *want* to be in love with him, to have the complete intimacy possible between a man and a woman. That intimacy will come from forsaking all others as you are about to vow.”

Zabel wondered if Jnana saw the doubt on her face.

“Come, we will talk while you bathe.”

Jnana sprinkled jasmine and myrrh into the steaming water. Zabel’s skin reddened as she immersed her body into the marble tub, hugging her knees while Jnana rubbed her back with a sea sponge.

“I wonder how Raymond feels about the bath being forced on him at this moment?” Zabel asked. They giggled together. “He had better be agreeable. I’ll not happily share my bed with a man who stinks of the sweat he’s accumulated over who knows how long.”

Jnana had placed satin covers beside the sleeping platform that would make up the bridal bed. Exquisite animal shapes: stags, gazelles, bulls, goats, and between them clusters of three pomegranates, were embroidered along the border in gold thread.

“Such luxury will be new to Raymond. He told me they have no running water or sewers to take away the filth. Can you imagine such a primitive place?” Zabel eased her back into the water. “Perhaps he’ll be offended he’s being asked to partake in our customs. He’s a man, after all. With a man’s pride.”

“When he knows it’s required in order to share your bed,” Jnana said, “He will be only too eager to do what pleases you.”

Zabel’s face turned serious.

“You said this marriage is what you wanted. Have you changed your mind?” Jnana asked.

"This child, this seed growing in me, *is* Siraj. The only part of him I have." A smile returned to her face. "But it's a sweet solution, like Russian honey from the hive, don't you agree?"

"What seems sweet at first can become bitter as it sits on the tongue. It is not wise to think you have solved all your problems with this wedding."

"Perhaps I haven't. But I've solved an immediate one. Fate has led me here. I must follow this path."

"You know life is a great circle that returns to itself."

Zabel frowned.

"But, we have become too serious. It's time for you to dress."

Zabel covered herself with a pink silk robe and relaxed onto the divan, feeling the warmth from the fire blazing in the hearth. Jnana sat on a small stool and painted intricate designs on Zabel's hands and feet with henna and outlined her eyes with kohl. She oiled and plaited Zabel's hair into bridal braids. Lastly, Zabel stepped into the gown she designed for herself.

Jnana fastened the long row of pearl buttons as coins jingled from the ends of several layers of the finest silk skirts. She clasped a gold bracelet high on each of Zabel's arms and secured the long veil with a narrow embroidered band, over which Zabel placed her crown.

"You're beautiful, Zabel. Look in the glass." Jnana's eyes moistened from the intense feeling of love she felt.

"Just one more thing," Zabel said. "Affix this peacock feather into the head band."

"The eye of the Great Mother."

Zabel nodded. "I wanted to be married outside where we could call the forces of Nature to surround us, but Bishop Scarfos mistakenly thinks the cathedral is the only sacred space. With this feather the Great Mother will be with me."

Six strong footmen lowered the takhteravan that was waiting in the courtyard of the palace. Jnana helped Zabel into the sitting compartment, leaning in to arrange the gown on cushions edged with beads of gold. She closed the curtains so only a shadow would be visible from the street as Zabel passed.

The square in front of the cathedral was filled with Zabel's subjects waving boughs of apple blossoms to ensure the fertility of her womb. They will be gratified on that account, Zabel thought, as she stepped from the litter.

Candles flickered through the haze of incense as Zabel approached the altar. She was pleased to see Raymond wearing the clothes she'd had made for him. He looked like a Turkish pasha with the turned up points of his leather slippers. His hair was freshly washed and his face clean-shaven. Instead of his coarse wool tunic and leather breeches he was resplendent in a red and green striped silk caftan and a cloak of deep purple. Zabel stifled a sob as she recognized the red silk coronation mantel that her father had worn. On the back, a date palm embroidered in gold signified the stalwart nature of the king who would nurture his subjects with the fruits of the land. Two lions were embroidered on the front. The king must possess the strength of a lion to protect his people. *I will ensure he possesses the required attributes.*

Together they moved under the silk canopy where Bishop Scarfos stood. Through her veil, Zabel saw the anger on his face when he noticed the peacock feather but could do nothing. She was pleased to be hiding her self-satisfied smile.

Bishop Scarfos slowly chanted the wedding prayers. He walked around the couple three times, waving an intricately carved incense burner, the fragrant smoke wreathing them.

At Raymond's request the ceremony included the vows of his Latin Church. So at the completion of the Armenian prayers, Raymond intoned, "With this ring I thee wed, with this gold I thee honour, and with my dowry I thee endow." He then placed a gold ring on her finger and the bishop rang a small bell. Zabel repeated the vow and the bell was rung again.

He has a kind face. It was the only word that described the lack of malice, the openness, she saw there.

Raymond lifted her veil and presented her with a cake of flour and salt. "It represents the flesh and blood of each of us," he had explained to her earlier. As they ate, they became blood kin, forbidden from that day forward from harming one another. They crossed their hands together, making the infinity sign. Joined forever.

Bishop Scarfos took King Leo's crown from the altar holding it above Raymond's head.

"Raymond de Gisor, by this marriage, you become King of Lesser Armenia. Do you vow to protect this land and these people with your life?"

"I do."

Raymond bowed slightly to allow the shorter bishop to place the crown on his head. When Raymond righted himself, Zabel recognized the transformation. The code of chivalry with which he was raised had prepared Raymond for this moment. It was his duty to protect women, children, his Church, and the land. He stood now with the commanding stature of a ruler, his chest forward and his mouth firm as he stared unflinchingly at the bishop.

Outside, two musicians playing silver trumpets, their clear sound filling the air, led the procession. Zabel and Raymond rode side-by-side, he on his large dark stallion, and she on her prancing Arabian mare. Each horse was adorned with a richly decorated saddlecloth and gold bit. The roaring approval of the crowds blended with the ringing of church bells as the couple approached the palace to consecrate the marriage before the wedding feast could begin.

Raymond's knights formed an honor guard up the palace steps, their lances bearing brightly coloured banners that snapped in the breeze as the couple ascended. They faced the cheering crowds and Zabel raised her hand to silence them.

"Today I give you a new King," Zabel announced with certainty. "I give you, King Raymond."

The crowd cheered.

When it again grew quiet, Raymond said, "You have my pledge of honour as your King to ensure the safety of Lesser Armenia. My new country. My new people. My new bride."

Another cheer, louder than the last, followed the couple as Raymond and Zabel entered the palace.

Zabel had ordered vases of red roses to be placed throughout the bridal chamber. She hoped their intoxicating scent would enhance the intimacy she wanted to achieve. An image of the cave she had shared with Siraj entered her mind but she forced it away. *I must think only of my new life, my new husband.*

Zabel and Raymond undressed one another.

"It is according to the ancient custom of this land, husband, that I anoint you with rose oil."

Naked on the embroidered sheets, Zabel mounted Raymond in the traditional posture of an ancient queen. As she lowered herself so he penetrated her, she prayed Jnana's deception would work. A bloodstain appeared on the sheets beneath them. Raymond had no idea that a fragile silk membrane, made taut with her blood, had just been broken. To Zabel, they became the goddess and the sacred bull.

Raymond lay wide-eyed in the dim light of the chamber, shy and innocent. It moved her. What must he be thinking of the woman he married who would position herself in such a brazen manner? She wondered if he knew that in the ancient days, he would remain king only as long as he protected the land and ensured the crops grew. When he grew aged, when his powers failed, the queen would have him killed in a ritual ceremony before choosing another who would take over the sacred duties.

Jnana presented the stained bridal sheets to Bishop Scarfos, verifying the marriage had been consummated. Now, the feast could commence.

As Raymond and Zabel seated themselves on the raised dais, above a floor that was a bed of rose petals, servants in red satin breeches and vests presented silver trays loaded with every delicacy. Platters of steaming lamb, roasted to perfection in olive oil and herbs were placed in front of the guests. Bowls of savory chickpeas cooked in cumin and garlic accompanied platters of figs and dates, tabouleh and yoghurt. Goblets of wine were passed to each guest. Hundreds of roasted lambs and other delicacies were distributed to the citizens who celebrated outside.

Zabel and Raymond toasted each other with wine in Venetian glass and sampled each dish. Jnana, radiant and content, sat at Zabel's side. But, as Zabel leaned over to talk to her, she noticed Raymond's brother Guy standing in the shadows. *He stood with Raymond in the cathedral, rode behind him to the palace, but as is his way, he keeps himself apart, always watching, calculating.*

"We must include that one in the circle dance," Zabel spoke softly into Jnana's ear. "He's my brother-in-law now, but I'm as suspicious of him as I've always been. His envy seems as sharp as the blade of a hunting knife."

"Indeed, he's like a caged tiger whose hunger and thirst have not been satisfied and is waiting for the door to be opened." Jnana paused, as if turning over in her mind what this might mean for her granddaughter.

"Perhaps we can find him a bride of great beauty who would relieve his longing," Zabel said, and the two women smiled at each other.

With a nod of her head, Zabel signaled for the orchestra to begin. A frame drum began to beat. She remembered the day of her initiation. The drum had beat then, too. This time she felt the presence of her mother, the woman of whom she had no memory, but had come to know through her beloved grandmother. Zabel rose, pulling Raymond to his feet.

"It is customary to have our families dance in a circle together. It shows we are united. Jnana will bring your brother." When he seemed to hesitate, she said, "Come. It's easy." She led him to the middle of the floor.

"I am familiar with dancing, my queen. In my homeland, our women are fond of this activity, so to honour them, all knights must become proficient."

The four joined hands, Zabel leading them in a simple step, crossing one foot behind the other to the beat of the drum. Then, as their timing became as one, the other instruments: the oud, the spiked fiddle, the flute, joined in and the rhythm became faster. They moved round and round, until breathless, they urged the assembled guests to join them.

The king and queen soon left. It was expected they would couple once more in marital bliss, but Zabel had another plan in mind. Tonight was the first full moon after the spring equinox. The peasants would be celebrating the lengthening days, the time for planting. Instead of heading for their chamber Zabel led Raymond to the stables.

Raymond seemed shocked that they were not going to bed. "Where are we going?"

Can it be that he is actually attracted to me? That this marriage is more than merely political? "You must trust me, husband. I have something special in store for you. You'll not be sorry."

The stables were empty; the attendants had joined the celebrations.

"Cover yourself with a riding cloak," Zabel said, as she pulled one about herself. "The night air is beginning to chill."

"What would take us from our wedding night? Can't it wait until tomorrow?"

"Be patient. You'll be pleased. I promise."

Leaving the sound of revelry behind, they followed the long trail of light left by the setting sun, riding into the countryside.

“It’s a beautiful evening for a ride, wife, but I think it’s time you explained why I’m being denied my nuptial pleasures.”

“Our peasants use the position of the stars and planets to determine the time for planting and harvest. Tonight the alignment is such that fertility is at its height. The ancient tribes knew crops would be abundant if men and women copulated under the stars to honour the Great Mother.”

“I have heard such an event takes place in Gaul. Our peasants believe the same thing, but I have never been present.”

Zabel noticed the stiffness with which he spoke. *Assuredly these Catholic knights have been told such beliefs are evil.*

“As King, you must understand the importance of these rituals for your people.”

He nodded. “Now that it is my kingdom, too.”

Zabel looked sharply at him, vigilant, for a trace of covetousness. It would take her a while to trust this stranger, even one whose face remained free of deceit.

“This ritual is in my blood, Raymond. You must understand; my mother was of peasant stock.”

“Your mother was a peasant?”

Zabel saw he hadn’t expected this revelation. “She died shortly after my birth, and my father raised me with the beliefs of the Armenian Church. But my grandmother made sure I learned the sacred ways of the Great Mother. Jnana showed me everything is created from Her. But it’s not just that Jnana taught me this. I spend time in nature. I watch. The seasons, tiny birds hatching, the colors in small stones that have washed down from the mountains. I feel Her. And I'm in awe." She paused. "I don't believe there is a god in heaven who created everything."

Raymond was silent in his turn, pondering her admission. Finally he spoke. "What about eternal life? Don't you want that?"

"No. Being alive in this moment is enough for me." Her eyes pleaded for his understanding. "I loved my father. Trusted him in every way. He was a Christian and my Armenian subjects are Christians. I respect their right to believe as they see fit. It is because I don't ever want to fight in a war, to kill another human being that I agreed to marry you. My father made sure I could lead an army into battle but my mother did not want me to do so. It is a great conflict for me. How to honor both my parents."

"What is it you want me to do?"

"Just to understand that I, and now we, have an obligation to both our peoples. You are a Christian, so there's no problem there, but you must honor the ancient ways of my mother as well."

"Then, I am happy you brought me."

They rode in silence to the base of a small hill. Villagers were converging, eagerly herding cows and sheep. The night was alive with the bleating and shuffling of animals amid the voices of people who called to each other with excitement, as the horde moved upward.

"We'll leave the horses here and walk the rest of the way," Zabel said.

He was surprised. "We're going up? It's blasphemous, Zabel? This ceremony, these people. We are putting Nature before God."

Zabel bowed her head to conceal her annoyance. Evidently Raymond wasn't as agreeable as he had indicated. She stepped back from her horse and as she did she bumped into someone.

"Oh, I'm sorry. I didn't see you behind me," she said.

"No harm done." The stranger was about to move on when he looked directly into Zabel's face. "Queen Zabel?" came his shocked inquiry.

"Yes." She waved him ahead, "we will follow you."

The farmer's look of surprise turned to one of disgust. "No, no, I will not be joining you and the others. I am a Christian. I have given up the superstitious ways of our ancestors." With that, he walked briskly into the darkness.

Zabel felt a pang of sorrow for him. He has lost much, she concluded. It redoubled her resolve to ensure she and Raymond would help those who worked this land to retain a relationship with the spirits, inherent in it. She took Raymond's arm but he balked.

"I'm not the only one who is uncertain about this rite."

She wouldn't let him refuse her. "Just today you promised to honor our people. These are our people, too. Not just the Christians."

She could see that the idea of honor had struck a cord with him and he trod up the hillock with her.

Twilight had turned to dusk by the time they reached the summit. The crowds, even the animals were hushed. Suspense filled this time before darkness. Zabel's breathing was shallow in anticipation of the great event to follow. In years past she had sat at her window and watched. Her father had never allowed her to leave the palace on this night of heightened sexual energy. But this time, she stood with her husband, able to participate in the rite. It was dark now, enveloping the people and animals. The only sounds were a few hushed comments. Then, a dragon's tongue of fire split the night. Zabel was barely able to see Raymond's face but his hand covered hers. The bonfire stack that had been prepared earlier in the day began to crackle in the light breeze. Raymond caught his breath as a dozen hillocks burst alight with the flame of bonfires.

Zabel sensed the shock of delight that ran through the crowd. Raymond's hand tightened over hers. In that instant they were connected like a word and its meaning, connected to each other, connected to Nature, to the patterns that appear in the smallest details: the budding fern unfolding, the precise arrangement of the seeds of a sunflower, the design of sea shells, the swirls in ammonite.

Zabel thought of the sexual attraction that assures the continuance of life. Fire is the energy, the lust to procreate. Fire, encouraging each erect penis to send forth the seeds of life, impregnating each female; each male and female orgasm a part of the energizing principle of the cosmos. Fertility, birth, life, death, regeneration, repeating in endless cycles.

Zabel pulled Raymond to an open area covered in thick moss. "We must lie together like everyone else. We will create our own new life."

She wanted him, wanted to have him, here, in Nature. "You will seal your place as king by producing an heir as soon as possible, Raymond. We will conceive a child tonight. Fertility is ripe in the land."

She stood close, her breath mingling with his. Zabel felt him stiff under his cloak. The ritual was having its effect on him despite his religious training. The very air was drunk with fruitfulness. She pulled Raymond down feeling the soft moss under her back.

The mysterious power of regenerating Earth awakened him. He welcomed her body as she lay beneath him. "We may burn in Hell, but at this moment, I don't care." His voice was husky with his passion.

His seed will be wasted but the fire in his loins is my delight, she thought.

As soon as they returned to the palace, Zabel ordered another bath to be drawn in her private chamber. The early spring night had become cold, the wind sharper. She was chilled despite the fur-lined cloak she had worn.

"Will not all these baths give us a fever?" Raymond asked.

She realized this must be the reason he never changed his clothes, never bathed. *How odd. The Franks are a curious people, indeed.* "Is that what you believe?" She couldn't keep the sarcasm out of her voice. "It has not been my experience, but to ensure that you don't become ill, I will rub you with a warm towel after the bath."

"As your king, I demand that you teach me all your ways without ridiculing me. That is your new role, Queen Zabel."

She felt relief that he had not caused an argument. "As you wish. First, you must give me your hand each time I enter the bath, to protect me from falling on the slippery marble."

Zabel slid under the hot, perfumed water and watched him enter. As he settled in the tub opposite her, the steam rising from the water made his dark hair curl. A long strand had fallen onto his brow. She reached up and moved it with the tips of her fingers.

"Zabel, I want you to know I came to the East looking for land. I had no idea I would find a woman such as you."

Ignoring his compliment, she asked, "I thought you were here to free the Holy Land. What do you mean?" Her muscles tightened with apprehension.

"Publicly, that is the reason. But we, my family, we have another more pressing reason."

"What is it?"

He squirmed in the water. "There are three brothers in my family."

Zabel gave him no chance to continue. "It is a fine time to be truthful. After we have taken our wedding vows." Then she wondered if she would ever be completely truthful with him.

"It changes nothing between us, Zabel. But it is important for me to tell you this. After all, you waited until after the ceremony to tell me about your beliefs."

She sunk deeper into the water hoping her flushed cheeks would appear to be from the hot water. "Point well taken. Please continue."

"My eldest brother, Alphonse, is to inherit the family estate. Guy and I were trained to help him protect it."

"Then, you remain part of the estate even though your eldest brother would be the overlord. Is that correct?"

"Not exactly."

Zabel's apprehension increased.

"My father decided that if we stayed at home, we

would become restless, perhaps initiate wars. He ordered us to take up the cause of the Holy Crusade but also to acquire new land. Here."

Zabel let his confession sink into her consciousness. She marveled at her situation. Sitting naked, in a bath, with a man who was virtually a stranger to her. One who arrived in her world for complex reasons of his own. She wanted to be angry with him. Thought of having the marriage annulled. Then the image of the bloodstained sheets filled her mind. There would be no chance of that. The dice had rolled. She gathered her strength. "You and I are forced by circumstances to be pragmatic, Raymond. Many people depend on us, on our decisions." The lock of hair had fallen loose again and she reached up to fix it as before.

"I wanted you to know," he said. "But, I also want you to know, I'm a fortunate man." Raymond took her hand and put it to his lips, his smile warm.

They rose from the bath and she dried him with the warm cloth as she had promised, rubbing vigorously. Lying on fresh bed linens that covered the mattress, Raymond fell asleep instantly, the effect of the long day and the hot water preventing further talk. He lay on his side, facing away from her, his breathing regular. She touched his back, noticing the thin layer of fat underneath smooth skin. There was security in the fact he was strong and healthy.

Zabel lay awake, feeling the night wind blowing softly through the open windows as she watched the moon, nearly full, move across the sky, its brightness lighting the room. She would never think of this man as she did Siraj. But he was pleasing. He was truthful, She liked him.

Chapter 16

Zabel and Raymond proceeded to the council chamber the next morning full of confidence. Each councilor stood and introduced himself to Raymond. Zabel wondered how they felt about this stranger, one who won his position by marrying the queen and committing his large army. Some surely resented it. She sighed. There was no use pondering this now; if there were resentments or fears, she would know about it soon enough.

The morning business proceeded. Venetians requested more docks be built at the port in Ragma. The number of Crusaders being ferried to the Holy Land through Armenia was taxing the present facilities to the point of frayed nerves and the occasional clash of weapons, as legions of knights and attendants vied for loading space. Figures were presented with estimates of the cost of the additional facilities. The councilors debated the various tax increases open to them. Zabel's head was swimming. She wanted to be anywhere but here. Raymond, on the other hand, was regarding each speaker with the utmost attention.

Then Zabel realized Guy was not in the room. He had agreed to be Raymond's assistant in these council meetings. *Where is he?* She wanted to leave these boring discussions to the men and was about to suggest Raymond summon Guy, when the heavy doors of the chamber opened.

Bishop Scarfos stormed into the room with Guy at his side.

The bishop shouted without asking formal permission to speak, "I demand to know if our newly anointed king and his bride were present last night at a pagan ritual involving fornication and fire worship."

Raymond rose to his feet and stared calmly at the Bishop, "What is the meaning of entering this chamber unannounced and bellowing in such a disrespectful manner?" Though his face remained still, Zabel could see Raymond had tightened his fists. He was as angry as the Bishop but fought to remain calm.

"The incident was reported by a farmer early this morning," the Bishop replied.

"It is my understanding that ancient customs exist here. I deem it necessary to support the continuation of such traditions."

"These 'customs' as you call them, have placed you in a state of sin," the bishop said.

Zabel noted Guy's manner was arrogant, his look, smug. *He's enjoying this.*

"I am King. The Queen and I will participate in any or all of these traditions as we see fit."

The Bishop's eyes narrowed. "We shall see about that. You are God's representative as long as you uphold the sacred teachings. And as a knight in the special service of the Pope in Rome, you took a vow of allegiance to the Church you serve. You are subject to her laws. I crowned you. Your blasphemous behavior allows me to remove you and your bride from the throne. I warned the late King Leo his marriage to a heathen would result in catastrophe."

Zabel's heart raced.

"My Lady and I are good Christians. You have no reason to chastise us. We have not diminished the teachings of the Church in any way. We merely acknowledge the long standing customs of our people."

The Bishop's face was scarlet. "Letting the peasants have their rituals is one thing. It keeps peace in the land, but participating in such a ritual is a heinous sin. You are worshipping idols."

The bishop stopped to recover his poise. He spoke to Guy for some minutes under his breathe as everyone present sat motionless. Finally the bishop spoke. "I was prepared to be lenient with this first offense, but it is evident that you, both of you, are unrepentant.

"With Armenia on the verge of war, you leave me no choice. I revoke your crowns.

"I will have neither of you here to bring the wrath of God on us. Your brother Guy de Gisor assures me he has no love of these heathen ways. Guy will be anointed King and we will find an Armenian woman to be his queen. You and your bride must leave for France on the next tide."

Zabel had been content to let Raymond speak for them until now but the word 'exiled' reverberated in her head, the echo becoming louder and louder.

"This is ridiculous. My father intended I rule Lesser Armenia."

"Your father was a fool," the Bishop shouted. "I warned him. To mix pagan blood with that of the royal house was nothing short of folly."

"You haven't the power to force us to leave," Zabel countered.

"Our Holy Church gives me that power. If you

remain in Armenia, you will be imprisoned. Do not attempt to return, for if you do, you will be put to death.

"First ministers, follow me to my chambers. The rest of you are dismissed until your new king reconvenes this assembly."

Bishop Scarfos and Guy left the chamber with the others trailing behind.

No one spoke. The only sound that of parchment being folded as the Venetians, too, prepared to leave.

When the large wooden doors closed Zabel felt as if she were sealed in a funeral vault, the silence was so complete. She and Raymond sat for some time, the Bishop's words reverberating off the arched pillars. She was chilled as if the blood had drained from her body.

Raymond took her hands. "Can he do this, Zabel? I am a stranger to your laws."

"Yes, I think so. My father accepted the power of the church. But I never talked directly about it with him...I recall hearing stories. Some of our predecessors were not as loyal to the Church as expected. They lost the throne." She paused. "Would your brother really do this? Take the crown from you?"

"He's as ambitious as the bishop is powerful, and he's always resented being the third born. He thinks himself the most capable brother." Raymond stared at the floor. "Perhaps he is more competent than I in political matters. In truth, he is more skilled in the arts of war. He would be better able to lead our armies." Raymond shuffled in his seat. "But you are losing everything. I pledged to keep you safe, and I know not what to do."

Raymond hung his head. "I thought if Guy were my advisor, we'd be safe. But things have happened so fast.

We've had no time to set things in their proper order."

"I must speak with my grandmother. She will know what to do." Zabel spoke the words, but for the first time her voice held no conviction. "The bishop has found a way to be rid of me that will seem legitimate in the eyes of the Armenian people. Convincing them will not be difficult. Armenians became Christians shortly after the time of Christ, a fact they acknowledge with honour. They lost their pagan ways centuries ago. To them our behavior *will* look blasphemous.

Raymond stood. "I'll go to my men to see how many remain loyal to me."

Zabel found Jnana bent over the herbs in her garden, plucking leaves. She was wearing a woolen cloak faded from many washings. The old woman straightened, gripping her lower back with gnarled fingers, as she saw her granddaughter approach.

"Are you as upset as you look? Did it not go well this first morning with Raymond in the chambers?" Jnana led Zabel to a stone bench beside a fountain. "Sit, we will not be overheard here."

Zabel raced through the story, barely taking the time to breathe, all the time feeling like a clay pot that had been dropped, shattering across the floor. Zabel's voice shook as she forced back tears of hatred and fear. "I cannot leave. This is my home."

Jnana gripped Zabel's hand as they stared at the bubbling water.

Finally Jnana spoke, "You made a decision to have a child, Zabel. For her sake, you cannot risk prison, or death."

The truth was as simple as that. Zabel knew the child growing in her belly must be her first concern.

She saddled her horse and left the walls of the city for the countryside, her mind moving faster than the swift horse beneath her. In spite of knowing Jnana was right, she railed against the unfairness of life. Her mother had been taken from her before she could know her, then her beloved father, and now, her land. Exiled to France? She had no idea how she would survive this new loss.

She slowed her horse as she reached a bluff overlooking the ancient landscape. The fields below were being tended with patient care. She rode down until she reached a small house. Tying her horse to the paddock fence, she opened a gate and stood amongst the recently born lambs as they ran, thrilling to the experience of being alive.

On the window-ledge of the house, in a small earthen pot, violets trembled in the spring breeze. Inside, she could see a woman kneading dough for the evening meal, her baby tied to her breast with a colorful shawl. The aroma of yeast working tugged at her senses. Would this scene of domesticity ever be hers? Weary from the complex emotions coursing through her, she sat on the earth and leaned against the firm mud wall of the farmhouse.

A lamb moved toward her and began to nuzzle Zabel's arm. The trust of this innocent creature finally caused the release of tears Zabel had been holding back. *How can I leave my beloved land? It's too much. It's not fair.* She sobbed, overtaken with despair.

The tiny lamb now worked it's way onto her lap. Zabel's tears mixed with anxious laughter. "You're breaking my heart, little one," she said.

She pressed the warm body to her. It relaxed onto

the warmth of her arm as she walked to the other side of the enclosure. The farmer was walking behind a plow pulled by two oxen. *In the fall these fields will be swaying with golden heads of grain.* The wind moved across the field, it whipped the newly turned soil into small spirals.

The Maulana said the peasants survive wars and the intrigue of the power-hungry. It matters little to them what tribe of people sit in the palace, surrounded by luxuries the peasants provide with the sweat of their brow. Their life will continue as it always has. They don't need me.

Zabel returned the lamb to its mother. Instead of remounting her horse, she led it, walking slowly back to the palace, absorbing the energy of the land with every step. By the time Zabel entered the palace she had accepted the truth. *Fortune is leading me to another life.*

Chapter 17

"You understand, I can't go with you," Jnana said.

At these words, heartache was added to the desolation Zabel already felt. About to protest, she saw the anguished look on her grandmother's face, and stopped herself. *She's an old woman and deserves to die in this land that has nurtured her.*

"There is no harsher sentence than leaving you. But I understand."

The two women spent their last day packing. Bishop Scarfos made it clear Zabel was to take only her personal possessions. Even her father's chessboard belonged to the state, he had declared. Zabel tried in vain to feel excited; to convince herself she was headed for an adventure.

She recalled bitterly how certain she had been when she talked with her father of fate and chance. In the last few weeks she had come to realize that change could be permanent, and events were not simply moves on a game board without consequences. She told herself she would return one day and everything would be as it had been, but she knew, deep in her heart, that was a false hope.

She leaned against the rounded pillar dividing the

arched window, drinking in the flavor of her country. The sun's rays caught the strand of a spider's web, reflecting light like a long slim mirror as it hung from the open window. Zabel reached over and swept the web away from the molding. *There is no certainty.*

This realization buoyed her spirits. She surmised it was the strange reaction to the freedom that came from the loss of choice.

Try as she might to slow the packing, her belongings were finally loaded. Thick, powerful oxen stood rattling their yokes, anxious to move. Zabel looked about for Jnana to give her a final kiss, but her grandmother was nowhere to be seen.

"We must be off if we are to leave on the tide," Raymond said as he rode up.

Zabel's voice strained with anxiety. "I've not said good-bye to Jnana."

Raymond was about to dismount to look for her when the older woman appeared.

She laid a heavy woolen cloak reverently into Zabel's arms. "I have made this for you."

Zabel hugged it to her body, smelling Jnana's familiar scent. The cloak was dark indigo with a wide embroidered hem.

"I hope it will comfort you as I have over the years."

"Nothing will replace you," Zabel said. "How could you even think such an idea was possible?"

Jnana touched Zabel's cheek, softly. "If you are ever in need, you must pay close attention to the symbols I have had embroidered on the hem. They will help you."

Zabel examined the stitching: golden snakes intertwined with silver crescents. Then she swung the cloak over her shoulders.

"I'll never forget all you've taught me. Never." She held her grandmother, shocked at how small Jnana had become. *I might have lost her soon even if I remained here.* Zabel tried to console herself with this thought. Tried to make the leaving easier, but it wasn't working. *Jnana, whose life is full of service. Jnana, who always experiences life as a continuous prayer of respect, the Spirits of Nature her friends. Jnana, this woman who is gratitude itself.*

The older woman pulled away, looking fiercely at her granddaughter. There was an urgency Zabel had rarely seen.

"Now, don't forget. Pay attention to that hem if you are ever desperate. Let your intuition guide you." She stepped back, taking in fully the young woman in front of her. "That is my blessing."

Zabel was sobered by the urgency in Jnana's voice. She managed to murmur, "I will do as you ask." Her grandmother looked satisfied, but as Zabel was about to mount her horse, Jnana's brown eyes clouded with concern.

"There's something else."

"What is it?"

Jnana's shoulders stooped, as if she were carrying the weight of the world. "Your initiation was not complete. There's much you don't understand."

"I'll find a way. I promise," Zabel said, wondering how that would be possible without her grandmother.

Jnana reached out and touched the ceremonial knife Zabel now wore prominently in her girdle. "You know I promised your mother..."

"There's nothing you can do now.   It's out of your hands."

"I know. But she was so determined that *you* would get a full initiation. She died before her own was complete."

Zabel read the pain in Jnana's eyes. "I'll find a way," now feeling she must. " Don't worry."   Zabel's voice was pleading now.   She wanted her last memory of her grandmother to be of the smiling woman she loved.

As always, her grandmother sensed Zabel's need. She pressed reassuringly on Zabel's arm, her face beaming. "I know you will. I have complete faith in you."

Zabel mounted her horse. She looked back at her grandmother as the entourage moved forward at the pace of the oxen, until it turned a corner. Silent tears streamed down her cheeks.

She forced her awareness onto the horse beneath her. Tambour was a fine Arabian and with a toss of its head, confirmed the pride of his bloodline. *I must act the same.* But she felt small, as insignificant as a stone under her horse's hooves. It was like death. This land, that had known her mother, Jnana, and all the women preceding them, back to the beginning of time, was her very soul.

She saw Raymond ahead. He was her life now. He and the child growing inside her. *I am no longer Queen Zabel.* She touched the ceremonial knife and pulled the cloak more tightly about her, shivering in spite of its warmth. *I carry my ancestors with me. Their blood has isolated me from my kingdom, but I hope it will connect me to myself.*

They neared the port of Regma. In the distance, Venetian ships were moored at the wharf. Broad shouldered men carried travelers' trunks, boxes, and bales of merchandise from the ships to the customs house, their muscular backs darkened by the sun. *The war in the Levant is bringing much extra money into our coffers.* Then she corrected her thought. *This is no longer my country.*

On the heights overlooking the sea they approached the remains of the ancient temple of Isis, protector of those at sea. *Great Mother, you are known by so many names. It was here, when this temple stood in all its glory, that Queen Cleopatra rode in her barge, the image of regal and feminine power, for her fateful meeting with Anthony. She could not retain her crown, just as I have not. For both of us, being queen was like finding a shell on a beach, the promise of sustenance, that is, in the end, empty.*

Zabel dismounted by the crumbling ruin, letting her horse graze on the grasses mixed with red poppies that grew between the broken columns. Against the wall an ancient grapevine clung to the sandy earth. She inscribed a spiral into the dirt below her feet. *There it is, the symbol I see in all my meditations, ever regenerating Nature, ever enlarging renewal that is always connected to what came before. Just as the grapes are transformed into wine, I can become someone else.*

Book 2

Chapter 1

The crew moved about the ship as if they were one man, so precise were the activities that readied the ship for departure. Finally the main sails caught the wind and the great ship quivered. Her wooden joints creaked and they were underway.

The mother-of-pearl fog that had been challenging the sun all day finally retreated, leaving a clear sky. Zabel was empty of all feeling as the ship slipped from its moorage. She stared at the cliffs above her spotting a cormorant nest cleverly constructed of seaweed and guano into a fissure of the rock-face. It would contain two chalky blue eggs. One of the pair of birds sat on the dead bough of a tree, watching, guarding the nest. She could make out the long hook-tipped bill of the bird, the sunlight reflecting off its glossy black coat. *I envy you. Your young will be born here.*

The sea journey to the port of Marseilles was to take one month, one cycle of the moon. The crew and other passengers were in the buoyant mood of a new adventure. Each night, with the wind cracking hard against the taut sails, Zabel stared up into the vast panoply of stars that moved about the heavens. The moon, in the first crescent to the half, lit their way, streams of light dancing over the ocean swells.

She and Raymond settled into a cabin on the aft deck while most of the other passengers slept below in airless surroundings. She was grateful the bishop had seen to these arrangements. *He's assuaged his guilt by seeing that I left in comfort.*

Raymond busied himself with the horses, settling them into their stalls. He did his best to keep them calm, grooming and exercising them by walking them round and round the upper deck.

But by the time the moon was going from the half to full, the horses began to act capriciously, stamping and whinnying, uncertain as to why they were confined on a moving piece of land. Salt spray coated their hides, the winds now more brisk than usual. Zabel took a walk with them each day, the dull routine on board starting to wear on her as well. Raymond's face had taken on a sallow pallor.

"You're not feeling well, today, my love?"

"A bit of seasickness. That's all." He smiled wanly as he struggled to control his stomach. The ship pitched suddenly as a rogue wave hit the vessel from the side. At the same time it rolled into a long deep trough. Raymond abandoned the horses and ran to the ship's rail. Vomit flew with the wind and sea spray, small specks clinging to his clothing.

Zabel had taken control of Tambour and Midnight, walking them to the rail. "I'll settle them below. Can you get yourself to our cabin?"

He glanced at her briefly and she saw his face had

reddened with embarrassment. It would have been more fitting if it were she who was sick and he caring for her. A vision of Siraj passed through her mind. *He would never let himself be incapacitated.* But she pushed the thought away. *Raymond is my husband and I must deal with whatever comes of that.*

Raymond lay on the bunk holding a large wooden bowl full of vomit. Zabel took it away and emptied it over the side. Back in the cabin, she peeled sweet lemons, pressing the skins against his nostrils to alleviate the nausea. He seemed grateful but spoke not a word.

The next day, he asked Zabel to exercise the horses. "This constant fighting off nausea has left me drained. I'm sorry, my dear, I don't have a seaman's stomach."

She wondered if that were the only reason. He was trained to be a knight and had failed to save their kingdom. She suspected this was eating away at him, adding to the motion sickness. To be betrayed by one's brother must be a terrible thing. She wondered if the three boys had once been close. What would he tell his father when they reached his home? She hadn't the courage to ask, and perhaps to weaken him further.

One day after leaving the horses, she found him playing backgammon with one of the other passengers. Memories of playing with her father flooded back. The pain of his loss filled her.

By the night of the full moon, Raymond refused the soup Zabel brought to him. He had lost much weight. The horses too, were indifferent to exercise. Zabel could do nothing more than keep them alive by feeding them each day. Raymond gave up the backgammon, sitting hour after hour staring at the emptiness of the relentless sea. She felt helpless. A storm hit one night as they were making for landfall on Crete. The sky wept rain as all aboard searched the black night for the lighthouse to guide them. The storm had, at least, provided fresh water, caught in barrels secured to the open decks.

Late that night as the ship's lines creaked against the dock, Zabel made a suggestion. "Raymond, what if we go ashore. We could begin a new life here. You're getting so thin. It's not worth continuing this journey if it's going to kill you."

"We can't do that. We have nothing with which to build a life. Believe me, I would do almost anything to be off this infernal ship, but I will persevere. Just be patient and things will be better." He smiled at her but without conviction.

By the thirteenth night of the moon's journey, Zabel's thoughts were at war with her very being. She regretted the rashness of marrying this Frank. Muddled guilt ran through her mind. *I have lost a kingdom out of fear of the unknown. I let myself be bullied by Bishop Scarfos. I stupidly took part in a pagan rite that has torn my kingdom from me. I naively thought I could be queen for my mother's people as well as those of my father's faith. Now I'm on my way to a foreign land with a man who is a stranger to me, and by the look of his countenance, is lost to himself. As this child grows inside me I must depend more on him, and it's unclear how strong he is.* Zabel began to shiver. *That's if I am with child. What if Jnana was mistaken? Then I married for nothing. If I'd had to, I could have led my forces into war. Jnana would have understood.*

A grey fog descended on the ship, its piercing damp augmenting her lament. By the next night dozens more negative thoughts filled her mind. Like the wind buffeting the ship, she became heavy with tumult. The horses, now sensing her confusion, were completely out of control, kicking their stalls.

The next morning, Raymond followed her to the hold of the ship.

Perhaps he's getting his sea legs at last.

"These animals have to be disciplined, Zabel. How could you let them get out of control?"

Shocked by his verbal attack, Zabel was lost for a response. He glared at her, his mouth set firm. *At least he's lost his lethargy. It's probably a step forward.* He moved to the horses, crop in hand and struck one of the animals. Zabel stepped in between. They faced each other in deathlike stillness. She grabbed for the whip and they wrestled for possession, falling on the straw together, rocking back and forth. The yearning in Zabel's soul was quickened by the feel of his muscular body. He raised her skirts, their thighs and lips tight. She wanted their lust to dissolve her deepest feelings of regret and sorrow.

With the passing of the full moon, and no moon blood, Zabel knew that she was with child. The weather had settled, the days becoming warmer. The clouds parted at times to reveal a warm sun. She stood on the deck and let its heat permeate her skin, filling her with hope. In her heart she looked forward to reaching Marseilles. The horses, too, felt the change. They became calm again and showed eagerness for their daily exercise.

When the moon reached the last crescent, Zabel felt fresh, like the breeze. *I will be a new woman in a new land, my child safely under my heart keeping me company.*

Their coupling was not repeated. Raymond was no longer seasick but his malaise worsened, Zabel now convinced he dreaded facing his father. She had hoped the sexual energy between them would work some magic on his soul, convince him life would go on, as it had done for her. But he was lost deep inside himself. She tried to excite him but to no avail. Then, during the three nights of the dark of the moon, she felt no desire for him. She was in a cocoon as if metamorphosing into a new person who would emerge with the appearance of the first thin crescent.

"Raymond, I am with child. You will be a father after another nine moons have passed."

He looked at her with vacant eyes. A small smile passed his lips and he turned and walked away. Zabel knew then she would be raising her child alone.

Chapter 2

As the ship docked in Marseilles, Zabel stood on the starboard side, crowded together with the other passengers, savoring her first glimpse of this land. Fish boats unloading their cargo gave off a pungent odor that permeated the humid air. But, Zabel was happy. It was a smell that one only experienced on land. *Land.* Any land would be better than the prison of the ship.

Zabel noticed the coarseness of the clothing worn by those on the road that ran past the harbour. The women were not veiled, and anxious to fit in, Zabel put hers aside.

Raymond languished by their crates, staring off into the distance, so Zabel looked for a wagon to take them north.

Away from the sea, the air was filled with the stench of animal droppings mixed with human waste. Fish offal and rotting fruits and vegetables lay in the hot sun. Zabel dabbed her silk scarf with the rose oil she carried and discretely covered her nose to avoid retching. *I should have prepared myself for this. I knew that Raymond came from an uncivilized place, but I had no idea.*

Zabel was grateful she spoke the language of the Franks but was surprised that here the tongue had peculiar variations. Somehow she was able to make herself understood, and secured a suitable cart pulled by two strong draft horses. The driver, Monsieur Mellon, loaded the crates and Raymond mounted his horse, tying Tambour to the wagon; she would be more comfortable riding on the wooden seat as there was a cover to shelter her from the intense spring sun.

Their small caravan headed out of the low marshlands sharing the track with other carts loaded with early spring produce. They crossed what the driver explained was an ancient Roman bridge, and then followed a winding river into ragged hills that bordered the coast. Here, Zabel was delighted to see orange and lime trees in blossom.

Raymond maintained the silence that had developed between them onboard ship. Zabel pondered what she knew of his life: an overbearing father...lord of an extensive manor who thrust expectations on his son, and Raymond's failure to keep the oath he made to protect Lesser Armenia and her. That it had all slipped through his fingers at the hands of his overly ambitious brother was something Raymond seemed unable to accept.

As the days went by he tied his horse to the rear of the cart and lay in the back with the crates. *If his deterioration continues he will be unable to give an explanation to his father. Perhaps that is the escape he seeks. The mind is a place of lonely mysteries. I remember how Jnana used to cull her beans before she planted them, telling me that some had a weakness that would not survive the first drought.* Zabel did not know what she could do for him, so she turned her attention to discovering the land as she slowly passed through it.

They proceeded north, in a valley with a great plateau along the west that was covered in the fresh green of newly germinating mustard; the only sound now was the occasional squeaking of the axle and the grating sound of stones crushed under the wheels.

"This will later be a vibrant yellow sea," the driver told Zabel as they plodded along. "You are lucky. You hit a dry patch. Spring rains usually make this road nearly impassable, but not much has fallen this year."

Zabel breathed a sigh of relief. She didn't need the complication of rain. She studied the little man beside her as unobtrusively as possible. When he spoke Zabel could see that only one tooth remained in his mouth, which made his face shriveled like a walnut. His head was as smooth as a leather polo ball, and his eyes were sharp like the knife in her girdle. She decided she would be safe in this diminutive man's care with or without Raymond's help.

As if reflecting her thoughts, Monsieur Mellon spoke, "But be aware, Madame, the countryside is filled with brigands. I will do my best to protect you."

"I am familiar with the use of weapons, Monsieur. I have a bow and arrow and can stop a man's attack from fifty paces."

"Keep them concealed at all times. Women are not allowed to bear arms in this land. However, I'm a practical man. I will welcome your aid should we need it."

Zabel pondered the custom of a land that would forbid weapons to women. *There will be much more to learn.*

A hawk in the distance, raking after its prey, took her attention. *Jnana always said that seeing a hawk should remind us to be observant.* The bird cried with a sudden shrillness. She could hear Jnana's voice, "A hawk has a great vantage point as it floats on the air, enabling it to discern danger. Hawk is patient, waiting for the right time to take action." With a husband who seemed to have given up altogether, she would have to be the one to pay close attention.

The dry weather failed to hold. As they neared Paris, the wind blew in squalls. Banks of storm clouds moved in over the hills. Thunder and vast sheets of lightning announced the weather had turned, and Zabel's intuition told her a turbulent change was about to enter her life. She sat under the canopy and watched a downpour soak the fields. Rain fell silently over the backs of the animals. A grove of oak trees disappeared before her eyes as the clouds lowered and thickened. The ridge of hills vanished.

Raymond refused shelter under cover; he stared with glazed eyes at the sky, letting the rain cool his fevered face. As Zabel looked back at him she noticed the cart was leaving deep tracks in the thick mud. They would be slowed down, Monsieur Mellon said, adding at least a day to their journey.

When they arrived at an inn where they would spend the night, the sky cleared, washed bright by the rain. Zabel shed quiet tears while Raymond slept. She allowed herself this luxury of purging her emotions, knowing she would need the endurance of the hawk to withstand whatever came in Gisor.

On the final day of the journey, they skirted Paris, the walls of which Zabel could just make out in the distance. Continuing northeast, they reached the forested rolling lands of the Gisor's demesne. The forest became cultivated fields, some newly plowed and others lying fallow where sheep grazed. Soon the road led them to a cluster of small houses with thatched roofs. A miller's wheel slowly turned as water from a small stream ran into a river that meandered among the fields.

Zabel turned to Raymond and touched his forehead. He was still hot. In one of his lucid moments he had directed the driver to this location and she sought confirmation from him that they were, indeed, at Gisor. She rocked him tenderly but couldn't rouse him. *I'll let him sleep. We'll find out soon enough if we're in the right village.* She indicated to Monsieur Mellon that they should pass through the opening in the wooden stockade where villagers transported goods suspended on poles carried over their shoulders.

Inside they rode along an avenue lined with ancient oak trees. The wagon wheels crunched on small stones that formed a semicircular drive in front of a two-storey chateau, with a profusion of chimneys emerging from a dark slate roof. Dark green ivy clung to its stone walls. Behind it, horses were visible, grazing in a clover-filled pasture. *Our horses will be happy here. But what about us? Raymond is in no condition to explain why we are here. Must I do it? What will I say?*

When she alighted from the cart the stench of a dung-heap reached her nose. From behind the house a pig snorted its way toward them, curious, perhaps to see the newcomers. *How terribly uncivilized. Why would they keep their animals so close to their lodging?* Zabel walked up the short flight of stone steps that lead to a large wooden door and pulled the cord. A retainer led her to the great hall where a fire blazed. The family crest, a large boar surrounded by acorns, hung above the fire.

An erect, aged man entered the room, his graying mustache followed the drooping lines of his mouth to his chin, giving him a sinister appearance.

"Are you Guillaume de Gisor?"

"Yes. And who are you?" Close-set, wary eyes studied her. He cocked his head slightly to the side as if to better hear her response.

"Your son has returned home," Zabel said, instinctively pulling herself to her full height so that she would appear strong before her father-in-law.

"My son? Which of my sons returns?"
"Excuse my omission. I should have named him. It is Raymond who has returned."
"And," the piercing gaze bore into her, "who are you?"

The look unsettled Zabel but she forced herself to exude a confidence she was beginning to lose. "I am Zabel, his wife."

"His last message said he was in Lesser Armenia, training with the future queen. Zabel was her name. Is that you? Why has he returned? I do not understand. Where is he?"

"There will be time to answer your questions later. Raymond is unwell. He lies outside, in the cart."

Guillaume rushed past Zabel calling for his servants. Raymond was carried up to his quarters where a fire was set at once and warm liquids brought.

"I expect you to give me an explanation later." He sneered at her. "While I arrange for the doctor, see that he takes some of this broth." Guillaume swept out of the room.

She persuaded Raymond to take mouthfuls of the steaming broth cooled with her breath. His eyes were glassy and his forehead still burned. Zabel rubbed him with wet cloths, wishing she knew what herbs grew in the area.

The fief's doctor examined Raymond. He announced that blood would be let. Zabel felt her heart stop. She was sure bloodletting had led to her father's death, but her protests were ignored without comment. Distain for the healing arts of woman seemed even stronger here than in Armenia.

She determined that in the morning she would walk through the surrounding woods in hope of finding some familiar herbs that could be added to Raymond's broth, undetected.

"His Lordship would like to see you now," said a servant who had come quietly into the room.

"I humbly beg his permission to wait until morning. I find myself overwhelmed by fatigue and worry. I would like food brought to my room?" She needed time to think.

The servant returned a few moments later. "Duke de Gisors will be happy to meet with you when you break your fast in the morning. And he hopes you find your rooms comfortable."

She longed for her marble bath with its hot scented water, but no such luxury existed here. She fell into a restless sleep on coarse blankets laid over a straw mattress. Her last waking thoughts filled with dread of the primitive society in which she now found herself. *What kind of life have I brought my child to?*

In the morning Zabel dressed hurriedly and made her way to Raymond's quarters. His condition had deteriorated during the night. She realized she had delayed as long as she could. She would now have to confront Guillaume.

The Duke de Gisor sat in the dining hall, his food before him. He rose courteously as Zabel entered. Once seated, the servants placed food in front of her but she waved it away. She was in no mood to eat.

An older version of Raymond entered the room. "I would like to introduce you to my eldest son, Alphonse," the duke said. He runs the fiefdom for me now that my maladies will not allow me the pleasure of riding my horses. There is something which always needs our attention, which I'm sure you can appreciate, Princess Zabel."

"Queen Zabel, actually. My father died a short time ago." In the month since she left home no one had referred to her by her title. She had almost forgotten that she had been a queen. *My title gave me much power. Without it life is going to be more difficult than I've ever imagined.*

She noted that both men were visibly startled by her admission. She must take advantage of the moment.

"I hope you're sufficiently rested to explain your sudden appearance here," the duke said.

"And to tell us what has happened to Guy?" Alphonse added.

Zabel recited her tale using Raymond and Guy's extreme rivalry as the pretext of her exile. They visibly relaxed. She had guessed correctly. The de Gisors relished the idea that fierce competition between the two siblings had resulted in Guy, the stronger of the two, winning the contest. They were obviously aware of Raymond's tender side, believing it led directly to his becoming ill. Zabel felt revulsion and contempt for the two men seated before her. It was this sense of rivalry and greed that led men to war.

"Raymond was conscious for moments last night while you were resting. He informed the nurse that you are with child. Is that true?"

"Yes."

He smiled, folding his bony fingers together. "This is delightful news, my dear." The old man broke off a crust of bread and tipped it into his small mouth. "Alphonse's wife of seven years has yet to produce an heir. Raymond's child will secure our dukedom."

His words horrified her. His withered fingers

pointing like an evil omen toward her unborn child. *Her* child who was to continue *her* line of women. "Secure it how?"

"You are a queen, my dear, Zabel," Alphonse said. "You understand hereditary succession. If I leave no heir, our manorial holdings will revert to the King of France."

Zabel felt faint. She had not considered this as a possibility. There was a very great likelihood that Raymond would not survive the bloodletting. She would be here alone among strangers whose customs she did not know. She put her arm on the table for support.

Both men leaned toward her in a protective manner. "Is there anything you need?" Alphonse asked.

"I'll be fine. Perhaps a bit of fresh air." *I need time to think. They both believe I am still Queen Zabel. It will serve me well until I decide what to do.*

"Now that we are aware of your condition, I am very annoyed that Raymond put you through the ordeal of the nearly impassable roads from Marseille. He knows the importance of a grandson to me," Guillaume said.

Zabel could hardly breathe. She wanted to scream at them that her child would never be theirs but she held her tongue. She felt the blood again rushing from her face

What else has Raymond kept from me? Then the image of the hawk came to mind. *I will be more secure if Raymond lives. I must save him.* "Perhaps I'll take a walk."

"Yes, of course. Our questions can wait." The duke turned to a servant. "Bring Queen Zabel some wine."

She took a sip of the wine and the blood returned to her head.

Alphonse motioned for the servant to remove his plate. "I have arranged for you to have a serving woman. It is all we can do on short notice. In the coming days we will add more attendants as befits the mother of our heir. For now, Louisa will accompany you."

"You needn't trouble her. I am perfectly capable of taking a walk alone."

"You could stumble on a root or large stone. We couldn't risk that. Louisa is a sturdy, peasant woman and can easily look after you," Guillaume said. "These woods are full of wild boar that will attack if surprised. We must keep you safe. Alphonse, you accompany her as well." A satisfied smile parted his thin lips. "Alphonse supplies meat for our table. No boar has escaped his aim."

She was trapped. What excuse could she use to justify digging up roots and picking the herbs she needed? She would have to wait and see.

Raymond grew steadily worse. That night, the sound of shuffling in the hall and the smell of incense woke Zabel. She called to Louisa to light a lamp just as a knock came to her door summoning her to Raymond's side.

The priest was giving the final blessing to the dying man. She held Raymond's hand, silently reliving their short time together. She felt a stab of loneliness that turned to anger and revulsion. *This would not be happening to me if I were married to Siraj. Raymond, you were trained as a knight, but you couldn't even save yourself. If you had but the courage to face your father, you would have realized you and I have the one thing he needs.*

They buried him the next day. Zabel felt empty as she walked to the small churchyard. It was as if she, too, were dead, such darkness had his family placed around her heart.

He is the third man I've lost. In such a short space of time. She shuddered as the wooden coffin was lowered into the newly dug earth. *What now? What will I do?* She wanted to scream. *How could this have happened to me?*

A hawk rose from the great oak that shaded the family tomb. Zabel watched as the bird hovered in order to survey the land below for a meal. *It is as if Jnana is sending me another message. The hawk shows much endurance and strength, she always said. I must keep my wits about me.*

Zabel steeled herself as she spread red and purple petals over the wooden box. *Raymond has joined the other silent bones. He can no longer speak for me or for this child.*

Upon their return to the chateau, the duke summoned Zabel to the main hall. Alphonse sat to his left gesturing Zabel to a chair opposite them.

"As you are new to these lands it is our duty to inform you of the Frankish laws to which you are now bound," her father-in-law began.

Zabel tightened her grip on the arms of the chair, wary.

"You must understand," he continued, "as Raymond's widow, the child you carry has become our property. Your dowry reverts to us. We are obliged to care for you; for your well-being, but you have no rights over the child. You will be allowed to visit him daily but his upbringing and care will be of our choosing. We will be obeyed in this matter. If not, we will use corporal punishment to gain your compliance. Do you understand?"

His eyes were cold, devoid of sympathy as he delivered to Zabel a decree just short of death. She stared blankly, unable to generate a response.

Taking her silence for acceptance, the old man continued, "You will remain in the room we have prepared for you until the child is born, at which time you will be moved to other quarters. At that time, the child will be moved to Raymond's former rooms where he will be attended by a wet-nurse of our choosing."

This child is mine. Mine. You will never have possession of her no matter what I must do. I have been caught in the labyrinth of another's life, and with that life gone, the string leading to my escape is becoming harder to see. But I will find a way.

Not daring to speak, Zabel rose from her seat, and left with as much dignity as she could muster. She felt their eyes piercing her back as she retreated, Louisa following her out.

In her room, Zabel wanted to pace, to try to intuit a plan, but she didn't want such action reported to Guillaume and Alphonse. Instead, she lay on the bed, feigning sleep while she thought. As dusk approached, outside her window, an owl called desolately. *The scavenger bird always appears after something has died*

Soon a plan emerged in her mind. She told Louisa she needed a chamber pot. When the woman bent over to retrieve it, Zabel leapt at her, knocking her unconscious. *I may not be able to lead an army to war but I can handle one unsuspecting woman.*

Zabel gagged her with a scarf and bound her hands and feet. She had only a few hours before Louisa would be expected in the kitchen.

She looked at the silk garments in her open trunks. Her beautiful things would have to be left. Zabel tucked her feet into soft leather boots and covered herself with Jnana's cloak. She concealed her mother's knife in her girdle, grabbing Raymond's money pouch and bread and cheese from her untouched lunch. A carrot would lure Tambour. Lastly she concealed her small bow and some arrows beneath her cloak.

Zabel opened the shutters that covered the small window letting in the cool evening air. She just fit through the opening, finding footing on the thick, sturdy ivy that grew up the walls. Carefully she worked her way to the ground. She moved slowly past the windows of the great hall, thankful the color Jnana had chosen for her cloak was the color of deep shadows, and made her way to the pasture where her horse grazed.

Zabel would have to ride bareback, an act she'd done since childhood. Tambour approached the offering and she coaxed it to the fence. Climbing to the second rail, she thrust herself onto its back. Zabel took hold of the mane, released the gate latch, and eased the horse forward with the pressure of her knees.

Keeping to the shadows cast by the large oaks flanking the lane, she guided Tambour to the main road to Paris. Raymond's family would presume she would attempt returning to her homeland and search the road south rather than west. With luck she could disappear into the anonymity of the city.

Chapter 3

By mid-morning Zabel approached the walls of the city. She realized the de Gisors probably had associates in Paris who, if hearing of a lone woman on a magnificent Arabian horse, would alert them to her presence. So, she slid from Tambour's back. *Go, my beauty.* She walked a few steps then gasped for breath as the loss of the animal overcame her. *What else must I lose?* She put her hand to her belly. *It's just you and me now, my child.*

Even though Zabel had no idea what to expect, she felt safer inside the city's walls. She had hoped Paris would be as sophisticated as Sisium or Tarsus, but it was nothing but a swollen market town with muddy streets. Never had she seen such filth. She longed for her palace, the clear waters that bubbled in its fountains. A great loneliness settled over her as she walked from street to street looking for lodging. *I feel no more than a stone in the street that has been kicked aside.*

She turned into a deserted alley with a series of doorways. A woman's voice rang loud and clear, singing, and Zabel decided to follow it. The alley curved, and she came upon a small woman dressed all in black busily scrubbing the brick stoop in one of the doorways. This attempt at cleanliness was reassuring.

"Would you have a room to let?"

The woman stopped her singing and studied Zabel from head to toe. "A small room, at the top. Is it just you?"

"Yes." She wondered if young girls from the country came to the city to look for work. She decided not to give more information than she was asked for.

Following the woman up three flights of rickety stairs, Zabel was shown into a cold and cheerless room tucked under the eaves of the roof. Light from the slate-colored sky entered through a dirty skylight. A small hearth with a hanging pot protruded into the tiny space, the only furniture being a straw mattress that slumped against the wall.

The woman, Madame Gilbert said, "The toilet for the neighborhood is at the end of the alley."

Zabel's heart sank. "Is there anywhere to bathe?"

"You wouldn't want to do that. You'll catch your death." Madame Gilbert ran her fingers under her nose to remove a drip.

The garret was clean, so she agreed to the price, not knowing if it was fair.

"My son will bring you wood for a few coins when you run out. I'll send him up now with some live coals to get your fire going. Best not to let it die out."

Zabel looked at the small stack of wood beside the stove, wondering how long that would last. The servants always took care of the fires at home.

Zabel walked to a near-by market avoiding the open sewer as best she could. The street was bustling with trade: mules laden with wool, goatherds tending their flocks and pigs swilling in the mud. A beggar with running scabs jostled her, leaving a smudge of slime she dared not touch. *Disease must be rampant here.* She pulled her cloak tighter about herself, feeling threatened at every turn.

She purchased some candles, a jug for water, a bowl, a small drinking cup and cheese and wine for a simple meal. A gray fog lingered over everything and her nose had begun to run. She wiped her face with her sleeve and saw that her fingers were filthy. *Oh my goodness. This is horrid, but I mustn't cry. Not here on the street.* A few blocks away, approaching her carrying two large containers was a water seller. She bought enough to fill her jug and carefully carried it home. She added a stick to the fire and then poured the water into the hearth pot. When it was heated she washed her hands and face and tried to scrub the filth off the hem of her dress; then she drank the wine. It warmed her.

Zabel collapsed on the straw mattress. The silence populated with her memories overwhelmed her and she wept with desolation. She thought of rose gardens, sweet wine and the colorful enamel tiles on the walls of her chamber. Her embroidered silk bed linens. *I was a queen only two short months ago. How I long for my clothes, my bath, warm fragrant water, and Jnana to rub my back.* At the thought of Jnana, Zabel's tears streamed down her cheeks. *Will I ever have a home again?* She looked up through the window longing to be swallowed into the vastness of the sky.

Day after day Zabel purchased her water and a meager allotment of food. She had no idea what to do, and felt her soul disappearing along with the money from Raymond's pouch into the emptiness that was Paris. Zabel's thoughts tormented her. The loss of Jnana was like hunger, gnawing at her. But then she would feel her belly, think of the child asleep in her womb, and strength returned. *I must make this life, here in Paris, sufficient.*

One afternoon she lay on the straw mattress under Jnana's cloak, breathing in the scent of the woman now lost to her. She moved her fingers over the gold and silver threads stitched so closely together they shone like pure metal. One of the moons seemed too thick. Was something in there? Zabel pulled the knife from her girdle and slit a tiny opening in the hem, moving the fabric back and forth between her fingers. A small round object fell onto the straw. It was a pearl, translucent in the dim light. She made another slit and out dropped a diamond. All about the hem, the full moons were thicker. *My jewels? It seems Jnana did not give all my possessions to Bishop Scarfos, but sewed them into this cloak. At great risk to herself. Oh, I hope she was never found out.* Her heart lurched at the thought her grandmother might be in trouble for such a daring act, but such courage gave Zabel hope. Tomorrow she would find a gem merchant and sell the diamond. For the first time since arriving in Paris she was ravenous. She made her way to the market to buy whatever tempted her in celebration of Jnana's love.

She returned with a lamb chop, some root vegetables, and herbs that she stewed slowly over her fire. *Goddess of the Earth, in my misery I have forgotten you. I forgot that I exist in your plenitude.* Zabel sunk her teeth into the meat, savoring the taste. The logs in the brazier began to heat the room. Zabel covered herself with the cloak clutching the diamond she had freed from its nest. Her dreams that night were of lush green fields surrounding a small farmhouse that she owned.

In the morning, Zabel wandered the warren of streets sure she would find a merchant who traded in gems. Her optimism waned after several fruitless hours before she found a shop with the words 'Gems Sold and Bought' painted in faded gold letters across a window that had not been scrubbed for some time. Nonetheless, Zabel ventured in.

The room appeared to be empty, but a short man wearing a visor moved from behind a high counter in a darkened corner. His clothes were gray with soot. He walked toward her, holding a magnifying glass.

"How may I help you?' he asked in an accent that suggested his first language was Hebrew.

Zabel had practiced what she would say, wanting to sound knowledgeable and confident. But, truthfully, she had no idea of the value of the diamond. Worse still, she had never had to bargain. Servants did that as well. She blushed and the more she tried to conceal her nervousness the redder she became. There was nothing to do but blurt out her mission.

"I am here to sell a gem. It's a very good one."

He said not another word.

Taking a deep breath, she placed the large diamond on a thick velvet cushion that sat on the countertop. It sparkled in the light from a candle.

The jeweler picked it up and looked at it through his glass.

"I will give you a very fair price, but before you accept it, you must take it to a number of other dealers so you will know I am not cheating you," he said, looking again at the diamond. "It is of exceptional quality."

He moved his fingers rapidly across his abacas. "I am one of those miserable creatures who was born with a conscience. I say 'miserable' because those without one make a much greater profit than I. But, I sleep at night after eating the supper I have earned in a fair manner. Yes," he sighed, more to himself than to Zabel, "I insist you do as I say and compare my offer."

"There are no others. I've walked the streets for hours and you are the only gem dealer I've found."

"Had you gone a bit further and turned into the next alley, you would have seen my shop is on the edge of the gem dealers' quarter."

Zabel did as he instructed, walking from shop to shop. The others were obsequious in manner, studying the gem carefully, but stated her stone was of poor quality. Each offered less than the original jeweler's amount. Zabel hurried back to the first shop. "I accept your offer." She smiled at him.

"It pleases me, also. One of my clients will be happy to learn I have finally secured what he desires. But, now, I insist you share a cup of tea with me. You look tired and you need your strength for the little one sheltered next to your heart."

Shock turned to appreciation. He was the second stranger who noticed her slightly protruding belly. Just this morning a fruit vendor had offered her a shiny red apple, saying she would need it for the child. "Tea will be perfect, monsieur."

"Call me Isaac," he said, a warm smile wrinkling his eyes.

Zabel was grateful for the chance to relax on a small chair Isaac produced from his living quarters. She sat, basking in a stranger's kindness, wanting to share her story with him. But she decided against it.

There was little chance for an awkward silence to ensue. The jeweler embarked on the story of his life. "I am an émigré from Catalonia." He poured tea from a pot heated on a brazier, loading her cup with milk and sugar.

The first sip removed all her weariness.

"The unrest there has recently sent many of my people in search of a place of peace."

"What unrest are you speaking of? I apologize. I'm unfamiliar with what is happening there."

The jeweler searched her face with the same intensity he had studied her gems.

"I... I've been traveling," Zabel stammered; still not ready to reveal her tale.

"The sheik decided we Jews were a danger to his realm. It's not a new story, as you may know. It seems impossible for my race to find a lasting home where we can live out our lives in peace. But that is how I came to be in the gem trade. Gems can be moved with ease. In bad times I have sown them into the hem of my cloak, smuggling them past authorities who would have been only too willing to relieve me of my burden.

We have something in common. Dare I trust him? Not yet. She decided to alter her story slightly, not a lie, simply a slight alteration of the facts. "I have recently arrived from Armenia. Brigands did release me from the burden of my other possessions. But, fortunately they never discovered my little treasures. They're all I have left."

Isaac showed no surprise. With his round, fat fingers, he handed her coins in the agreed upon amount. "Life can unfold many surprises. But happiness is always possible, and with patience you can discover a sign that can lead you to your destiny." He held Zabel's hand in a warm gesture of reassurance.

Tucking the coins into her girdle, Zabel headed back to her loft, less anxious than she had been since her arrival in Paris. The days passed and she waited for a sign to present itself as the jeweler had suggested.

She bought a measure of coarse wool and thread to make clean skirts, longing for the silks she'd left behind, but could not dare to wear now. On her daily trips to the market she became aware of the people who shared her building. She wanted to befriend the women but no matter how much time passed, she was still concerned someone might know Raymond's family. Perhaps a reward had been offered. So she kept to herself.

Many of the women sold their bodies as the girls in the caravan had in order to eat and to look after the infants who arrived as the unwanted outcome of their work. One day she passed a woman on the stairs who coughed incessantly, black spume showing between her lips. Zabel was frightened a disease could be passed to her and her child. She instinctively pulled her scarf over her nose. The woman was only a few years older than she was, but life in cold, damp lodgings had taken its toll. *Bless you, Jnana. Without you this could be me.*

Zabel's coins were running low, so she returned to the gem dealer, this time with a large emerald.

"Have you settled comfortably into the city?" he asked.

"No. My room remains cold and damp, even though I heat it with wood each day. Perhaps I need to move on. But I am at a loss as to where I should go."

The jeweler pointed to the chair. "Please. Sit."

Zabel gratefully accepted the tea Isaac again offered. As they chatted, she shared more of her story. Warmth emanated from him, reminding her of the Jews that inhabited her homeland.

She began to visit the gem dealer as part of her daily routine, resting each time for half an hour or more. He was learned, so the conversations included philosophy and the sharing of poetry.

One day as summer was coming to a close, he said, "Zabel, I think you should move to an area in the south called Languedoc."

"But why? I landed in Marseilles. It was as smelly as Paris, although, I admit the weather was better. Besides, I would miss you, my dear friend." Zabel smiled, hoping he appreciated her sincerity.

The jeweler took Zabel's hands in his. "That is just the point. A young woman needs more than one old man to keep her company. Montpelier was Muslim during the time Islam spread to the West and so Muslims and Jews fleeing the troubles in Spain have settled there. Their customs would be familiar to you. And many returning crusaders who took a Muslim wife, are settling in the region. What I am trying to say is, it would be comfortable for you. I have friends in the area. I could arrange a meeting for you."

Zabel stirred more sugar into her tea contemplating what he said.

"It is the most literate area in the Frankish domains," he continued. Philosophy and other intellectual activities flourish. Poetry is extolled. Greek, Arabic and Hebrew are studied enthusiastically. Averrole, the famed Arabic scholar, is a citizen. It will be like home. There is an easy religious tolerance. Surely, you must find this Catholic city too stifling for someone of your experience and intelligence. I would go there myself but I have work here other than the gem business that precludes it. Besides," he gushed, "you owe it to your child to be around your own kind. And Paris, as you must be aware, is a dangerous place for a widow on her own."

Zabel had heard tales of widows being burned as witches. The thought was terrifying. "It is true, I don't feel at home here." Zabel realized if she were to travel south she must do so before her belly grew much bigger. Later, she would be unable to endure the long journey. "Who are these friends you would introduce me to?"

"They are Cathars, a sect of Christianity that recognizes the feminine principle in religion as you learned from your grandmother. They repudiate the dogma of the Catholic Church, relying instead on personal knowledge obtained from a mystical experience apprehended first hand. Does this sound similar to your understanding?"

Zabel felt hope lift the gloom from her heart.

He leaned in closer to Zabel. In the stillness she could hear the candle on the table sputter as it burned. "I have friends who would keep you safe on the journey. A sect of knights whose organization stretches from here to the Holy Land. They will help you if you will but grant them one favor." Isaac cleared his throat as he adjusted his position in his chair. "I am afraid we must all pay our dues...in one way or another."

"Who are these knights? And what could a pregnant woman possibly do for them?"

"In the course of their duties the Knights Templar has amassed a great fortune. Their wealth has made Paris the financial centre of Europe. At this time, some money needs to be moved to the South without the authorities knowing."

"Are you suggesting that I carry money to Languedoc? Wouldn't that be extremely dangerous?"

"A knight would ensure your safety. You and he would pose as a married couple; your expanding belly would make that believable."

It occurred to Zabel that if Raymond's family were still looking for her they would never suspect she would be travelling with another man. She began to warm to the idea. "I no longer have a horse. Could we go by cart? Or donkey? A slow trip would ensure my child's comfort."

Isaac patted Zabel's hand, as her father might have. "I can arrange that for you."

"I met these Templars at home. They were always honorable. And I've heard much of their military prowess. I could trust them. And you, I especially trust you." Zabel sat in silence for some minutes. "I'll do it."

Isaac beamed. "I'll inform the Templars and my friends in Albi."

"Albi? You said I should go to Montpelier."

"Albi is but a short distance away. It's where you'll leave the money. You can rest there a few days after your journey and decide if you want to stay. If not, you can reach Montpelier in a few hours."

Zabel relaxed into the chair, at peace now that she had decided to act. "That sounds fine."

"We've talked long," Isaac said, "and you mustn't be out alone after dark. Hurry along and I'll send word of the time of your departure."

Once again Zabel felt her life being shifted by forces she could neither see nor understand, but this time she was leaving on a more hopeful note. Back in her room, she bound the hem of her cloak with some homespun wool to conceal the intricate embroidery, and waited. Two days later word came that she should go to the gem shop the next day when it opened for business.

She met her companion, Hector de Villiers, a tall, slim man wearing a plain woolen cloak over breeches and long boots, scuffed like those of a simple peasant. He had chosen two sturdy donkeys to which he strapped the meager possessions she had acquired. They set off immediately, blending into the flow of people leaving the city.

Outside Paris, the journey took on a slow deliberate rhythm, the days of late summer moving one into the other. The warmth of the sun alternated with the shade of the elm trees they passed under. Hector spoke little, but seemed as content as she to ride through the warm countryside that was now heavy with Nature's bounty. They passed serene cows pasturing on yellowed grasses that were to her as sacred as any icon in the cathedral in Paris.

Golden wheat fields moving in waves created by the soft breeze surrounded farmhouses protected behind high earthen walls. She could just make out the tops of apple trees, their fruit ripening in the hot sun. Zabel held her belly, feeling the child gently kicking.

At other times, low stone fences divided each field, grape vines growing between rows of fruit trees dotting the hills. She felt safe in this luxuriant countryside with Hector at her side.

But one night, as they entered an inn where they would spend the night, Zabel noticed one of the patrons had been in the inn where they'd stayed the night before. *What are the chances that a man travelling alone would be moving at the same speed as Hector and I?* When she caught his eye, he turned away quickly. Too quickly. *I won't say anything tonight. I'll see what happens tomorrow.*

That night Zabel got little sleep, sure the stranger was a spy sent from the de Gisor family. She and Hector left just after dawn. In the next village they stopped to buy cheese and a loaf of bread. Zabel saw the same man. He was talking to the town blacksmith, but he was watching them. *I must tell Hector.*

She tugged at his sleeve. "Can we stay here a bit longer? I'm feeling a bit out of sorts today. Perhaps we could take a place for the night."

Hector looked concerned. "Yes, of course. This plan mustn't endanger you or your child. Wait here, on this hay bale. I'll make arrangements and come back for you." To Zabel's horror, the stranger followed him.

Her heart raced. She must warn Hector. She hurried after him and as she turned the corner, she crashed into the stranger. He and Hector were talking, their heads bent together. "What, the..."

Hector grabbed her arm and hurried them down the road. The stranger left quickly in the direction of the market. "What are you doing, Zabel? I told you to sit and wait." She was surprised to hear anger in his voice.

"That man. Who is he? Why were you talking to him? He's been following us. I've noticed him everywhere we stop." Hector's mouth formed into a broad smile.

"Oh," she said. "He's one of you, isn't he?" It all made sense now. The tension drained from every muscle.

"Yes. Given our precious cargo, both living and financial, my people would never leave us to fend for ourselves."

"No, I suppose not. But you could have told me. I've

had a terrible fright."

"We thought you would act naturally if you didn't know; not be looking around all the time for the others."

"Others? How many others are there?"

"There are three of us." He inspected her carefully. "Are you really feeling faint or were you pretending?"

"I wanted to see if he would remain here if we stayed. Once I was sure, I would have told you. When I saw him follow you, I had to do something."

Hector let out a hearty laugh. "You are a most courageous woman. If our order accepted females, I would recommend you."

"I'll take that as a compliment," Zabel said. "Now, let's be on our way."

That night during their evening meal at an inn, a young man strummed the strings of a lute. The troubadour's ballad filled her with memories of evenings with her father.

"We have entered the lands of the South. You are in for many beautiful surprises," Hector said.

They ate lamb that had stewed all day in wine and the thyme, rosemary, oregano and juniper berries that grew wild in the hills through which they had passed. Zabel dipped bread, flavored with olive and onion, into the rich sauce. A mixture of ground walnuts and sugar in a crust completed their meal. Relaxed now from the food and wine, Zabel said, "Can we stay the night at this enchanting inn?" Her back muscles ached from supporting the weight of child.

"We must travel a bit further."

"I was just enjoying a moment of weakness. Let's begin."

They wound their way up a hillside, the donkeys picking their way among exposed roots. The horizon, cleared dramatically of the clouds that had settled there most of the day, revealed an empty plain bordered by mountains turned purple by the setting sun. They arrived on a granite plateau sparsely covered with grass and fissured with steep ravines. Zabel heard the tinkle of bells in the distance from a herd of goats. In this region, walls made of stones gathered from the hills sheltered the farmhouses and barns. White cranesbill poked out from any cracks. Further up the hill, terraces filled with olive trees were underlain with lavender. The gray-green color of trees and the subtle smell of the grove sent a sharp pang of homesickness through her body. *Everything in this area reminds me of home.*

They turned off the road onto a small trail leading to a barn just as the wind came up. "This will be our shelter for the night," Hector said as he opened a heavy pine door. He led Zabel to the straw that would be her bed. "It's the farm of a friend. Don't worry. We're safe."

Chinks in the ancient walls allowed the wind to penetrate the small enclosure. "They call this northwest wind the Tramontane," Hector said. "It blows more than two hundred days each year and has been known to drive some people mad."

Zabel pulled her cloak more tightly around her. *I have too much to be hopeful for to be driven mad by a wind.*

Chapter 4

At mid-morning the next day, Hector pointed to a hill in the distance, "that spire you can just make out is Albi."

After a rather arduous climb in the hot sun, they rested outside the walls of the village. A falcon flew high above the surrounding pinewoods. *It's a messenger bird,* Jnana used to say. *Perhaps there's information for me here.*

They entered through a gate in the wall and were met by the cacophonous sounds of town life, harsh compared to the tranquility of the land through which they had passed. Zabel recognized the hard metal ringing of a smith at work. Cattle moved freely about the streets adding an earthy barnyard smell to that of human excrement and garbage. An open doorway revealed a carpenter constructing a long table, the sweet smell of the pine resin relieving the harsh smell of the lane. They climbed until they reached a small dwelling near the top of the hill where an austere looking couple, Monsieur and Madame Le Blanc, welcomed Zabel.

"Lunch is nearly ready, my friend," Madame Le Blanc announced, but Hector said, "Not for me, I must reach Montpelier today."

He turned to Zabel, "You are safe here amongst these people. But before you decide where to live you should make the short journey to Montpelier. You might feel more at home there. But rest first. We have arranged for your room and board here for as long as you wish. And remember, the Knights are forever in your debt." He mounted his horse. "Oh, I almost forgot to tell you. Your donkey has been traded for a fine horse. You'll find him in M. Le Blanc's stable."

Tears welled up. Hector had become a trusted companion, one who had looked after her with every consideration. She was about to lose another friend. "I can't tell you how grateful I am to have another horse." She reached up and touched his hand. "Good luck to you, my friend. I hope I will never need your assistance, but I feel less alone knowing you're there."

He bowed low and was gone.

Back in the house Madame Le Blanc said, "Allow me to take you to your room where you can rest before lunch. You must be very tired after such a long journey."

Zabel followed Madame Le Blanc to a bedroom at the top of the stairs. Wooden shutters were nearly closed, keeping the room cool. Small brightly colored rugs were scattered over wide plank floors. Zabel removed her cloak, now layered with dust, and lay on the thick goose-feather quilt, falling into a deep sleep as a slight breeze moved the air.

A soft rap at the door awakened her. "Lunch is served. Please join us at your leisure." Mme. Le Blanc's stern voice belied her thoughtfulness. Zabel rose immediately, unwilling to disrupt their routine. As she descended the stairs, the aroma of fish cooked in garlic and herbs aroused her appetite.

Madame Le Blanc carried over a steaming bowl of

chowder to the bare polished table where Zabel sat. "It's a family recipe. My husband travels to the port of Sete to purchase the seafood. Each time I make it, it is slightly different. Today I've added early ripening beans," she said in her monotone way.

Zabel filled the wooden spoon and tasted the broth. "It's delicious."

Preparing a fine meal always brought Zabel joy, but Madame Le Blanc reached for a covered earthen jar filled with herbs and crushed a handful indifferently into the pot hanging from the hearth. She ladled only a small portion of the soup for her husband and herself.

"Isaac informs us you are Armenian. This is of interest to we Cathars. Our faith had its roots in Armenia in the seventh century."

"You are a Christian sect. Is that correct? You must explain it to me."

Monsieur Le Blanc spoke slowly, articulating each syllable as he spoke. "We Cathars live in anguish in this world." He extracted the meat from a clamshell and dropped it into his mouth.

Zabel found his words alarming. She had hoped to find people who shared her joy of life.

"We are enslaved to our human bodies, to time, and to the world in general. We humans are entangled in evil, constantly threatened and defiled by our existence. Our only desire is to be delivered from it. We are part of God and like Him are strangers here, for God cannot exist in this evil. We believe He could not have willed all the suffering we witness daily. Therefore, there must be a separate principle opposed to the God we love. As I said, our only desire is deliverance from evil."

Zabel said nothing, compressing her lips. *They live surrounded by the gifts from the Mother, but do not know Her. How could Isaac have thought I would feel at home with these people? They are against the human body, against all of Nature. Our views are completely incompatible.* Had Isaac merely used her? She didn't want to think ill of the man she considered her friend, but she felt empty. She ate her meal but its taste had gone flat.

In the days that followed Zabel met more Cathars. They lived simple lives; each person welcomed her, treated her with respect, but she knew she could never make a home among them. Unlike them, Zabel relished her walks in the nearby woods, discovering plants, trees and animals that were familiar to her and opening herself to what was different. The spirits of the land spoke, coming to her in the flowers along the road, in the flowing water of a stream so clear she could see each small stone along its bottom, and from the stars and constellations sparkling quietly above in the still of the night.

One day, she past a field with peas and beans growing from the brown earth. In another a peasant was slowly cutting summer wheat with a sickle. Walking past a field lying fallow, she followed a stream hoping to find its source. It led her up a small hill dotted with dark green beech trees. Further up, fragrant herbs grew in abundance beside the stream and she bent for a drink. *It's* warm. *Is there a hot pool near by? I would give anything to immerse my body in warm water.*

As she hurried along, the trail disappeared at times, indicating it was seldom, if ever, used. This thought made her more determined. She was forced to backtrack several times before she found herself standing in front of the mouth of a cave, similar to the yoni shaped one at her initiation ritual.

An unusual shape on the ground caught her eye. Pushing aside some stones, she beheld a small stone figure. It was a naked, pregnant female holding a notched bison horn in her raised hand. The figure's other hand pointed to her vulva. Zabel counted thirteen notches on the horn. *Did someone use this figure to keep track of time?* She could see traces of red ochre that had once covered the entire figure. *The sacred red of fertility and birth.*

She ran her fingers over the carved indentations made by a person who believed as she did. Its mute message speaking of the silence from which everything begins and ends. Her heart raced with excitement as she entered the cave but she could see nothing in the dark. Afraid of falling and injuring herself or her unborn child, she retreated, vowing to return the following day with an oil lamp.

Early the next day Zabel entered the cave and circled its perimeter, lamp held high until she found an opening in the wall just large enough for her to slide through. She entered a large chamber where faint images of women in birthing postures covered the walls. *An ancient birthing cave.* She felt a rush of elation.

She saw another opening at the rear of the chamber and could hear water running. To her delight she discovered the stream had eroded the limestone making a pool. Sulphur vapors filled the still air. Zabel removed her clothes and descending steps that had been roughly hewn in the rock, she immersed herself in the water. Its warmth caressed her body, the Earth Mother embracing her.

She was overcome by a wave of homesickness, tears falling into the water. She lay back, remembering. Slowly, a feeling of connection came over her. *The Goddess is everywhere. Surely I will find people here who know her as I do.* She thought of what Hector had said about going to Montpelier. He had known she would not stay with the Cathars. *Montpelier.* She said the name out loud letting the rich sounds echo off the walls of the chamber.

Zabel took her leave of Madame and Monsieur Le Blanc the following morning, the sacred carving tucked into her saddlebag. A gentle summer shower during the night had momentarily turned the dry landscape green, and as she rode, Zabel savoured the juicy melon Madame Le Blanc had packed.

The road led through a dry ravine where her horse's hooves rang on the stones laid down by Romans. Birds flew up, startled by the sound. *Siraj, your spirit is free like these birds. Do you ever think of me, wondering if there might be a child?* She pined for the intensity of feeling she had experienced with him, the lifetime of emotion that was compressed into a few brief days.

Chapter 5

Zabel saw the outline of Montpelier ahead and was soon crossing a moat that surrounded the stone walls of the city. She stopped to admire a pair of elegant swans gliding toward the drawbridge. She heard Jnana's voice saying, just as the brown cygnet turns into a beautiful swan, you must be willing to accept whatever the future holds.

Butchers, bakers, potters, and weavers were at work as she passed through the labyrinthine streets of the city looking for suitable lodging. Finally she was directed to an inn outside of the walls in the lower town adjacent to the port.

Zabel settled into her room alone, alarmed that her child was due in three months in an unfamiliar city where she was without a friend or acquaintance. *I must stay calm. The fates would not have brought me so far from home, to lead me to destruction.*

She took to wandering the streets on foot, talking to merchants who explained that Montpelier was a seat of great learning. Arabs and Jews had established a university to transmit the great wisdom of the East, especially medicine and philosophy.

Zabel overheard students at the vegetable market

sitting and dipping almond cookies into hot mint tea, discussing the philosophies she had studied. *Isaac was right, after all. This place feels like home.* But, now that she was alone again, she found she still feared the de Gisors and would not engage the students in conversation.

As the days turned into weeks, the coins in her purse dwindled, and she had no idea how to support herself and her child. The gems would not last forever. Impatience became her constant companion. *Maybe Isaac was mistaken. Maybe there's nothing for me here. Maybe I'm destined to be poor. No, I can't accept these negative thoughts. But what will I do?*

Early one morning Zabel arrived at the stall where she purchased fresh fruit each day. Sitting on a wooden crate she peeled an orange, its juicy sweetness making her mouth water as she savoured each segment. The owner of the stall, a small, dark-skinned peasant, was busy and paid Zabel no heed.

The sun, already hot enough to evaporate dew from the freshly picked fruit, warmed her back as she watched the local women buying vegetables. She became absorbed in the sounds of the bartering, the shouts of men moving crates of produce, and the laughter of small children who ran about the legs of the vendors. She felt her own child kick gently under her rib cage and loneliness enveloped her again.

A mendicant friar walked from behind a waiting cart and stood across the alley from Zabel. Holding his begging cup, he tried to engage the passersby in conversation. When no one noticed him, he turned his face to the heavens as if asking what to do. Then making only a slight adjustment to his stance, he stood perfectly still with his begging bowl held out. A merchant, about to mount his horse, stopped and stared at the friar. Without a word the man reached into his silk topcoat, produced a coin, and dropped it into the bowl. The friar made no gesture of acknowledgement. Next, a woman loaded down with her purchases happened by. She too, stopped and dropped a coin into the bowl. Again the friar made no sign of acknowledgement.

Soon, a legless man pushed by on a wooden platform that had been mounted on wheels. The friar stooped to talk to him. The invalid tried to put a coin into the friar's pot but the friar stopped him. He asked the man something to which the invalid shook his head . The friar stood and straightened his robe. He turned to the vendor behind him who was roasting lamb on a brazier. The friar emptied his cup to pay for some meat and a large mug of beer.

He offered the food to the invalid. They sat together while the man ate. The invalid kissed the friars hands with tears of gratitude and went on his way. The friar resumed begging.

What had she just witnessed? She had never seen such an act of compassion from the priests at home. *Siraj talked of how little Buddhist monks took from their society and how much they gave. This friar, like them, had taken the gifts of strangers to pass on to someone in need. His way wasn't to barter one thing for another. He wasn't selling a way to heaven or using rhetoric to ignite guilt and fear in those with the means to give. He simply stood with his bowl outstretched. The friar kept his vow of poverty while he bestowed gifts. A circle without obligation.*

Zabel knew she learned something vital to her life. Perhaps if she looked for a way to be helpful, Chance would provide the opportunity to sustain her. But a question entered her mind. *Am I standing in the right place?*

Chapter 6

After the monk moved on, Zabel meditated on her problem. The idea came to her that the answer would have something to do with the sea. She had learned Montpelier was an important centre for trade in the much-valued spices from the East: cinnamon, cloves, and nutmeg. Salt was evaporated from seawater along the southern coast in great saltwater pans. She rode to the dock and day after day she stared out at the blue Mediterranean listening to the sound of the gulls, looking for her opportunity. But nothing came.

Towards the end of summer it had been continually overcast but at daybreak one day the clouds began to break up as Zabel wandered along the quay. She envied the fishermen who were pulling their nets; engaged in useful work to provide for their families. The seer, Mazora, foretold she would travel, and she had, but what had she gained? She was depressed. Her life was nothing but empty hours of wandering and waiting. She longed for the love and friendship she'd experienced in Armenia. In spite of Isaac's glowing account of Languedoc, she had not let herself make a friend. Loneliness aggravated her worries.

The hot sun accentuated the heaviness of her belly so she found a quiet place and hung her feet over the side of the dock where barnacles clung to the pilings. A duck and drake floated toward her, their feet an orange blur in the water as they dipped their bills for food. The green feathers of the drake reminded Zabel of the emeralds she continued to sell. She had never felt so frightened.

She pushed her feelings aside and focused on the scene about her. Men with enormous muscles wrestled crates off ships onto waiting wagons. Fishermen wheeled barrows piled high with shimmering fish along the wharf. Their wives cleaned and sorted the catch on the beach. Zabel envied those women, talking and laughing together. No matter where she looked, each scene reminded her of home.

She recalled a poem the Maulana had recited. Something about: if you are in a tavern, you should drink. *But drink what? I am here, on this dock. I sit. I'm patient. But nothing is happening.* Zabel watched ripples hit the pilings, opening, becoming something else, and yet remaining water. *I'm ready but The Fates have abandoned me.*

Zabel gazed out to the horizon. The white canvas of a ship still far at sea, reflected the suns rays. *What had been empty space just moments before is now full. I mustn't give up.*

The ship, closer now, changed tack. It flew the flag of the Sultan of Damascus; a great merchant ship, an Alexandria, it was named after the port where it was built. *It may have docked last in Armenia. Perhaps it's laden with spices that Siraj brought from the East.* Zabel touched her swollen belly.

She heard the sailors calling in Arabic as the ship drew near. She moved behind a large barrel to give the sailors room to berth their ship.

A man on horseback, wearing a tight fitting velvet

jacket trimmed in gold braid, trotted toward the gangway. "Well, Captain, you've finally arrived. The wives of Languedoc were becoming anxious. Their husbands complain of bland dinners. If the women have been beaten, the fault rests with you."

The captain, a stocky man with a full beard, and wearing a thick wool tunic tied with a hemp cord, walked down the gangplank. His woolen pants were tucked into high scruffy leather boots. "We are fortunate to be here at all. The Kurdish general, Saladin has overrun Damascus. This war is interrupting the spice caravans. What little supply there is, is priced beyond what anyone would pay. Instead, I have brought Syrian silk. And, at a good price."

"You fool. I would have paid you anything you wanted for the spices. Silk. Wives cannot season their food with silk. I'll find another captain with some sense. Our arrangement is over." The merchant urged his horse toward the shore.

"What am I to do with the silk? I'm not a merchant," the captain called after him.

"That's your problem," the man replied as he hurried away.

The captain stared after the merchant. His shoulders slumped. "I'm ruined," he said to himself.

Zabel was shocked, thinking Siraj could be in the midst of the troubles. *I can't worry about that now.* She moved from behind the barrel, addressing the captain in Arabic, "I think I can be of some assistance. I couldn't help overhearing your conversation." The captain's stunned expression made Zabel smile. "What's the matter, captain? Are you surprised a stranger, a woman stranger, speaks to you?"

"It would not happen in my country, but here the customs are different. I try to accept such things."

"I have an idea that will help both of us. I've been waiting for you, captain."

He stared at Zabel, blinking with incomprehension.

Zabel pointed to a small building at the end of the quay. "You must take me to that tavern where you will buy me my noon meal. I've become very hungry sitting in the hot sun. There we will discuss our new partnership."

Too stunned to object, the captain followed her.

The tavern was crowded but they found a table in a dark corner. Zabel gave her order to the serving girl. "With all this noise, we'll not be overheard."

The captain emptied his pockets: a book of Persian poetry, a knife, and a compass, onto the table. Then he removed his outer jacket and rolled up the sleeves of his tunic.

Zabel asked, "Have you read much of Al Arabi?"

He nodded his assent. "Do you know this poet?"

"Yes, I have read much of this mystic's wisdom. He revered the female principle insisting that the supreme deity was a woman. For this he was accused of blasphemy."

The curious look on the captain's face turned to astonishment. "I am Abdul al Boumeni, a native of Damascus, the greatest city in all the world," he blurted.

Siraj used the same word to describe the Syrian city. "I am Zabel."

"Zabel from where?"

"That, my friend, must wait for another time. But I confirm what must be obvious to you. I am expecting a child. What is not so obvious is I am a widow. One with no family close by."

"I am devoted to a loyal wife in Damascus, and am the proud father of three delightful children."

Zabel laughed. "You're worried I'm interested in you in a lustful way. I assure you, I have a much more interesting proposal for you."

"It would be interesting enough for me if we continued to talk of poetry. On my voyages I have much time to read and contemplate, but no one with whom I can discuss my thoughts. You are a gift from Allah."

The serving girl brought two steaming tureens of oysters, scallops and clams to the table along with a jug of ruby-hued wine. Zabel poured two glasses. It tasted of the verbena that grew in the hills.

Zabel clinked his glass. "Here's to much enriching conversation. But now Abdul, regarding your problem. You have a cargo of fine silk but no means to sell it."

"You said you had a proposal."

"I will buy your silk if my conditions are met."

"I do not like conditions," Abdul said. "It usually means I will lose money. As I mentioned, I have a wife and three children in Damascus to support."

"You won't find these conditions onerous." Zabel returned her goblet to the table and leaned closer to him. "I have learned it is very dangerous to be a wealthy widow in this part of the world.

"But, how can I help you. I am married."

"I don't want you for a husband, I want you to *pretend* to be. Your profession takes you away for much of the year. It will explain why I am alone most of the time. You must find me a shop with living quarters above. The women of Montpelier have a taste for silk garments and I have a talent for creating them. My shop will be very successful. You will see. I will share the profits with you. But each trip here, you will have to live in the shop a few nights. I will make a private space for you."

"My wife will be most unhappy with that arrangement although she will undoubtedly be pleased that I have a new means of making money."

"It is a mark of your fine character that you keep nothing from your wife. You can assure her I will not compromise you. Our arrangement is too important." Then, seeing a look of disappointment cross Abdul's face, Zabel added, "It's not that you're unattractive. You *are* a most handsome man."

They laughed together, the friendship getting off to a comfortable start.

"I have no desire for another husband, so our pretense has the added advantage of keeping suitors away."

"Your requests are within my power to grant. But do you know the value of the cargo. It's worth a king's ransom."

Zabel smiled to herself only too aware of its value. *I may not have a king's ransom, but I have a queen's.* "I will have your money in two hours. Meanwhile, you must locate a shop in the grandest part of town where the wealthiest citizens will shop. I will have this shipment sold by the time you come back with a new one."

Chapter 7

When Zabel returned to the inn with the gold, Abdul was not there. Her stomach tightened. *Perhaps he's had a change of heart, deciding not to proceed with the plan. There's nothing to do but drink spiced tea and wait.*

After the second cup Zabel's stomach felt queasy and she was depressed. Then, Abdul burst through the door, slightly out of breath.

His face was glowing. "You won't believe our luck. Thanks be to Allah. I arrived at the busiest part of the town just as a vacancy sign was posted. There's not another like it in all of Montpellier. Living quarters above a bright room large enough to hold the bolts of silk. I've paid the landlord. You will see. It's perfect."

Zabel and Abdul rode over the cobbled streets behind the wagon loaded with the brightly coloured silks. Zabel, still appalled by the open sewers, told Abdul to try to dodge slops that had been tossed from second storey windows. "I've lived outside the city walls where the worst smell is rotting fish," she said, pulling her scarf over her nose.

Trying to abate her disgust, Abdul said, "You will be safer in town. Each night a curfew bell is rung ordering everyone home and all hearth fires extinguished."

"But, why?"

"The authorities believe only the enemies of peace are abroad after the curfew. Such rascals can then be easily apprehended." Abdul smiled, satisfied all would be well.

Zabel warmed to this man who was so protective of her.

Abdul urged on the horse, a smile stretching across his face. "It is just around this next corner."

He was so excited Zabel held her breath praying the space was as he described and she would not have to disappoint him.

They stopped in front of a row of shops, each with living space above. The empty one was exquisite. Strong diagonal timbers supported earthen walls. A heavy pine door opened to a large square room where glazed windows filtered the sunlight. Protruding from one wall was a stone hearth that could be lit on cool days.

Broad pine planks absorbed the sound of their feet as they crossed to a door that led up a small flight of stairs. There was another stone hearth, this one flanked by stone benches. Open shutters revealed a walled garden shaded by a tree, yellow with ripe lemons.

Back downstairs Zabel relaxed. "This is my home, Abdul. Thank you." She touched his arm in gratitude. *He couldn't possibly understand how much this place means to me.*

Abdul carefully stacked the bolts of cloth along the wall, while Zabel shopped for food. She returned as dusk fell, the room now dark. The two partners sat on the floor sharing a loaf of bread and cheese, a candle between them.

Zabel decided she would have to trust this man. She him of her life.

"I'm grateful you didn't reveal your identity before. I wouldn't have made this arrangement had I known," Abdul said scanning the shop. "It's a humble place for a queen."

"But don't you see?   Here I'll be queen in a world of my own making. And you, my friend, have made it possible."

Abdul drove her to the inn assuring Zabel he would be back with another shipment in two months. He returned to his ship to ensure all the other cargo had been off-loaded and then to make preparations for a morning departure.

The next day Zabel engaged a local carpenter to build pine trestle tables stained the color of dark red wine. It was on these tables she would roll out the brightly coloured fabric, enticing the ladies of Montpellier. The carpenter built wooden racks along the walls to hang the bolts. She chose the night of the new moon to hang a sign depicting a fashionably dressed woman. She hoped prosperity would enter the shop, just like the moon fills with light after three dark nights. On either side of the entrance, she planted orange trees in large brass urns that were the shape of her rounded belly.

The carpenter also built a smaller version of the wooden tables in the shop where she would take her meals, and sturdy chairs to encircle it, to seat the friends she hoped to make. Zabel searched the market for cooking pots, the most important being a large cauldron to hang in the hearth, where she would always keep a stew simmering. She found where to obtain the wood pruned from grape vines that the townspeople used for heat. *This hearth will then be aglow with the Spirit of Fire.*

She discovered glassblowers in Montpellier who had learned their trade from the Venetians, glass so pure that when she held it up to the window it caught the sunrise. She bought an embroidered linen coverlet, choosing a down mattress instead of straw, and a bright Persian carpet for the floor. She hung heavy curtains to partition off her sleeping area and another for Abdul. Finally, she lined a wicker basket with a soft fleece and silk. Here she would lay the child when it was born. Zabel felt like a bird building its nest twig by twig.

Now she needed to find a midwife. One afternoon she visited the apothecary whose shop was across the cobbled square. "Good day, monsieur. I am Zabel, your new neighbor. She pointed across the square. "My husband, Abdul, and I have just opened our shop. We sell the finest Syrian silk."

"When your sign went up, I must admit, I was upset with the temptation you have offered my wife," he said, smiling warmly. "I am Felix Marmoutier." He bowed slightly with this admission. "I see your child is due. Are you experiencing any problems?"

"No, I'm well. But, I desire a midwife for the birthing. I was hoping you'd know of one."

Monsieur Marmoutier fiddled with some jars on the counter. Zabel saw her request had made him uncomfortable.

"My wife knows someone. She will arrange for Madame Noirfor to call on you."

The late afternoon sun through the open doorway was the color of honey. Zabel was returning bolts of silk to the racks after a busy day of meeting the demands of her customers. The local gossip had passed the word that a new shop carried exquisite silk, and the owner, an Armenian woman, offered creative suggestions for the tailoring.

A melodious voice called her name. A woman, as round and full as a melon in autumn, walked into the shop, her broad feet splaying outward as she advanced. The long robe she wore was held together by nine wooden toggles carved with the sign of the yoni. *Just as Jnana wore.* Zabel knew instantly she wanted the woman to assist at the birthing. Montpelier did, indeed, offer everything she needed to feel at home.

Zabel moved her embroidery from a chair so the woman could sit. "You must be the midwife, Madame Noirfor. We'll have tea."

Picking up the needlework and softly running her fingers over the threads, the midwife said, "You do beautiful work."

"It helps to pass the time when no one is in the shop. Women with no patience for this art are happy to pay me to embroider their purchases," Zabel said. She placed her hand on her belly. "This is my first."

Madame Noirfor examined the pattern of lavender sprigs Zabel was creating. "I see you are interested in herbs. But we will talk of such things later. You must have questions for me."

"I assume you're very experienced."

"I have delivered many of the children you see playing in these streets. It is a profession handed down to me by my mother. I am descended from generations of midwives."

Zabel suddenly longed for Jnana. She brushed a tear from her eye, willing herself not to breakdown in front of her new acquaintance but the emotion was too strong. She sobbed, and the midwife drew Zabel to her ample bosom, comforting her.

"I'm sorry," Zabel said as her tears dried. "You remind me of the grandmother I had to leave behind in Armenia. And my husband is a sea captain. He's away most of the time." She straightened and wiped her eyes. "Usually I can control my emotions better than this."

"It is understandable, my dear. I can only imagine what it must be like to be so far from your people at a time like this. I will do my best to feel like family and I'll bring some of my friends to meet you. Don't worry," she said, patting Zabel on the back as if she were a small child. "You won't be alone when the baby comes. I promise."

How fortunate I am to have met this generous woman. She is like the Earth herself.

"My grandmother wore the sign of the yoni just as you do," Zabel said, suddenly having a need to make herself known to this woman. "My mother died shortly after giving birth to me. It was in the ancient ways of women that my grandmother raised me. You are just like her." After the words were spoken, Zabel felt afraid. Had she spoken too openly to a stranger, even to one who seemed so loving?

Madame Noirfor eyed Zabel critically. "Worshipping the Goddess is seen as a danger to the faith by the church fathers. We've been accused of offering children to the devil in magical baptisms. You must be very careful with whom you speak of such things. It can be very dangerous."

Zabel's heart sank. She recalled the stories she'd heard in Paris; that midwives were burned as witches. She had hoped to be able to follow the ancient ways without interference, but, to her horror, the long tentacles from Rome reached here as well. "I would not want to put you in danger."

Madame Noirfor was silent for some moments. "New edicts from the Church demand women seek the aid of male doctors to deliver their children. These men are anxious to see women scream in pain during childbirth as the Bible says they must."

A shiver ran through Zabel at the thought of such treatment. "How is it you're still able to practice your craft?"

"I am allowed to be present at births when the local doctor is busy. But even though I know which herbs will ease birth pangs, I am not allowed to administer them."

"I will be made to endure great pain, then?"

"Don't worry, when your time comes, I will give you the herbs. But you must act your part, cry out for the whole neighborhood to hear, or we'll both be in grave danger."

Zabel nodded in agreement, but she was angry with the church; angry that women weren't left alone to deal with women's matters.

Madame Noirfor looked about the shop. "You'll need someone to help you after the baby comes. I know just the person. She is the middle daughter of my cousin. Their farm is but a short ride from the city gates. Brigit is a delightful girl, her father's pride. She's used to the hard work of the farm as well as tending to the needs of her younger sister. She's assisted me at some births, being intuitive in the healing arts. And she'll keep your hearth-fire burning." Madame Noirfor laughed heartily. "Best of all, she has the soul of an artist. She has made some beautiful tapestries. She would be an asset to your shop."

"Why would her father let her work for me?"

"My cousin dreams of buying his land. For that reason and that reason only, he will allow it. He knows such an able young woman can earn him a great deal of money."

“I’m not sure I can afford her.”

“You can negotiate with him. Remind her father that with you she will learn the skills required to run a shop. No one in the family has such knowledge and the town is expanding. She could someday have a shop of her own. It would be like paying for an apprenticeship.”

Chapter 8

The next day a young woman with large brown eyes entered the shop, fixing Zabel with a sure, steady gaze. She curtsied holding her skirts wide with long delicate fingers. "I'm Brigit Cantellon."

Her skin, the rich tan color of the surrounding hills, indicated a Middle Eastern influence in the bloodline. Zabel instantly felt comfortable in the girl's presence. "Are you able to negotiate our arrangements or must we speak with your father?"

Brigit flushed and Zabel wondered if this girl resented she was not master of her own fate. *If that is true, I like her even more.*

"It is my father who will decide. He has asked that you meet him at our farm on Sunday after church. I can come for you in our wagon. It would be more comfortable for you, don't you think?"

Zabel thought of the mistake she'd made upon becoming queen when she allowed Bishop Scarfos to summon her. Should she worry about Brigit's father? No, she decided. Monsieur Cantellon was not a bishop and he held no power over her. As much as she liked this young woman, if his terms were too onerous, she would refuse them.

It was hot when Brigit arrived in a wagon pulled by a shabby plow horse.

"You needn't worry about being jostled. This old mare is steady and true."

They took the road to Albi.

"I have acquaintances in Albi by the name of Leblanc. Do you know them?"

"He is my father's liege lord," said Brigit. "It could help our cause."

"What have they to do with our bargain?"

Brigit maneuvered the horse around a pothole in the road. "In this region, it's law that the liege lord must give his permission for such a contract."

Zabel said nothing, but thought, *I risked my life to deliver money to them. I'm sure they'll feel obliged.*

Before the hill leading to Albi, Brigit turned the mare into a dirt lane worn smooth by time. Laden olive trees and vines heavy with purple grapes filled the fields.

They stopped beside a thatched cottage shaded by tall cedars. Brigit's mother was bent over, working amongst her leeks, beets, and cabbages. She straightened as the wagon approached shading her eyes with a brown hand encrusted with dirt. As they approached, Zabel saw she had planted herbs between the vegetables. *She lays out her garden as Jnana does.*

Madame Cantellon put her arm about her daughter. "Brigit is most anxious to work in your establishment. She has talked of nothing but silk."

Zabel felt a pang of envy. *To be loved by your mother. Brigit does not know how blessed she is.*

"But it's my husband you must convince. He has great plans for this one; our most talented child." She lifted her daughter's hand and stroked the long fingers. "Her slender fingers, and graceful appearance is a sign she is to rise in the world, don't you agree?"

"I certainly do," Zabel said.

"She's already worked in the castle, for the Lord's wife, learning the arts of women. But her father will tell you all that. He's newly arrived from his fields and awaits you."

Madame Cantellon led Zabel inside a room with low ceilings and a dirt floor tamped as hard as tile. It was immaculate.

Brigit's father sat formally at the end of a rough-hewn table looking uncomfortable. *He's probably unused to being in the cottage before dusk; his farm must require his continuous attention.* He nodded to his wife to pour wine for each of them. Zabel took a sip, letting it relax the muscles in her back.

Monsieur Cantellon smacked his lips, examining the amount of tartness in his wine before he began to speak. "Brigit has a way with animals. Since she has become a maiden my cows have never gone dry."

Zabel took his abrupt beginning to mean the bargaining had begun. "I am willing to pay you well. Madame Noirfor says Brigit will be worth every penny."

You see, " he paused to take another sip of wine, "We are Basques. Recently settled here from beyond the mountains to the west. It was a time of trouble. The

Basques were accused of witchcraft."

Zabel felt a shadow cross the room. *This talk of witches is everywhere.*

"In this region we can own land. But a high price has been set. Brigit's been promised in marriage to the son of a local family. Such an alliance will strengthen us. I will postpone the wedding so Brigit can earn extra money and we can purchase the land sooner. As is the custom, I have received permission from my liege lord. It was easier than I expected. He tells me you are a valued friend."

"I'm grateful they have not forgotten me." *Is this how the Great Mother designed her world, where one good turn keeps bringing rewards?*

Brigit's father bargained over every detail but in the end, Zabel decided his demands were fair, so the arrangement was sanctified over a bowl of thick cabbage soup and newly baked bread. Brigit packed her meager possessions into the wagon, promising to return it to her father the next day.

"Can you ride?" Zabel asked.

"Yes, of course."

"Then take my horse with you tomorrow for your return."

Zabel sewed Brigit a silk gown and began to instruct her in the art of selling. It was soon apparent that Brigit's natural grace made the customers comfortable. She began a tapestry: a tree of life that each customer vied for the right to own. She gathered reeds from the shallows at the coast and wove beautiful and sturdy baskets in which to keep the vegetables she brought from her mother after each weekly visit. Yet with all her talents Zabel found Brigit remained unaffected. Her company was as nourishing as the bread she baked each morning.

Each night, Zabel slept contented with her new life, clutching under her pillow the carved fertility figure she'd found, and waited for her child to be born.

One Sabbath she awoke yearning for the warmth of the sacred spring: to feel the strength of the Great Mother before her lying in, and to savor the luxury of floating free of the weight of her belly. She decided to have Brigit accompany her after early mass. That way they could then still have lunch at the Cantellon farm as usual.

They soon were heading into the limestone hills to the place where the trail through the bush began. They tied the horse so it could forage and they entered the pine woods. Zabel relaxed as she always did when she entered untouched Nature, the realm of the living Goddess.

Birds flickered from branch to branch where mottled sunlight touched the translucent green of the leaves and the burnt gold of the earth, comforting after the hectic bustle of Montpelier. They sat, leaning against a log, and looked up to the vast cloudless sky, Zabel hoping her child was absorbing the energies of the Spirits that surrounded them. Sleep overtook both women.

Zabel was nudged awake. She thought it was Brigit, but when she opened her eyes she beheld the face of a deer. It stepped over her, continuing it's grazing, undisturbed by their human presence.

Zabel sat up, holding her belly. *This glade. The deer. It's like the dream I had that prompted Jnana to begin my initiation. But now its real.*

Her senses heightened. Zabel rose, touching the rough furrowed bark of a pine, keenly aware of the sharp fragrance of its needles. *The Spirits are woven into the very fabric of this place.*

She woke Brigit and they continued up the hill to the cave; the remains of the fire she had lit on her previous visit were undisturbed, reinforcing her belief that no one else knew of this place. Zabel lit the torch she brought, leading the way to the birthing chamber. Brigit gasped, as the images painted on the walls were illuminated.

"My mother told me stories of these places," Brigit said as she ran her fingers over the symbol of the yoni.

"What stories, Brigit?"

"In the times before my mother was born, women gathered in caves like this to birth their babies. There was much joy and celebration. But now doctors...the men have taken over. I'm sure Madame Noirfor has told you. The church wants women to experience pains as it states in the Bible they must. To suffer for Eve's sin."

Zabel muscles tensed at the thought of uncontrollable pain. "Madame promised to help me."

"But only if other women need the doctor at the same time," Brigit said. Otherwise the doctor will attend you. Madame will be there of course, but she won't be able to give you the potions to ease your agony. You understand, don't you?"

Zabel read the concern on Brigit's face and pressed her arm. "If it comes to that I will have to endure it. It will be enough to have someone who cares by my side." *I'll have to trust that all would be well.* "Come deeper into the cave, Brigit. I have something else to show you."

They entered the chamber with the pool, mist rising

from the water. Brigit knelt and submerged her fingers. "It's warm."

"It's why this cave was chosen as a birthplace. It is the womb of the Goddess from which all else flows. Have you ever bathed in such water?"

"Never." Brigit's eyes widened. "Will you enter it?"

Zabel removed her clothes. "Come in. I promise, it is the deepest bliss.

"But I've never taken my clothes off in front of another person."

Zabel laughed softly. *The people here train their young to be ashamed of their bodies.* "In my country, everyone bathes. The men, together in large pavilions; while we women share tubs of warm water, scented with fragrant oils, in our private rooms."

"I've never heard of such a thing."

Zabel slid into the water and felt the welcome caress of its minerals. Brigit's curiosity soon overcame her shyness. She entered the pool, her smile revealing her pleasure.

"If I could choose, I would birth my child here in the presence of the Great Mother."

"I would give anything to make that happen."

But Zabel sensed the power of the Church, intruding through the hands of a compassionless doctor. She shivered in spite of the warm water.

Chapter 9

It became Madame Noirfor's habit to accompany Brigit and Zabel each Sabbath to the Cantellon farm. As the conversations grew more intimate, Brigit and Madame revealed to Zabel their shared worship of the Goddess, immanent now in the flaming red and brilliant gold leaves of autumn.

One Sunday, Zabel sat in the wagon as they rolled past cottagers preparing for the barren season. At the farm, Madame Cantellon placed a sturdy chair in the warm sun so Zabel could watch the family gathering acorns and beechnuts to feed their pigs over the winter. In the distant fields Zabel could see Brigit's cousins harvesting wheat, their scythes moving rhythmically in the orange light of the setting sun. She stood waist deep in the field of undulating wheat, conjuring the aroma of the fresh bread Brigit baked each day.

The grape harvest began the following week. This time Zabel sat amongst the vines in a wagon that was loaded down with an enormous oaken barrel. She watched Brigit, her hair tied back with a bright red scarf join the others who climbed wooden ladders to gather the ripe clusters of fruit. Once the baskets were full, the pickers balanced them on their heads, and walked to the wagon, dumping their grapes into the barrel.

When it was full, Brigit climbed onto the bench beside Zabel, wiping her brow with her scarf and urged the old mare to the crushing yard. The warmth of the day and the physical activity had caused a soft sheen to appear on Brigit's face and neck giving her a flushed appearance. "I've been thinking," Brigit began. "There's an ancient custom of our people. A ritual, to determine the purpose of the life of a child about to enter the world. Would you like to have such a ceremony?"

The aroma of fallen fruit crushed by the rush of feet stirred in Zabel the memory of a recurring dream, in which she was Dionysus. A man in the dream announced he knew her fate. She just had to roll the dice he said. Then she woke up. Her fate remained unrevealed. The dream always brought images of Armenia, of her father, of chess, of Jnana to her mind. Now, almost nine months since she left, she was sure she had found her destiny, and a new family.

She'd never heard of such a ceremony for an unborn child, but it sounded intriguing. "I would be honored."

"You must remember the Church is against our rituals," Brigit said, grasping Zabel's arm. "You must promise to tell no one."

"I understand the dangers, Brigit. I'll not betray us."

"Tomorrow night is the full moon, the best night for the ceremony," Brigit said, her usual confidence returning.

Dew sparkled on the meadow at dusk. They would stay at the farm overnight, as the gates of the city would be locked at curfew. Zabel was nervous. The energy of the full moon brought great potency for the ritual, but it could reveal them to curious eyes as they proceeded to the sacred site.

Brigit turned the wagon into a small lane that wound through an almond orchard, nuts littering the ground. *Each nut has grown safe, nestled in the branches, washed by rain and rocked gently by summer breezes, finally letting go, plunging to the soft, moist Earth, ready to regenerate in the ooze while covered by a blanket of leaves.* Zabel rubbed the child in her belly. *Like the almond, my child, we will take root in this land, pushing deep into the Earth.* Zabel imagined the tree inside each nut, just as she could see the woman she was sure grew inside her.

They entered a cypress forest where the lane narrowed to a footpath, just as the light was disappearing amidst low-gathering clouds. Brigit carefully helped Zabel from the wagon and they proceeded on foot, the moist fall air aromatic with the scent of the trees.

In the grove, a cow, decorated with bunches of grapes and sprigs of fall leaves, was encircled by eleven women. With Zabel and Brigit they would be thirteen, the sacred female number. Each woman in turn told Zabel her name then hugged her with the warmth of deep friendship. *It is as if I have known these women forever.*

As the moon began to rise, Madame Noirfor indicated Zabel should take her place in the centre of the circle beside the cow. "This animal is a symbol of the force that supports all living things." Madame began. "I call the Spirits with this hawthorn wand, the sacred tree of fertility." As she called to the four directions, each woman raised her arms above her head in a circling motion, and then rested them together at her heart. The women stood silently in contemplation, watching the newly risen-moon bring the heart spirit into the grove.

One by one the women entered the centre and placed their hands on Zabel's belly. Returning to her place, each sat, meditating on the message she had received from the unborn child.

The last to approach Zabel was Madame Noirfor, who after receiving her message, indicated Zabel should sit in front of her. With her eyes closed Zabel became acutely aware of the silent strength of the trees that surrounded her, of the dark loam made from a thousand leaves decomposing, providing nourishment for each new tree. Life from death.

As if reading her thoughts, Madame said, "The Great Mother is ruthless with her sacred laws. When autumn comes, no leaf is spared though it may be of singular beauty. No flower, even if of wonderful fragrance. The circle is always completed, death following birth, birth preceding death. We live in endless time. Each living thing dies, but Life, goes on. The ancient night sky has cast it's light upon the continuous creation of the Mother, connecting us to her deeper wisdom. Each has a place in Her realm. Speak, child, what is the purpose of your incarnation?"

Madame sat, her hands pressed to Zabel's rounded belly, meditating on the energy of the new life. Finally she announced, "The child is ready to speak through me."

"I am coming to keep the ancient rituals. The dark time is not over. We humans will do much harm to Mother Earth and all the things upon her. I am one who will hold the memory, who will bring the knowing forward until we reach an age in the far distant future when it will once again be safe to freely and openly celebrate the Earth and all the Spirits."

A gentle murmur of agreement echoed around the circle. Then sistrums and castanets sounded to accompany a frame drum whose steady beat was that of Her living heart. The women rose and moved to the strong, even rhythm, each one holding Zabel in turn, pledging herself to support the new life that would soon be among them. Then Madame said, "May the mystery be completed in your body, by your blood turning to milk to nourish this child."

Once again Zabel thought of the dream where she had been Dionysus. Transformation of grapes to wine. Of blood to milk.

She saw Jnana's face in her mind's eye and took a deep breath. Here tonight, with this group of woman, she was keeping her promise to her grandmother to continue her initiation.

Witnessed by the slate colored sky, the women shared a meal around a small fire. They talked in the easy way of women when they deliberately set themselves apart from the world of everyday existence, ignoring the patriarchal laws outside the grove. Zabel felt nourished, not only by the food, but also by the love expressed by these women, strangers, who accepted her as one of their own.

As the fire burned down and the shadows deepened, Madame released the spirits from the sacred circle and the grove became profane once more. Zabel shivered. She sensed the contentment the women shared could be shattered in the most horrific of ways. And it could turn in an instant.

Chapter 10

Madame Noirfor walked across the tree-lined square to the silk shop as she did each day now the birth of Zabel's child approached. Golden poplar leaves lay scattered at the open door as she hurried inside. Zabel was standing with her hand pressed against the small of her back in an effort to ease her discomfort. *Awkwardness encourages women to look forward to the birth. Otherwise, I might want to hold the child inside forever.*

"Zabel, have I told you why it is fortuitous for your child to be born now?"

"To save my back from breaking?"

Madame Noirfor sat down in a chair and removed a scarf from around her neck. "No, no. It's a special time of cosmic significance. Did your grandmother explain this is the time of year when the thirteenth sign of the zodiac used to appear in the heavens?"

"Yes," Zabel said. She recalled the night of her initiation. "The Snake Goddess."

"Perhaps with the birth of your child we will be ushering in an age when men's rule will end. When the Goddess can once again appear in the night sky."

Zabel's emotions had been unsteady for the last few days. She felt irritated by Madame's positive attitude. "You know my child will be born into a world of oppression. I can't even birth her without a man being present." Zabel cried into her hands.

"Come, let's go out back," Madame said, leading Zabel by the arm. "Brigit," she called, "come down here. Zabel needs you to take over in the shop."

The garden was quiet and the scent of fall lavender settled Zabel's nerves, until a sudden stabbing pain in her back doubled her over. Madame steadied her.

"Walk, Zabel. These could be birth pangs. Just keep moving."

As she walked, Zabel thought of the last few days. Her new friends had visited. They brought loaves of bread and freshly harvested vegetables to keep the stew pot full. They massaged her back and limbs with scented olive oil after walking with her around the square each day.

Another pain wracked her body, more alarming than the first. "I need to sit."

"Rest for a bit, but it's better if you keep moving. For now."

The pains continued, increasing in frequency. The process of birthing had begun.

"Brigit, tell the apothecary we need Dr. Lafevre now," Madame said.

Zabel looked at Madame with terror in her eyes. "Don't worry, my dear. I'll be close by. But you understand. It is the law. He must deliver your child."

A tall, thin man entered the enclosure. His grizzled beard covered a pink complexion dotted with many dark spots. "Get her inside. She must lie down," was all he said bypassing introductions. Madame and Brigit helped Zabel into bed. As another pain convulsed Zabel's body, Dr. Lafevre placed his hand on her belly. Zabel was horrified to see his nails were encrusted with dirt. She recoiled instinctively, not wanting his hands touching her or her child.

Another sharp pain forced a cry from Zabel's lips. She wanted to get up, to move, but she lay still, as ordered. She glanced to Madame, silently pleading with her to do something.

Madame could do little but offer comfort with a smile and a nod. "Brigit, bring some damp cloths to wipe Zabel's face."

Brigit, who hated to witness suffering, looked as shaken as Zabel. These births, where the doctor was in charge, were always hard on the girl, Madame had told Zabel.

The hours passed. Zabel called for wine. "To relieve my dry mouth," she said.

"Get her some," the doctor said. "She must keep up her strength. This looks like it will be a long and painful birth."

Brigit was appalled to hear pleasure in his voice. She followed Madame into the kitchen. "You have to do something. I can't stand this. He's a brute. We could give her something to ease the pain."

"You know we can't. I want nothing else. But he would discover it, sure enough."

"I know," Brigit said, resignation on her face. Then

her look changed to excitement. "Can you stop it?"

"Stop what?"

"The labor?"

"Of course I can, but why? What good would that do? It would only start again later and she would have to go through the pain twice." Madame poured a small draught of wine into a goblet and walked toward the door.

Brigit grabbed her arm, splashing wine on the floor.

"What are you doing?" Madame said, her eyebrows rising. This isn't like you.

"Put something in the wine to stop the contractions. You'll see. My plan is a good one."

From the other room, Zabel screamed.

"Just do as I ask."

"All right. But if anything goes wrong, we'll be in grave danger. Dr. Lafevre has much influence with the authorities. He's brought grief to other midwives who have disobeyed him. Terrible things. You don't want to know."

"But she's terrified of him." Brigit's face remained firm. "If he figures it out, I'll tell them I did it. No trouble need fall on you."

"Don't be foolish. I love her as much as you do." Madame reached into the pouch she wore around her waist. She pulled out a small vile and added two drops of dark green potion into the wine.

As dusk turned to evening Zabel's pains eased until finally the doctor concluded her labor had ceased for the moment. Zabel would not have her child this night. "Call me when the pains resume. Perhaps she is waiting for her husband to return. Some wives do this. Whatever the reason, she'll sleep now and so will I." He wiped his hands on Zabel's bedclothes and left.

Zabel was shaking with exhaustion. "Madame is something wrong? Why did the pains stop?"

"No, nothing is amiss." Madame tucked the blankets about Zabel. "But I'll stay the night to make sure you sleep. Rest now. Brigit, make us some tea. I'll join you as soon as I'm sure she's asleep."

The aroma of mint and spices filled the room as Madame pulled a chair to the table where Brigit sat. "Now tell me. What is this plan of yours?"

"Tomorrow is the Sabbath," Brigit said. "Each week I've taken Zabel to the farm to be with my family. You and I will take her tomorrow, as always, but before we get there, she'll deliver her child. These things happen. There will have been no time to get the doctor."

"You stupid girl. She cannot simply have her child by the side of the road. She could die. We need water. She'll want privacy. If anyone sees her in labor they'll fetch the doctor. Your plan has only succeeded in putting her in more pain." Madame had worked herself into a fury. "What ever possessed you to propose such a preposterous scheme?"

"What you don't know, you tiresome old woman," Brigit said with a smile, "is Zabel has found a cave with markings on the walls to indicate it was once a birthing site. Zabel can have her child there with you as mid-wife."

"It is a noble idea but fraught with dangers."

"If it makes you feel better, we'll let Zabel decide tomorrow when she wakes. If she doesn't want to have her child in the cave, we'll call for the doctor."

“A birthing cave. I’ve heard of them. From my grandmother. They were places of much joy for women.” Madame poured herself more tea. “It will be worth the risk to experience such a place once before I die. I’ll do it if it’s Zabel’s wish.” She swallowed the last of her tea. “We must sleep now, too.”

Zabel woke in a fog, the residue of the sedative still in her body. Brigit was beside her, already dressed, her hair in braids that she’d wound around her head.

“We need to talk,” Brigit said. “Is your mind clear?”

“Clear enough,” Zabel said, attempting to sit.

“Just lie back. I’ll get Madame.”

The older woman came in carrying a bowl of warm broth. Brigit raised Zabel against the cushions and Madame began to spoon the clear liquid into Zabel’s eager mouth.

“We’re taking you to the farm today,” Brigit said.

Zabel remembered it was the Sabbath. “But, can I do it? Can I travel, Madame?”

“Last night I gave you a potion to stop your labor. Brigit has convinced me the ideal place to birth your child is in the cave you discovered.”

“It crossed my mind as well, but I put the thought aside. I won’t endanger you and Brigit.”

“I’m an old woman, Zabel. I want to deliver just one child in the ancient way. Brigit assures me it is unlikely anyone will find the cave. I would be the only one going against the law and I’m willing to take the risk.”

Brigit hid the basket Zabel had prepared for the child in the back of the wagon, and the three women rode from the walls of Montpelier.

Soon they turned off the main road and after following the small path they reached the trailhead where they secured the horse and wagon. Zabel felt a surge of energy as she moved upward.

The labor pains began soon after they settled inside. Zabel let out a howl as one intense cramp seized her. She panted as beads of sweat formed on her forehead.

Madame gave her a tincture of herbs to swallow. "These will help, but my grandmother told me the babies were born under water with ease. Your pains are very close together now. I'm sure the water will help. Let's all get into the pool."

Brigit and Madame helped Zabel down the steps. She leaned against Brigit. The tightness in Zabel's back eased, buoyed by the warm, caressing water. There was a cramp, a pause, and then another cramp, but she was so relaxed they were nothing like the pains of the previous night.

Soon she felt the head of her child between her legs, a swirl of Divine Energy unfolding through her.

Madame reached down and supported the head as the child emerged from Zabel's body. Only the cord held them together. "It's a girl," Madame said.

My child. You've been living in darkness in my belly, in the salty water of my womb. Our blood is to be separated forever. Now there will be you and me.

The two women helped the mother and newborn from the water and onto a blanket on the floor. Brigit held Zabel's sacred knife.

"Cut the cord. My daughter is ready to begin her

life."

Madame tied the cord and Zabel watched as the blood settled between mother and child and then Brigit cut. They placed the tiny infant on Zabel's bare skin; two separate people joined by an unbreakable bond of love.

"What will you name her?" Brigit asked.

Zabel thought of Siraj as she stroked the fine black hair on the tiny head, amazed at its silkiness. She could honour him for the gift of his seed by naming the child after him. But she didn't. "She will have my name. Izabel. The first of a line of women born of me in this new land."

Izabel was hungry and soon latched onto Zabel's breast, feeding ravenously. The three women laughed through tears of joy at the loud sucking sound the child made. Zabel was overcome by an intense feeling of pleasure, security and warmth. They lit a fire and Zabel envisioned the couplings of her ancestors that had led to her, and now to her daughter.

They wrapped Izabel tightly in soft blankets. She lay awake, a beautifully formed child with smooth chubby cheeks who seemed relaxed and already sure of her place in the world. Zabel felt as though her heart had leapt out of her body and attached itself to this new person, the daughter she'd prophesized. *Siraj, if only you were here to see her.*

Zabel kept the child warm under her cloak, as they drove to the farmhouse in time for the family dinner.

"Let me hold her." Brigit's mother took the infant into her arms, joy spreading over her face. "She's a grandchild, Zabel. If you wish her to be."

Zabel was overcome with emotion. "It would be my

honor." These people, strangers but a short time ago, were family now. She wiped away a tear.

"Brigit, I've prepared some herbal tea for Zabel. There, in the small pot," she said, pointing to the long table. It will restore her strength."

Zabel sipped the infusion. "What will we do about the doctor? We must make sure he believes our story." She felt a chill in spite of the warmed glass between her hands.

"You must call him in when you return. To check the baby," Brigit's mother suggested. "Tell him the child was born here when the rest of us went to Mass. He will accept that."

"But the lie, the story would involve you as well. I don't think we should do that," Zabel said.

"We'll stick together, as always. It's our way."

Zabel choked back tears. Fortune was smiling on her.

The next morning Dr. Lafevre arrived. "The gossips have been busy. The child was delivered at the Cantellon farm."

"Yes." Zabel looked quickly to Brigit. The girl was calm.

"Shortly after we arrived my labor began. Madame Noirfor would have sent for you, but the pains came so strong and fast that there was no time. My water broke. Ah, the pains. They were terrible. Would you look at her now, doctor?"

Madame entered the shop as they were proceeding upstairs. Dr. Lafevre walked toward her. "So, you have delivered another infant without my help, have you, Madame

Noirfor?" He looked down at her with his deep-set eyes, his face menacing. "Perhaps you would like to be admitted to my honored profession, is that it?"

"Oh, my goodness, no. I'm only glad that on occasions when you are otherwise busy, I can lend some small assistance to the mothers, especially those like Zabel who delivered her first child. I only tried to keep her calm when she was wild with pain. I always pray you'll make it on time, but as you know, some of these souls are most anxious to come into the world."

"What Montpelier needs is another doctor. The population is expanding faster than I can manage," Dr. Lafevre said as if he were talking to himself. He followed Zabel to the sleeping infant where he unwrapped her roughly and looked her over thoroughly. Izabel didn't like being awakened in such a manner and screamed.

"She appears to have healthy lungs. She will be a fine child," he pronounced. "Congratulations." Then he was gone.

Zabel gave Izabel her breast and the child was soon asleep. The three women returned to the shop and Brigit poured tea from the simmering pot. "We are safe this time. We must have said all the right things," Madame said.

"I'll never forget what you both did for me," Zabel said.

Chapter 11

Abdul arrived in Montpelier five weeks after Izabel's birth and acted the part of an ecstatic father. "Come outside," he demanded, "I have a present for my daughter." Tied to a post in front of the shop was a handsome horse. "Well, what do you think?"

Zabel recognized a pure blooded Arabian.

Abdul's eyes sparkled. "An excellent gift for a child soon to possess her mother's riding skill, don't you think?"

Zabel ran her hand along the animal's glossy chestnut coat, and its supple limbs. "It's a majestic beast," Zabel said, noticing the long elegant tail that dusted the ground.

"I bought her in Damascus. A military horse, trained to play polo. She is called Grace."

"Abdul, how did you know? This is a gift we will cherish."

Abdul bowed deeply in acceptance. "When I saw her in the market her very attitude reminded me of you. Feisty, sure, good blood lines. I knew she was meant to belong to this child. Of course, you will have to ride her until Izabel is somewhat older."

"With two horses, Brigit and I can visit her family without Brigit having to ride out to borrow the wagon."

"Go for a ride," Brigit suggested. "I'll watch Izabel."

"No, I'll take her," Zabel said.

Zabel strapped the child to her body with a long silk scarf, mounted the horse and they trotted out of town. The motion soon put the baby to sleep so when they reached the open rode Zabel gave a small indication with her heels and the animal raced toward the sea.

She rode the mare along the shallow foam of the surf, water splashing, and the wind passing her body. Her senses heightened, as they always did when she was atop a horse. The horse had been well trained, responding to her slightest movement. Images of polo playing, of her father, of Raymond, and of Jnana went through her mind. *Once these memories brought nothing but feelings of loss, but now, with my new family, I think of those I have left behind without sorrow. Just love.*

Zabel returned as the long afternoon shadows stretched across the street. Abdul was sitting by the fire, reading philosophy. The scent of anise and garlic filled the room from fish chowder Brigit and Madame had prepared. Soon they greedily tore chunks from the bread Brigit had baked, dipping it into the savory broth.

Izabel woke, hungry. Zabel moved to a chair by the fire and nestled the babe to her breast. She nuzzled for the nipple and after she had latched on suckling enthusiastically, Zabel felt the glory of her part in Nature.

Madame and Abdul shared a warm conversation, gesturing and laughing as they exchanged tales. Brigit cleared the dishes. Light from the fire cast a warm glow over the room, reflecting off the copper ewer from which Brigit poured their tea.

To match the elegance of the newly arrived Jews and Arabs to Montpelier, Zabel began to wear a gold girdle over her silk gowns, tucking her ceremonial knife into the rolled fabric so that the jeweled handle gleamed in the glow from the oil lamps that lit her shop. As her customers examined the luxurious silks, deciding on the colour and possible styles, she engaged them in conversations about the places they had lived, especially enjoying the explanations of their customs. Occasionally, women who had traveled to the Holy Land on crusade with their husbands bought her fabrics. She would sometimes feel homesick but more often than not she was able to push the emotion aside.

One morning, Brigit rushed into the shop, breathless, carrying a basket of fish and winter vegetables she had procured at the market.

"Eleanor of Aquitaine has just arrived from the Holy Land. I saw her. Then I overheard her asking where she might get some dresses made and everyone spoke of you. She and her ladies will arrive any minute." Brigit rushed about the shop, replacing bolts of fabric that had been left on the tables. "Eleanor's court at Poitiers is famous as a centre of poetry. They say it is frequented by the most famous troubadours who celebrate and refine the lore of chivalry and the mystique of courtly love."

That sounded to Zabel like the Persian poetry recited in her father's court. Then she remembered how her councilman, in trying to persuade her to marry Raymond, had used Eleanor as an example. She had arrogantly compared herself with the French queen. Things were certainly different now. But she couldn't help but wonder how Eleanor had held onto her lands after marrying King Louis.

Some time later a woman entered the shop with four ladies-in-waiting. She was of such noble bearing there could be no doubt she was the celebrated queen. Gold circled her wrists and pendants hung from her ears, heavy with rubies. *She is one who understands her power and how to use it.*

Zabel and Brigit unrolled bolt after bolt of the finest silks Damascus had to offer; while the late afternoon sun streamed in through the windows, lighting the fabrics as if they were gems set in gold. At last satiated, the buzz of voices from Eleanor's ladies subsided. The queen looked hard at Zabel. *She has been stealing glances at me all afternoon.*

"Leave me," Eleanor commanded her women, "I wish to speak to Zabel alone."

"If you wish, we can retire to my apartment Your Highness."

"Very well." Eleanor followed Zabel up the stairs.

The queen seated herself by the fire, "There is something about you, your name, perhaps, that reminds me of a story I heard while traveling in Armenia. Their queen was deposed by one of my husband's countrymen."

Zabel's heart quickened, sure this knowledge could bring nothing but trouble to herself and Izabel.

"I remember now. Her name *was* Zabel."

Thankful she was stuffing mint leaves into the pot, Zabel had time to compose herself.

"I think you are she." Eleanor raised her hand to stop Zabel from speaking. "Before you try to deny this fact, as I am sure you will, understand I know the politics of this land and fully understand why you would not want your identity revealed."

"I have no reason not to trust you, my lady."

"We are both queens. You may call me Eleanor."

Eleanor's smile seemed heartfelt and Zabel relaxed.

"But tell me, where is the Frank? Is he here, in the south with you?"

"No, he died shortly after we returned to his family." Zabel felt the prick of tears for what could have been. "His father told me that under the Frankish law they would have custody of my unborn child. I fled. Here in Montpelier, the people believe I'm married to the Arab sea captain who supplies me with silk."

"A husband who is conveniently away most of the year is a believable lie."

The understanding that Eleanor displayed put Zabel more at ease. "I've told no one but Abdul who I am."

"I will keep your secret. And because you are Queen Zabel I know you understand the difficulties women in our position face. I want someone to confide in and I have decided it will be you."

Zabel poured simmering water onto the leaves. When Eleanor reached for her cup, Zabel noted Eleanor's hands and wrists were large, the bones of a sturdy woman.

"I am about to tell *you* something that I would tell only my closest ally," Eleanor said. "I trust you will hold it in the greatest confidence."

Zabel nodded.

"I am planning to have my marriage to Louis annulled."

"You have children. The Church will not permit such a thing."

"I am a vital woman. Being married to Louis is like being married to a monk in spite of him fathering my girls." Eleanor paced about the room.   "He believes that his piety ensures the salvation of his subjects, so he spends his days praying to God. I find this a ridiculous superstition. I will have my way. We are masters of our own fate because we have free will, don't you agree?"

Zabel thought of the discussions she'd had with her father. Was it chance that moved us swiftly across the board of life, or could we carefully design our life by pondering every move? Whichever way was true, the result was always uncertain.   But, being sure Eleanor did not desire a philosophical debate, Zabel simply agreed.

Eleanor continued, "When I was in the East I heard of a Sufi woman. She was a freed slave girl from the city of Basra, a mystic, with an immense love of God. She was seen each day in the streets carrying a torch and an ewer of water. Why do you think she did that?" Eleanor asked.

Zabel was given no time to respond.

"Her purpose was to pour water on hell and burn heaven so people would love God for his own sake, not to save themselves. I couldn't agree more and I will go one further. I think these damn wars are all vainglory for the priests, who are hiding from themselves the fact that the only true power in this world is the power to create life. Nature is supreme and we women are Her vehicles."

So, Eleanor is one of us.   What an amazing

revelation.

"I have had time to consider many possible plans on the long sea voyage, but I will not attempt anything that is sure to fail. What I want to know is how you lost your crown." She returned to her chair waiting for Zabel to answer.

She has told me something that could endanger her life. She trusts me. "No one but my grandmother knows the entire story. But, as we seem to be kindred spirits, I'll tell you everything."

The shadows from the setting sun reached across the full length of the room as Zabel finished her story. "I wanted my life to be as random as these bits of dust floating in the light, and Fortune has provided me with situations I could never have imagined. But now, I'm content."

"You are wise to accept what can't be changed. But, I still have the power to alter my life."

"I hope for your sake you can. But may I be so bold as to ask why you married Louis?" Izabel woke and Zabel picked her up and fed her. Eleanor seemed indifferent to the child.

"My father, William, was on a pilgrimage to the shrine of St. James of Compostela in the north of Spain. He drank some contaminated water, but before he died, he made his will, bequeathing his domains to me and appointing Louis' father, King Louis VI, my guardian."

"Why would he do such a thing?"

"I was fourteen, and because I was the richest heiress in all of Gaul, he knew I would be the most desired. In the will my father commanded his vassals to swear homage to me as heiress of Poitou, Aquitaine, and Gascony.

"Would their vow not been enough?"

"My vassals are a self-serving lot. They would have thought nothing of trying to wrest my lands from me. I needed a strong and powerful husband to force them to stay in line."

"I have heard tales of you. You're a strong and capable woman. Did you want to marry?"

"You must understand, our lands are held together by an ancient system of allegiances. Each duke owes forty days of fighting to his liege lord."

"I have heard of this custom."

"As a woman, I could not perform this function."

"Were you not taught to fight and ride?" Zabel asked.

"Yes, but realistically, to ensure I had heirs, my first duty was to produce children. Once I was with child, I would not be available for battle."

Zabel was in awe of this woman who sat before her. At fourteen Eleanor had understood her place in the grand scheme of power. *I only wanted to ride and shoot for pleasure, to enjoy my days. I thought my father would rule forever. Had I paid more attention to my position, perhaps I would not have acted so impulsively.*

"My father anticipated this eventuality, making me ward of his overlord, Louis VI, with the view to my marrying his son Louis. He is the only king in all of the Frankish lands. That fact alone gave him enough power, status, and authority to protect my inheritance and safeguard my interests."

"You were fortunate your father had time to write his will before he died. But, like me, you still had to marry a man not of your choosing."

"I was determined to make the best of it. I have given birth to three daughters, but truth be told, I find mothering rather tedious. So when Louis announced he had taken the cross and would journey to the Holy Land, I decided to accompany him.

"Louis said he wanted the knights and nobles of my lands to heed God's summons and join him. In actual fact, he didn't want to leave power-hungry vassals at home while he was away in distant lands. He needed my help to persuade them, as they still owed allegiance to me. I agreed if he consented to let me join the crusade." Eleanor rose from her chair again and moved about the room.

"My ladies and I dressed ourselves in white tunics emblazoned with red crosses, plumes on our helmets, and our feet encased in red leather boots. We looked the very picture of Penthesilea and her Amazon warriors with our hair blowing free in the breeze. We held tournaments to attract brave knights. My troubadours composed songs in the spirit of the adventure."

I can imagine her on a great white horse, pendants floating in the breeze, and the vigor of youth issuing from every pore of her body.

Eleanor paused, a thought darkening her face. "We crossed Armenia on our way to the Holy Land. I brought this grief to you."

"The outcome of such actions is not in the control of any one person. I hold no resentment."

"Perhaps not, but my pursuit of pleasure robbed you of your country. An act not to be taken lightly. I will find a way to repay you."

"I don't need anything. As I said, I am happy with my

new life. Please continue your story. How will you get your marriage annulled?"

"Because I have only given my husband daughters, Louis can persuade the Pope that our union is sinful."

"What does having daughters have to do with sin?"

Eleanor drained her tea, refusing Zabel's offer of more.

"Louis and I are cousins. God has seen fit to punish us by not supplying Louis with a son to secure the succession of the French throne. At this moment, he needs an heir more than he needs my inheritance. His bishops will curry favor with the Pope."

"But because you're married to him, isn't Aquitaine his?"

"It's rather complicated. Even though my father willed that his estates would remain in my hands when I married, by the laws of France, had I produced a son, Louis would have been able to retain Aquitaine. Having daughters has prevented this eventuality."

"But what about the military duty you owe the King?"

"I am not the child I was when my father died. I can deal with my dukes until I find a husband more to my taste."

"You'll marry again?"

"I am a woman of great appetites. I relish both political power and intimate relations with a man." She rose and moved toward the stairs. "I have left my ladies waiting long enough. They will soon become ill tempered. And you, my dear, have answered my questions. I will proceed with my plan."

Eleanor hesitated before moving down the stairs. "One last thought. Although you think you've found a paradise here for you and your child, I've heard of a movement afoot to rid this region of all heretics. The Pope wants to consolidate his power over all Christian lands here as well as in the East. He will not tolerate dissent. It could be a bloody time, so before it begins, you must leave. Your dark hair alone will single you out as different from our light haired peoples. And if his troops discover your beliefs, you will be seen as working in league with the devil."

"Leave? But where would I go? I can't return to Armenia."

"As you may have heard, it is my pleasure to surround myself at court with noble, intelligent women. You are welcome in Poitiers." She pointed to the table. "Give me that parchment and quill. I will have my clerk supply you with a letter of safe passage in Aquitaine. Leave when the troubles come, Zabel. And I must repeat, they will."

Eleanor touched the smooth silk of Zabel's tunic. "Next time your *husband* is here you must command him to bring mulberry trees and silk worms from Syria so we can produce our own silk uninterrupted by the wars of greed. I've come to believe women cannot live without this fabric."

Chapter 12

Yule was approaching. The shortened days were often overcast; with chill rains falling intermittently. One day, in spite of the weather, Zabel tied Izabel to her with a red silk shawl, and rode with Brigit into the forest in search of holly and mistletoe.

"What is their meaning?" Zabel asked. "We don't have these plants in Armenia."

"To the church they represent the body and blood of Christ, but to our women the holly berries are the color of the blood of life and the mistletoe's is the white of sexual juices that reproduce life."

Brigit clamored high into the branches of a hazel tree and cut the mistletoe. She let it fall to the ground and Zabel gathered it into a basket. Then they harvested the holly, trying to avoid its sharp edges. Izabel slept contently, her nose sticking out from the red fox lining of Zabel's cloak.

When they returned home, they decorated the apartment with their treasures. Then they prepared some carrots in an herb sauce to contribute to the solstice celebration Madame and the other women had planned.

"The Church forbids us to celebrate the renewal of light after the shortest day. You understand...we mustn't talk of it," Brigit said.

"It was like that in my homeland." Zabel said. She shuddered, remembering it was her attendance at such a seasonal ritual that caused her exile.

Brigit's countenance brightened. "My mother is preparing the roasted pig. She'll put a shiny red apple in its mouth, bringing the fruit of the Great Mother to the table.

Zabel was warmed by the girl's enthusiasm.

But the next morning Brigit was subdued as she kneaded her bread dough.

"What's troubling you? Are you not excited about the celebration tonight?"

Brigit wiped a wisp of hair that had fallen in her eyes, leaving a dusting of flour on her forehead. Her face showed fear, an emotion Zabel had not seen in Brigit before.

"Something is afoot," Brigit whispered. She paused, seemingly not having the courage to speak further.

"What's wrong?" Zabel's senses heightened. 'Afoot', was the same word Eleanor had used to indicate there would be troubles.

"We'll have to be cautious going to the grove tonight. Take a circuitous route."
"Why? What have you heard?"
"It's not so much what I've heard, although there've been whisperings."
"Stop this. Tell me what's happening."
Zabel's tone shocked the girl enough to force her to explain. "Early this morning when I exercised Tambour, many of the cottage doors I passed were hung with fennel."

"What does fennel have to do with us going to the

grove? People dry fennel to aid their digestion after the overeating at Christmas.”

Brigit stopped kneading and pulled bits of the dough off her fingers. “We are hunted as witches because of our use of herbs. The Christians think we cast spells. That we harm them.” Her words came in gasps. Her body convulsed and tears flowed down her cheeks. “By hanging fennel, they believe they can prevent us from harming them. They burn witches, Zabel.” A paroxysm of fear seized Brigit’s body, nearly doubling her over. “Why are we so persecuted? The Great Mother gave us herbs to make people well.”

Zabel moved round the table and pulled Brigit to her. “Why? Because the local priest has whipped his parishioners into a frenzy. He knows we worship the goddess freely in the groves, without need of a priest. We are, in the Church’s view, a danger to social order. It is the same here as in Armenia except here there’s a reason to single out widows. The law permits the property of a witch to be given to the one who accuses her. It has caused many an innocent woman to be tortured until she confesses to powers she does not possess. Men can be that desperate.”

But what I don’t want to tell her is that, in my opinion, celibate priests, denied the pleasures of sex, enjoy inflicting pain on others; burning their flesh, in the name of purifying the victim’s soul to prevent evil rising from their blood. These men deny the relevance of women; deny it so vehemently that they refuse to copulate with us. It’s madness. Religious law is not sacred law. Without the deception I maintain with Abdul, I could be one of the persecuted. The truly evil among these priests make the children of a convicted witch watch their mothers burn; are made to hear her torments. Brigit is too sensitive to survive such an event. I can say none of this to her.

Zabel walked to the shuttered window and yanked it

open, so stifled did she feel by the weight of the church.

"Don't worry, we'll be careful. Of course, if you would rather stay here tonight, I understand completely. You must do as you see fit."

Brigit was silent for some time. "I'll come. I must continue to honor the Great Mother even if they kill me."

They were in a somber mood as they rode to the grove taking a route that doubled back on itself so they could see they weren't being followed. The horses' breath formed clouds around their heads as they moved through the chill air. They crossed an old Roman bridge. A crow landed on top of the stone arch and looked at Zabel, first with one eye, then the other. *I remember Jnana telling me that if you look deeply into a crow's eyes, you will find the gateway to the unknowable mysteries of creation. Crow is keeper of the sacred law and in the understanding of our people there is no heaven or hell, she'd said. 'These are illusions created to make us obedient.*

But others did believe. Fennel hung from every door. Even at the Cantellon farm, Zabel was surprised to see that Brigit's mother had secured it to their door.

"It gives the appearance she fears witches as well," Brigit said.

Life is shifting off-kilter. The higher order, the harmony of the universe is out of balance.

The fields darkened as the afternoon faded over the distant hills on this, the shortest day of the year. The grove bustled with activity, but the women wore fearful expressions. Izabel stirred as Zabel dismounted. She found Madame's arms immediately about her. "Give her to me. My most recent miracle."

Zabel loosened the silk scarf and handed the child to Madame. But Izabel would have none of it. Her small face compressed and she let out a scream. It was the breast of her mother she wanted, the warmth and nourishment of Zabel's milk. *It will never cease to amaze me I can keep her alive with my body.*

When the sun set the women sat in a great circle silently honoring the darkness, darkness that allowed the Earth to rest. But their energy was subdued. Zabel guessed each of them had seen the fennel.

One of the women lit the small pile of dry sticks in the centre of the circle. In its warmth everyone made an offering of food to the fire. Then they shared each contribution, a communal blessing. Brigit's mother spoke. "With this fire we honor the sun that will appear in the sky longer with each passing day, warming the earth and releasing the seeds from their winter sleep. This longest night of the year will now lead us to spring and to a cornucopia of gifts from you, Great Mother.

"It is in the darkness of this, the longest night, when pure Spirit is visible to us, we honor the mystery of creation. We acknowledge our fear. We are afraid of the powerful one's who no longer understand. They have the means to hurt us. But we sit in a circle to remind ourselves all is movement in Nature. We suffer if we fail to remember that nothing lasts. Our own power will return to us."

Madame held Izabel as Zabel joined the others, dancing frantically around the fire; each woman trying to release her sense of doom.

Chapter 13

The next day the apothecary's wife, Adele, entered the silk shop, her face ashen.

"What's wrong?" Zabel asked.

Adele was a jovial woman who usually had a warm smile for each person who approached her. Today, however, she looked terrified, haunted. "Last night when Madame returned from the ceremony her neighbor was waiting for her with the sheriff. He accused her of being a witch. You know what that means."

Brigit gasped and fell in a swoon to the floor. Zabel quickly waved some fennel under her nose to revive her, aware of the irony; it was this herb that was supposed to protect the faithful from witches. They carried Brigit to her bed.

Adele left to inform the others. Zabel sat by her fire and stared at the steady flame that moved over the log. She had never seen a witch burning. The idea horrified her. What's more, it was disgusting how people flocked to the executions, relishing in the torments of another. She remembered once hearing the screams of a victim echoing through the stone streets of Montpelier. She and Brigit had beat their frame drums and danced around the shop in order to drown out the sounds of agony. They had fallen into an exhausted heap unable to keep their feet moving for as long as it took for the woman to die. Now it was Madame who would be made to scream on the pyre.

Anger gnawed at Zabel, each breath she took increased her terror. She could imagine herself in the fire, tied to a stake, skin melting from her bones as life was drawn from her body. Bile forced its way into her throat, and she spat into the hearth.

She went to Brigit's room. "Are you able to get up? I need to go to the farm. To speak to your father.   I have a plan. Are you well enough to look after Izabel?"

"I'll be fine. I'm sorry for being a nuisance."

Zabel mounted Grace and rode out of Montpelier knowing the part she was about to play meant she would soon have to leave Languedoc for good.

Before daybreak Brigit and Zabel packed some torches and flint, bedrolls, food and herbs. Zabel's plan was to rescue Madame and rendezvous with Brigit and Izabel at the birthing cave where the women would wait three days before they proceeded north to Eleanor's castle. Because there was the possibility the plan could fail, Brigit promised she would take Izabel to Poitiers and raise her. Before they set out, Zabel gave Brigit the cloak Jnana had made, with replacement gems sewn in place. She had expelled breast milk she stored in a wine skin. It would stave off the child's hunger if she woke before Zabel and Madame reached the cave. If the worst happened, Brigit would have to travel to Poitiers alone and there find a wet nurse.

"There's enough of a dowry here for both you and Izabel. And I have written a history of my family. Izabel must learn about her roots. I trust you will teach her about the Great Mother."

Zabel watched Brigit and Izabel ride off. There was the dreadful possibility she might never see them again.

Dressed in men's clothing borrowed from Brigit's cousin, she strapped her quill of arrows and the bow over her shoulder. Grace sensed the danger, her nostrils flaring as Zabel mounted the mare. Sensing the spirit beneath her, Zabel tried to absorb the horse's power into her being.

The square was jammed with the good citizens of Montpelier. Brigit's cousins were already there as planned, in the centre of the crowd. They sat on the wagon in which she had so often ridden. Now two enormous bulls were snorting in the back. The wind whirled in eddies as she halted under one of the archways that led into the square. She steadied her nerves as she watched the priest arranging the fire he would soon ignite. *If my plan doesn't work, I will be the next one tied to a stake in this square.*

The crowd hushed as guards brought Madame forward. Another priest carried a wicker basket in which Zabel recognized Madame's cat, Isis. She was a longhaired beauty, silver, with kohl-lined green eyes. Zabel's heart sank. She had heard of the custom of also burning a witch's cat, supposedly her ally in all the evil deeds a witch performed.

Madame's mouth was forming words but the sound emitted was as vacant as the look in her eyes. To Zabel's horror the crowd's whisperings became a roar as excitement rose, each person jostling for a better position to see the spectacle.

I am ashamed to be a human being.

Then she looked once again at Madame's face. Instead of the fear Zabel expected to see, Madame, in a moment of lucidity, looked on the crowd with pity. Seeing Madame's humanity was all Zabel needed to relieve her dark mood. Her resolve returned. The plan would work. It made no sense for Madame to die this horrible death.

The guards moved off the stand and the priest came forward to say a prayer. A smile passed his lips as he stooped to ignite the blaze.

Now charged with loathing Zabel hadn't known she possessed, she gave the signal and on each side of the wagon holding the bulls, a gloved hand reached up and released the leather thong of the gate. The bulls were instantly aware of their freedom and bolted down the lowered plank. Those standing nearby were pushed to the ground by the huge animals. Screams arose and panic caused hundreds of feet to stampede to the safety of the streets beyond the square as the animals snorted and pawed the ground, deciding which way to run.

Zabel urged her horse forward. Such an animal as this, trained as a polo pony, was not afraid to move among the scattering citizens. Zabel was playing chess, and this time, her opponent was Fate.

She threw back her cloak and loaded her bow. As she pulled back the string, an image of Siraj came into her mind. He had said a warrior was at peace if he did not act from personal hatred. She took a deep breath and stilled the seething energy within. She let the arrow fly as she approached the platform, aiming for the knee of the priest. He fell, clutching his limb in obvious pain. She reloaded as a guard ran up the steps, and he too fell, as Zabel released an arrow with accuracy.

A gloved man swiftly cut Madame loose, picking her up and the wicker basket containing the cat. He moved effortlessly to the edge of the stage. The guard who lay on his side grabbed for the man's foot. The man avoided him, shoving his boot at the arrow sticking out of the guard's leg, causing him to scream in pain. The priest lay simpering on the wooden floor, blood seeping from his wound; his dark eyes sought to identify the man, but to no avail.

The second gloved man rushed forward leading Tambour by his halter. The two men quickly tied Madame and the basket to the saddle and threw Zabel the reins. The horses needed little urging as they raced over the drawbridge before the general alarm was even sounded. The two gloved men followed across the moat and then slowed, riding in the opposite direction to draw the duke's soldiers away from the route Zabel took with Madame.

The previous night after visiting the farm, Zabel had ridden to Albi. The Knights Templar had been true to their word. She had risked her life to help them and they honored her by joining the rescue plan. They also agreed to intercept Abdul and inform him about the disastrous turn of events. They were to give him the money Zabel left for the cargo of silk she would never claim and make sure he knew to never enter Montpelier again as the authorities would be sure to apprehend him.

As Zabel rode, clouds formed across the sky, darkening the landscape. Forked lightning could be seen in the distance, followed by the rumble of thunder. The Tramontane wind crossing the plain picked up and suddenly they were inundated with driving sheets of rain. *This rain will help to conceal our route if anyone should be following.*

Zabel turned the horse off the main road and once in the woods, they had to proceed at a slower pace. She was chilled now and shivering. A large pine had fallen in the storm forcing her to concentrate as she urged the horses over the obstacle. *The tree of life has been uprooted.*

Chapter 14

As Zabel worked her way up the hill she could see the valley below, and was certain she was not being followed. She was nonetheless relieved when she reached the sacred cave. Brigit rushed out to help loosen the ropes holding Madame on the horse, the rain pelting down around them.

"It would have been better if we'd ridden camels," Zabel said, as they struggled to slide Madame off the horse. "She would be closer to the ground as the camel couched."

Izabel was sleeping beside the fire that blazed under a natural vent in the cave's ceiling. When Madame saw the flames she cowered in fear.

"How stupid of me," Brigit said. "I should have made only a small fire until Madame realized she was safe."

Zabel talked softly to Madame. "Brigit set a blaze to welcome you and to keep you warm. These winter nights are cold and we are hidden in the birthing cave. Do you remember it?"

Under her breath Zabel assured Brigit, "It is not your fault. I didn't think of it either. And to Madame, "Come lie on the bed Brigit has prepared for you. We're safe. You can rest now."

Brigit and Zabel removed Madame's wet clothing then her cap. To Zabel's horror Madame's head had been shaved.

"They believe removing the hair reduces one's ability to resist torture," Brigit said.

Zabel forced down the vomit that had risen into her throat.

Madame hands brushed against the woolen sheet on her bedroll and she shivered with pain. Her hands were burned and oozing.

Zabel saw that a cold sweat had broken out on Brigit's forehead, but she didn't flinch, pulling instead a tincture of burdock and bran she'd prepared for such an eventuality. She drew some warm water from the spring making a viscous salve to cover Madame's hands. Then as Madame had taught the girl years before, Brigit began the process of the laying on of hands to foster the healing. Madame's feverish body relaxed and she fell asleep.

"You must rest too, Brigit. We'll need our strength in the coming days."

Brigit lay on the straw mattress with Madame on one side of her and Izabel on the other. Zabel couldn't sleep and wandered outside into the starless night, her bow at the ready. Out of the darkness came the hoot of an owl. She watched it take flight noiselessly with huge wings spread as it lifted itself from its nest in the hole of a dead tree. *It is using the darkness to find its prey. Has someone noticed the light from our fire and approaches without a sound?*

She heard Madame moan and moved back into the cave. In the glow of the embers Zabel sat transfixed. The memory of sitting with her father in his library came into her mind. She longed for the innocence of those days.

Zabel poked the embers with a stick and a sudden small flame burst forth then died back. *I chose this way of life. I must live with the consequences.* She placed another log on the fire. *What it really feels like is that I'm caught in the vortex of a mighty river, the force inexorably drawing me to some centre. Where I'll find what? Death? Eventually, but surely not yet. Have I traveled this far only to succumb to an untimely end? And perhaps that of my child and my dearest friends?*

Madame woke and moaned piteously.

Brigit heard her and sat up. "I'll try to get her to take some mead. She needs nourishment if she's to recover her strength for the journey."

But Madame refused to open her mouth, turning her head from side to side in resistance.

"Let me try," Zabel said, moving to take Brigit's place on the mat. She lifted the moaning woman into her arms and holding the cup to her lips. "She won't open her mouth."

"She'll die if we don't get her to drink," Brigit said, clenching her fists. "I hate those people. Hate them. Why did they do this to her?

If Brigit succumbed to hysteria, Zabel couldn't look after two women and an infant. *Fortunately Izabel is sleeping, oblivious to the drama going on around her.* Zabel felt dampness on her hand. *My breasts are leaking. I need to feed her, but not now. Stay asleep, my darling.*

Then it came to her. Zabel lifted her tunic, exposing her breast. She began to rock Madame gently, soothing her wrinkled face and shaven head that in the soft glow of the fire looked like that of a newborn. Zabel hummed softly the way she did when she wanted Izabel to nurse.

Madame turned her head, nestling closer. Zabel

pushed her distended nipple toward Madame's cheek and her mouth opened. Zabel continued to rock back and forth and Madame began to suck.

Brigit's dark eyes filled with tears, her fears melting. Zabel wiped away her own.

"Go back to sleep, Brigit. I'll stay up with her for the rest of the night." The girl stretched out beside Izabel and fell into steady breathing.

Zabel was dazed and exalted by what had happened. She cradled Madame and from the nourishment and warmth of Zabel's body, Madame, too, began to breathe quietly.

In the morning, Madame was sufficiently improved to take the mead Brigit offered. With the first crisis past, Zabel slept. She was awakened when she heard a squeal of joy from Brigit.

"What is it?" Zabel asked, raising herself up on one elbow.

"The fever has broken."

"The Spirits are with us," Zabel said. She placed her hand on Madame's forehead and Madame's eyes opened. "You will be fine, now. We're in the birthing cave. Do you remember? No one will find us here."

Just as these words of reassurance left her lips a dark object raced toward Madame, landing on her stomach. Brigit stifled a scream and Madame covered her face with her hands.

"It's Isis," Zabel said. "She's come back. When we first arrived we let her out of the basket, and she ran into the forest. We thought she was gone for good, making her way back to your cottage. She certainly looks happy to see you, Madame."

"You saved her, too." The words that came from Madame's throat were choked with gratitude.

"We know what she means to you," Zabel said.

Madame convulsed into tears. Zabel held her to prevent a relapse. "We'll have to rid her of the emotional scars before we can think of moving her. "Go outside and find a stone the size of a loaf of bread. It must be smooth and round like a ripe womb."

Brigit was back quickly with a perfect piece of granite. "Clean it in the water and keep it submerged until it's warm."

Zabel laid Madame back onto the mat and taking the wet stone that was glistening in the reflected light of the fire, she placed the stone on Madame's belly. "I call on the Spirits of the stone to take the negative energies from our friend, Madame Noirfor. Zabel waved her hands in a spiral motion over the stone. "Relax, Madame. Let the memory of the horror flow from you into the stone."

Madame closed her eyes, meditating until her breath became even and her limbs relaxed. Zabel picked up the stone. "I give thanks to you Great Mother for taking this anguish from one of your daughters. I give the stone back to You to destroy the negative energy it now contains."

With that, Zabel dropped the piece of granite into the still water and it disappeared below the surface making rings of widening circles. Then the movement subsided and the surface of the pool was smooth once again.

"She's fallen asleep," Brigit said.

Chapter 15

Zabel screamed. "No, no. I can't leave them."

Brigit rushed to her side. "Zabel, wake up. You were dreaming."

Zabel opened her eyes, disoriented, her heart pounding. She pulled her hands through her wild hair, curly now from the moisture in the cave, trying to still her throbbing temples.

Izabel woke at the same time, crying. Zabel drew the infant to her, baring her breast and the child latched onto it eagerly. Brigit and Zabel laughed together, momentarily forgetting their fears.

"I've had the same dream many times. It always ends the same way, with my mother and uncle killed by a tribe of marauders."

"No wonder you were screaming." Brigit said, shivering.

"It takes place in a town where my grandmother told me our ancestors lived and it always ends with the death of my family."

Brigit stirred the fire under the kettle. "I'll make tea and we can eat our bread. I've never asked about your family. How rude of me.”

Zabel shifted Izabel to the other breast and said, “I was raised by my father and grandmother. My mother died shortly after my birth. Jnana, my grandmother was a midwife like Madame. She was a gifted healer, like both of you.”

Madame moaned in her sleep, and she opened her eyes. When she recognized her two friends she smiled. Brigit lifted Madame’s head and began to spoon warm mead into her mouth. After a few sips, Madame waved the cup away and fell back to sleep, Isis curled up at her side.

“It’s best if she sleeps as much as possible. The healing will be faster,” Brigit said.

“She’s responding to your touch.” Zabel was relieved. They wouldn’t be able to travel until Madame could ride her own mount.

When Izabel fell back to sleep, Zabel said. “Remember the papers I gave you, Brigit. I hastily wrote down my history.” Zabel reached out and touched Brigit’s arm. “I now realize how important it is for me to be more thorough. When my mother died, my grandmother took her place. She told me the oral stories of our ancestors, and, although you and I share much, there are things we’ve never talked about. So I’ll complete the document when we get to Poitiers.”

Brigit had gone white. “I didn’t want to worry you before the rescue, but I don’t know how to read.”

Zabel was shocked by this revelation. Brigit could do so many things, and do them well. It had never occurred to Zabel that the girl couldn’t read. “When we reach safety, I’ll teach you. If I don’t make it to Poitiers, there will be someone in Eleanor’s court who can. But I want you to raise

Izabel. You'll teach her your love of the Great Mother. I know that."

"You honor me, Zabel. I'll do as you ask. But I'd still like to hear about your life. From you."

"I can start by telling you my dream. It feels more like a memory than a dream. I have a strong feeling I once lived in that village, but it's not possible." Zabel shifted her position on the flat limestone rock. "Some believe we live more than one lifetime. Perhaps I have."

"The Catholic Church is very strict," Brigit said. "They say we have one soul that will pass into eternity." She poured some seeds from her pouch into the pestle and mortar. "But your church, in Armenia. Is it the same?"

"Yes, but my grandmother said in the ancient days, before Christianity, it was known that the soul circled back. That each of us has lived many times, although it is unusual to remember other lives."

"Did you ask your grandmother about the dream?"

"No. I regret that now; I was trying to sort it out for myself. And then it was too late. I left Armenia."

Brigit looked up from the mortar in her hands. "Tell me your dream."

"I am a young girl and I have just awakened with the first light. I climb up a ladder to the roof of our house. In the distance are twin volcanic peaks. I know these volcanoes spew black obsidian rock that provides my mother's brother with work. My uncle lives with us and helps my mother and me. My mother has no husband. These facts, like all the things in the dream except the deaths of my mother and uncle are things Jnana told me."

Izabel began to fuss so Zabel burped her while she

continued speaking. "In the dream, my uncle makes sharp blades from the shiny black rock and attaches them to large handles made of wood. These axes are used by the men in our village to cut trees for fuel and for the underpinnings of the houses our women cover with clay they've worked with their feet, just as they still do in Armenia.

"The obsidian is the heart of our community. The spirit in the volcano spews her black milk nurturing us the way mothers feed their infants.

"I feel the happy abandon of childhood as I enter my uncle's room to wake him. On his wall is a painting of the two volcanoes and our village with the fields surrounding it. Day after day I had watched the artist mix her pigments with soot she scraped from the bottom of our cooking pots.

"My mother provides all our food. She is a confident woman and I'm very proud of her. She laughs and dances in rituals. Often in the night I hear her intimacies with men from the village she chooses for her sexual delights."

"You're sure you've never been to that village? This dream has such detail," Brigit said.

"No. But before I came here I traveled to the modern city of Konya, near which I saw the twin volcanoes from my dream." Zabel stopped for a moment, contemplating. *It's odd. I didn't think of the dream when I was in Konya, but now I'm sure it is the same place.*

"Later in the dream, I'm walking in the village. I pass a shop where men are butchering a large cow with large curved horns. Enormous horns. The people in my village honor the cow for the milk that it gives. Many cows keep the tribe strong.

"Jnana told me these Auroch cows once roamed the flat plains near Konya, but are extinct now. She said our people followed the herds from pasture to pasture, but when our ancestors wandered into the land of the twin volcanoes they discovered barley and wheat growing wild. It seems the right amount of rain fell at the right times. The women discovered how to turn the golden heads of grain into flour, which they baked into bread. After that, the women of our tribe were no longer willing to follow the herds.

"But we missed the meat we'd been accustomed to eating, so the women figured out how to keep wild pigs around the village by feeding them some of the fruits and nuts they gathered from the nearby woods."

Brigit's voice rose in excitement. "It's just as my mother has told me. It was the women who did all this."

"Perhaps your ancestors came from a similar village."

"Or the same one. But go on with your dream."

"Then I'm in the pasture behind our house. It is early spring and the lambs have just been born."

"They had sheep, too?"

"Yes, but I know my mother worries about this. Herdsmen and their families who still follow the sheep are agitated with the boundary stones our people set up to mark our land."

Madame shifted in her sleep, moaning in pain. Brigit gave her a sip of willow bark tincture. "It will lessen her pain."

Zabel waited for Madame's breathing to become regular before she continued. "Then I'm with my mother, helping her pour grape juice into large wooden vats to ferment over the winter. I hold a large pigskin over the vat to filter the juice as my mother pours. We finish and I'm free to amuse myself.

"I wander to the paddock to check the newly born lambs, our dog following close at my heels. Jnana said it was the women who tamed the wild dogs. Without them the sheep would not have stayed together when they were moved into their winter pastures. In the dream the new lambs jump and run with the energy of new life. Some nuzzle their mothers, looking for milk.

"My attention is taken by a low thundering sound. A cloud of dust obscures the sun rising in the east. Men on horseback approach carrying shields and weapons. I hear screams coming from the far end of the village. My mother and uncle rush toward me yelling, run, Zabel, run into the woods.

"The panic in their voices makes my feet move automatically. But as I run I bend and scoop up a lamb, stuffing it into the sleeve of my tunic as I tear across the field. As I get to the edge of the woods I turn and look back at the village. It is in flames. Villagers run screaming in all directions pursued by the horsemen. Bodies lay scattered on the earth. Someone reaches for my hand and pulls me into the forest. I open my mouth to scream but I recognize our neighbor. She shoves me in front of her pointing up the path. As I run I keep looking back for my mother and uncle, but we reach the honey cave before I see them.

"Then it's morning and I stand at the edge of the forest looking at the smoldering destruction that had been our village. The faces of the dead are locked in hideous contortions of fear. The pens are broken down and all the sheep and pigs are gone. There is an eerie silence as the golden sun lights the scene. At the end of the dream it is always the same. I am standing over the dead bodies of my mother and uncle. My mother's arm is stretched out with the fingers of her hand clawing the ground as she tries to pull herself to safety and to me. Then I start screaming."

"The dream is always the same?"

"Yes. It's so real, I know that it really happened to me, to my mother, but my mother in this life died shortly after I was born. I never knew her."

Sometime soon Zabel knew she would have to reveal herself to Brigit and Madame; explain that Abdul was not her husband or Izabel's father. But not now.

Zabel picked up a stick from the fire and drew patterns in the ash. "It is so frightening to me. Everyone dead, all the animals gone." She threw the stick in the flames. "I have never experienced war except in that dream but it's why I hate even the thought of it. My mother did, too. She made Jnana promise I would never learn to use weapons."

"Did your grandmother ever explain why some of the people became warlike?"

"There was a drought. A long, constant drought. So the tribes who had had space to pasture their sheep were forced to live closer together to have water for their animals. Then famine came and the people turned upon each other. That was the beginning of war."

"But it is a good thing you knew how to use a bow and arrow or we wouldn't have been able to rescue Madame."

"Yes, but I only maimed those men, I didn't kill them."

Remembering her actions, the cave now seemed cold. Zabel pulled her cloak more closely about herself.

Zabel helped Brigit feed Madame small sips of the herbal

wine throughout the day. But her hands were still oozing.

Our food will only last one more day. And I can't risk leaving them here while I go for more. We must only leave once and that is when we are headed to Poitiers. The Templars will have led the sheriff away from this cave, but when we leave, we'll be completely vulnerable.

Zabel fell into a troubled sleep. Tomorrow would be decisive.

Chapter 16

Zabel woke to the sound of Brigit's voice. "What...what did you say?" Zabel asked, her voice still heavy with the sleep that had finally come just before dawn.

"I was talking to Madame."

"To Madame. Oh." Zabel leapt from her mat. "Madame, do you think your hands are healed enough to ride? We'll be safer when we reach Aquitaine."

There was confusion on Madame's face.

"Eleanor warned me things would get dangerous for us in Montpelier and has offered us asylum. We can never return to Languedoc."

"You dear girls saved me," Madame said, trying to sit up on her own. "I'm not sure how well my hands will work, so we may have to go slowly at first." She looked at the herbal mash smeared on her fingers and palms; then she sniffed the ointment. "Just what I taught you to use in such cases, Brigit, but I had no thought I would be the beneficiary of my teaching."

"I wish it were otherwise, Madame," Brigit said, her face shining from the compliment.

Brigit and Zabel packed the horses and secured the angry cat back in its cage. Brigit tied Izabel to her chest and mounted her horse. Zabel wore a cloak she had made for Abdul, having padded the shoulders in order to conceal her bow and arrow. It reinforced the image of her being a man traveling with his wife and aging mother.

The morning was cold, the sky a hazy light as they made their way down the trail. Madame was cheerful.

Perhaps this is what happens when you come that close to death. I hope her enthusiasm lasts for the whole, long journey.

The main road was full of merchants delivering their crops to market after the harvest, and by the end of the day they were well within Eleanor's domains. Brigit carried the letter Eleanor had given Zabel, affording them safe passage, but Zabel never stopped looking back over her shoulder each time she heard an approaching horse or wagon.

Zabel took in the features of the countryside through which they moved. The village houses in this part of Aquitaine were made of yellow and white limestone cut in roughhewn blocks while others were half-timbered wattle and daub with steep stone roofs and first stories that hung over the winding streets.

Each village and town had erected a stone watchtower to survey the surrounding countryside. Eleanor had said battles for supremacy had wracked her domains, and peace had come only after she married Louis. Zabel shuddered involuntarily as she recalled the masculine power of the house of Gisor and acknowledged Eleanor again for her great insight and courage.

As darkness approached, Zabel suggested they find

an inn in the next town where they could rest for the night.

"No," Madame countered, "we must stay in an abbey."

"But why?" Brigit asked, unable to keep the fear from her voice. "The church is after you. Perhaps the monks have been told to watch out for us."

"My dear Brigit. Monks are no fans of the Pope. They need the great pontiffs blessing to begin an order, but once that is achieved, these men and women have their own ideas about how to run their communities. Besides, they must give us sanctuary once we are within their walls. It is the custom."

In spite of Madame's certainty, Zabel's heart was pounding as they entered the abbey grounds. But as they dismounted she felt a sense of profound peace from the sanctuary the monks had created to escape the profanity of the outside world. It seemed unlikely these men would care about the events that had caused a few women to flee Montpelier.

The evening meal was taken in a low refectory lit by enormous candles placed in sconces along the walls. The tables were set with cloths and a novice had been sent to wash their feet. One young monk attended a roaring fire. Others, laden with vegetable dishes from produce grown on the grounds, entered from the kitchen.

Zabel noticed no dish contained meat. *They deny that life lives off life.*

They ate without talking, honoring the vow of silence. Zabel was grateful for this custom, fearing her voice would give her away. After the meal, the abbot led them along a stone passage to the room they would share.

The old abbot spoke for the first and only time, staring at them with pale blue eyes from a withered countenance. "Dusk is the time when danger commences. It is then the devil is abroad. No monk is allowed to be alone, and lights will be burning all night." The abbot pushed open an arched pine door and the women passed into a room that contained three cots. A small crucifix on the far wall was the only adornment. Then he closed the door and left them.

Zabel took Izabel from Brigit and fed her, luxuriating in the pleasure of nursing her child. By the time Izabel was full and sleeping peacefully, Brigit and Madame were already asleep; Isis curled up on Madame's belly. But Zabel's mind would not rest. She stood in the glow of the last sliver of a waning moon thinking about the monks. *They devotedly tend productive fields but at night when men and women couple in the dark, find pleasure in each other in order to create new life, these men keep the lights on, afraid of their natural instincts. The atmosphere here in the cells feels stifled and congealed, as if an ooze has settled over everything.* A shudder passed through her. *How ironic these good men go to such trouble to deny themselves the pleasures of this life in the hope of achieving eternal pleasure in heaven.*

Zabel was only too glad to be on the road again early the next morning. As they passed through the many villages and towns, Zabel worried they were still being hunted. Even though the church would have already confiscated Madame's lands, she doubted they would ignore the loss of their victim.

They rode through gentle lake-strewn pastures with herds of cows that alternated with recently harvested wheat fields. All looked prosperous. Zabel wondered why Eleanor's nobles constantly fought when life seemed so plentiful. *Does no one ever have enough?*

Further along the road, gorse-tufted hills rose from warm humid valleys, until finally, at nightfall, they entered the town of Perigueux. In an abbey surrounded by stands of oaks, they feasted on truffles, rich with the sensuous scent of Earth.

Next day they were ferried across the Dordogne River, much to the delight of Madame and Brigit who had never been on any contrivance that floated. The poplar-lined river was awash with boats of commerce. The boatman explained that wood, fruit and wine were heading for market towns along the river.

On the far side, the houses and farm buildings were different again. They formed a three sided courtyard with the forth side open to the road. *This must be a sign that here peace has reigned for some time. They appear to have little need of defense.* Zabel began to feel cautiously optimistic.

Late in the afternoon, they reached Tremolat, where the road first ran parallel to a millstream running through the village, before rising up a hill. From a vista they saw a warren of roofs atop ochre-colored houses amidst well-worn lanes and bountiful gardens. A Roman bridge crossed the river leading out of town. As they climbed toward the local abbey that occupied a steep, uncultivated rocky slope, they saw expansive cultivated fields. But in the distance a great cloud of dust indicated that horses were being ridden hard. Someone was in a hurry.

Zabel was grateful when they reached the safety of the abbey; she hoped that Brigit and Madame hadn't noticed the riders.

At the door of the church Zabel was dismayed to see a carving of St. George. *The dragon represents the power of rebirth. Even here in Eleanor's lands, the church has usurped the power of the Great Mother.* Zabel fell asleep that night with a heavy heart.

The next day the women moved into an open countryside with undulating hills and warm valleys. They passed small lakes, windmills for grinding grain, and cattle grazing on lush grass. They were now but a half days ride to Poitiers. Zabel picked up the pace still worried about the riders she'd seen the day before.

The cottages in the next village crouched below a great manor house as if in fear of the lord within. But as they rode past, Zabel saw the reassuring sight of a village matron tending a large herb garden. *They still know the secrets of the Mother here.* Amongst willows that bordered the river Dronne they found the monastery. The monks had their own mill, the wheel being turned by a section of the river that flowed with small waterfalls and cascades. Inside the walls was a forge from which they made cannon and cannon balls.

"We'll surely be safe here," Zabel said.

The women planned to eat and carry on to Eleanor's castle, but the midday meal was over. The abbey was quiet for the afternoon rest period.

"Could we have a small portion of bread and wine so we can continue on?" Brigit asked the monk who came to greet them.

"But, you must not risk the forest at dusk," he said, as he helped Madame from her mount. "It is populated by brigands. You'd best stay the night and travel with first light tomorrow."

Agreeing this would be prudent, the woman were led to their quarters, passing a large kitchen where the monks would soon prepare the evening meal. A well-stocked wine cellar indicated the vineyards were productive.

Lodging was a cell in the limestone caves behind the main abbey structure. Madame and Brigit wanted to rest before dinner, but after feeding Izabel and laying her to sleep beside Brigit, Zabel decided to walk. At the end of a particularly deep cavern, oil lamps lit a large fresco painted on the flat limestone wall. It was a scene of the Last Judgment. In the upper-half, winged angels welcomed souls into heaven. Each of the saved wore a beatific expression, eyes focusing ever upward. Each figure lacked the bulk of a corporeal body; spirit was all that mattered.

The lower half was a scene of hideous tortures. Monsters bit off the heads of those condemned to everlasting hell. Fire consumed others. Devils with whips struck others whose mouths gaped in agony.

Fear is the means to control people. Zabel watched the shadows cast by the wavering light move across the wall.

I fear death now that I have Izabel. The thought came as a shock to Zabel who felt her understanding of the ways of the Mother made her immune to such fears. *I want to raise her. To be the one to teach her all Jnana has taught me. Brigit would do a thoughtful job. She loves Izabel as her own. But...* Zabel became aware her breathing was shallow; her palms were sweating. The image of Madame tied to a stake, about to be roasted alive, came into her mind. *I just want to live my life in my own way.* She thought of her child, a soul so pure and fresh, asleep in a distant cave. *One false move could consume Izabel with grief and terror; cause her to experience the hell that can exist on Earth. I do not fear their hell. I fear them. People who have the power of life and death over me. But I promise you, my little darling, I will do all in my power to keep you safe.*

Zabel again studied the depiction of the souls rising toward heaven. *How odd it is to be in this cave inhabited by men so skillful at reaping abundance from the Earth to fill their larders. But who are blind to the Spirits that provide that abundance.*

Somewhere in the depths of the caves a bell sounded, its echo announcing the evening meal. Zabel hurried to join Brigit and Madame, helping to tie Izabel to Brigit. Abbot Roule had invited the family, as he perceived them to be, to eat with him in his private dining hall.

A pompous man with affectedly grand manners, the abbot wore a robe of fine wool covered with a fur-lined cloak. His appearance surprised Zabel. After observing the scene of tortured souls in the painting, she expected all the monks to be meditating on achieving the rewards of heaven. Instead, they sat at a table covered with a cloth of finely woven linen. *I wonder if the other brothers are eating in such elegance.* The meal consisted of a sumptuous soup made of chestnuts, mushrooms, and cabbages in a garlic sauce, as well as bread from finely milled grains.

"I hope this meal will satiate you. We do not eat of the flesh of animals." The words flowed from the abbot's lips like unctuous oil, seeming insincere.

"We are grateful that you let us share in your bounty, Abbot," Madame said.

The man's conversation recounted the worldly activities of the region, more political than religious or spiritual.

Emboldened by the hypocrisy before her, Zabel said, "How is it you are armed here in the abbey and yet brigands keep good folk from traveling through the forest at will?"

The Abbot shuffled in his chair. Zabel saw the flash of anger in his face. "Ah, I see you are but a young man, freshly out in the world with your wife and new child. It is only God's will that removes such villains."

"But God has given you the means to make the forest safe. You have a forge. You make cannon. What do you use them for?"

The Abbot sat for a moment, wiping up bits of sauce with a piece of soft bread. "You are a polemical young man, but I maintain my position is on the side of scripture."

"My point is not to make an argument; it speaks to effective management of Eleanor's lands."

A shocked Brigit cleared her throat. She had never seen her mistress in such a mood.

A loud knock that was heard on the great oak door of the abbey prevented Abbot Roule from responding. Male voices were heard, demanding to be let in.

The abbot rose. "You must excuse me for a moment. I have been awaiting these men."

Zabel tried to conceal the fear she felt, but it was Madame who spoke. "Perhaps it is the determined riders on the road behind us. They've caught up at last."

Brigit gasped, her face had gone white. Zabel clasped her arm in an attempt to calm her. "No one can take us from here," Zabel said. *I am doubly wanted. Once for saving Madame. Or the Gisor family has found me at last. Is this why the abbot did not want us to proceed?*

The abbot returned accompanied by an intense looking man, clean-shaven with long curly hair. "We will be joined for dinner by Lord Bertrand of Toulouse."

A servant appeared, relieving the stranger of his dust-encrusted cloak and to wash his feet. The abbot poured Lord Bertrand a large goblet of claret that the man downed in one gulp.

“A fine young family I see. Which way are you travelling?” the man inquired.

“To Poitiers. We have relatives there,” Zabel lied.

“I must reach there tonight. My liege lord, Duchess Eleanor, is pledged to marry Henry of Anjou.”

The abbot poured more claret and said, “Duchess Eleanor, now that she has taken back the running of her estates, is renewing grants and privileges to religious houses. We who ship our wine and salt through Toulouse have a vested interest in discouraging this marriage. Nothing must interrupt our trade.”

“Why would her marriage interrupt your trade?” Zabel asked.

The abbot took a sip of claret before he said, “You will find, Bertrand, that this young man is full of questions and firm opinions.”

Zabel’s only thought was to reach Eleanor and warn her of their intent.

“Perhaps we could ride with Lord Bertrand tonight. It would be safer for my family to be accompanied through the northern forest by a gallant knight.”

Bertrand chuckled. “A wife with a babe in arms and a grandmother in tow would surely slow me down. Another time I would gladly relinquish one of my knights to escort you, but I need my full contingent in Poitiers. Eleanor is headstrong at the best of times. Who knows what foolishness she will get up to with this marriage?”

The abbot said, “It is our opinion Lord Bertrand would make a better husband for the Duchess. We have every intention of making that happen. Unfortunately we have heard other suitors have covetous eyes on her vast inheritance. There may be attempts to abduct her. Lord Bertrand is not averse to using arms if required"

Zabel felt as if a cold blade were being held against her throat. She did not want to contemplate unwanted changes to Eleanor's court. She felt as if the floor had fallen out from under her; she had so much depended on Eleanor's help. All she could think to say was, "Eleanor would surely have considered these things. She has her own knights to protect her."

Madame tapped her napkin to her lips and rose from her place, bringing the conversation to an end. "As enjoyable as it is to share your table, Abbot Roule, I must return to my room. You see, I had a small accident while cooking and the pain now and again returns to my hands." She held out her still blistered fingers. This visual reminder of the danger they were in shocked Zabel into silence.

The Abbot was still visibly annoyed. His bushy eyebrows knit together. "I must repeat, it is lack of submissiveness to God's will is what brings evil into this life. Do not meddle in what is not your concern, young man."

Zabel felt the words enter her like sharp knives. "Your belief has robbed you of the ability to use your eyes and see the truth about you," she replied.

Brigit grabbed Zabel's hand and yanked her into the arcade. "What were you thinking? He could be upset enough to make us leave. We mustn't go through the forest at night."

Shaken by her own reaction, Zabel walked the long corridor in silence for a few minutes. "As these trees are barren with winter, this faith lacks the soul of Nature. I cannot sit idly by. I brought my daughter into this life. I must do something to warn Eleanor."

Brigit stared at her mistress. "You may do as you wish once we reach Eleanor, but think of us now. You risked your life to save Madame. Surely you don't want to spoil everything by having us thrust into the forest at night. We can only hope that the offering of sanctuary will be upheld. We are not yet out of danger."

Brigit had never spoken to Zabel in such a manner.

Zabel took a few deep breaths and said, "Forgive me. I have risked our lives needlessly."

As they entered their cell, the sound of men's voices raised in Gregorian chant filled the stillness. *Vespers prayers.*

Zabel said, "Give Izabel to me. I will nurse her while you get some sleep." She clasped Izabel to her chest, a single tear falling onto the cheek of her sleeping child. *I vowed to take care of you. This will never do.*

Soon she heard the sound of Lord Bertrand and his men leaving.

Chapter 17

Zabel was awake before dawn. She collected fresh bread and cheese from the monks in the kitchen before rousing the others. As they left the defensive walls of the abbey Zabel could see anxiety written on the faces of Brigit and Madame.

The forest was cloaked in the gloom of winter, the first light formed shadows that took on various shapes, becoming images of a living menace; a highwayman hiding, waiting for the opportune moment to reach into his cloak, retrieve a knife and slit their throats. Zabel's breathing was slow and shallow as she tuned her senses to interpreting each form she desperately hoped was only the play of light and dark.

The sound of horse's hooves, gaining on them, broke the silence. The person or persons must have been hiding in the woods, entering the road after they passed.

The three women turned and saw a man, his black cape roiling, like a sinister sail in the wind.

Zabel's breath caught in her throat. She was barely able to make an audible command, "Go fast," as she slowed her own stead.

The rider was upon Zabel too quickly for her reach her bow. A powerful arm reached around her, grabbed the reins from her hands and pulled her horse to a stop.

Zabel looked into a face hidden by a grizzled beard.

Her stomach turned as the stench from his open mouth choked her. She tried to pull the reins from his hand and the effort loosened the hood from her head, releasing her long hair.

The attacker's eyes turned from fierceness to lust as he realized he had hold of a woman. He gave out a throaty chortle and grabbed her off her horse, ripping at her cloak.

The man loosed his grip slightly to look down at her bosom. His lust became Zabel's friend.

In that brief instant, Zabel pulled the knife from her belt.

She plunged it deep into his belly, upward in an effort to reach his lungs as she had been taught.

Her assailant's grip slackened.

"Forgive me mother," Zabel murmured; sure the knife had never been used for such a purpose. She plunged it into the man again, higher this time, and causing a massive spurt of blood from his neck to splatter her.

A dumbfounded look crossed his face. He opened his mouth to speak but no sound came, just a trickle of blood that flowed over his lips onto her chest.

Zabel felt him lose his balance. She tried to pull away but he held her, staring with luminous eyes that were now riveted in death. The two tumbled heavily from the horse onto the hard ground of winter. All went black.

When she returned to consciousness, Brigit and Madame were looking at her anxiously. Zabel blinked, touching her face to ensure herself she was indeed alive. "Where...where is...?" Zabel attempted to ask for her child when she felt the warm feet of her baby kick softly against her. "Ah, all is well. We have all survived."

Zabel lay back for a moment, with her eyes closed, savoring their victory. "Where are we?" she asked.

"In Poitiers. In Eleanor's castle," Madame replied.

Instead of the relief Brigit and Madame expected to see, Zabel's face became distorted. She sobbed, her body writhing in agony.

Brigit's arms were instantly around her friend. "What is it? What's the matter? We're all here, safe."

Zabel was shouting. "I did what I swore I would never do. I killed a man. I broke my pledge to my mother."

Izabel began to cry, startled by her mother's screaming. Zabel picked up the child and thrust her into Brigit's arms.

"Take her. I am not fit to be her mother. Leave me. I want to be left alone. I'm a hateful creature," Zabel shrieked.

Brigit and Madame stood in shocked silence.

"Get out, get out," Zabel yelled.

They left carrying the screaming infant with them.

Day after day Zabel refused to eat. Madame located a wet nurse for Izabel and she and Brigit sat with Zabel trying in vain to comfort her. Zabel lay facing the wall, refusing to acknowledge their presence. They could do nothing but watch the life force slowly ebb from her body.

Then one day, the door to her room opened. Zabel heard Madame's voice acknowledge the presence of the queen. "Lady Eleanor."

"Leave us," she said. Eleanor leaned over Zabel. "Won't you turn around? I wish to see your face."

Eleanor's words were spoken with such compassion Zabel was unable to refuse. Through dimmed eyes she saw the regal Eleanor, splendid in a long red gown covered with a shawl loosely woven with golden threads.

"I've been away. There has been much diplomacy necessary to secure my next marriage."

She's so strong, so sure. I see now that Eleanor takes no heed of either the Fates, or Chance. She chooses the outcome she wants and works to achieve it. I have been buffeted about by Chance, choosing only from options presented to me. Never planning what I wanted. I'm weak. Incapable of keeping to what I believe in. I killed a man. I am nothing but an ugly blot on the earth.

"Brigit tells me you are ill because you broke a sacred vow you made to yourself, is that correct?"

"I have dishonored my mother and grandmother. I'm not fit to raise Izabel."

"We'll see about that." Eleanor touched Zabel's head, lightly.

Chapter 18

When Zabel heard her door gently open, she saw a woman with long auburn hair that fell over narrow shoulders. Piercing deep blue eyes gazed intently at Zabel from an ivory face, translucent in the flickering candlelight. It was impossible for Zabel to turn away.

"You are suffering," the woman began, her voice the clear tones of water running in the high mountains. "My name is Evangeline and I am going to make you well." She sat on the bed gathering Zabel in her arms, like a mother holding her child.

"We're going into the country."

Zabel gave a start.

"Don't worry. I assure you, I will take care of you."

Her voice beckoned with such warmth, Zabel did not wish to resist. The woman had stirred some small desire in her to live.

Evangeline helped Zabel dress in a warm woolen shift and cloak. She was carried downstairs and bundled onto a wagon pulled by a single horse. They drove out of Eleanor's courtyard and over the moat. Soon they were on a small path that led to a rude thatched cottage enveloped in grape vines, bare now in winter. Inside, a huge fire burned in a hearth blackened from the smoke of untold years.

"Sit here," Evangeline said, helping Zabel into a chair in front of the fire. The woman wrapped Zabel's feet in a blanket, and then moved to the cooking pot. She lifted the lid and the rich aroma of herbs filled the room making Zabel's mouth water. Evangeline sat on a three-legged stool and fed Zabel, as if she were a child, one delicious mouthful of rich beef broth after the other. Zabel felt her body absorb the nourishment.

"Now you must sleep. In a few days I have a task for you that will set you right." She helped Zabel to stand and move to the bed built into the corner, and then covered her with a thick down comforter. Zabel fell asleep instantly. The routine continued for several days until Zabel's strength returned.

"We must take a short ride," Evangeline announced as dusk deepened the shadows in the cottage. She placed a long woolen cloak lined with the curly wool of a black sheep over Zabel's lighter one and pulled the hood over Zabel's head. Then she handed Zabel deerskin gloves and boots that were lined with a soft white rabbit fur. Evangeline led the way to the barn where the horse and wagon stood in readiness. They drove under the starry night of the new moon. Two hanging lanterns on either side of the wagon lit the way through a vineyard.

Presently they stopped in a grove of leafless oak trees, their limbs spreading sensuously from gnarled trunks. Evangeline steadied Zabel as they walked to a clearing alight with candles. The tapers created a pattern that appeared to be a path.

"This is a labyrinth, Zabel. Are you familiar with

them?"

"No," Zabel answered, mesmerized by the flickering lights. "What is it for?"

"It is an ancient way of healing that was passed to me by my mother."

"Healing?" Suddenly, to be well, seemed possible. "What do I do?"

"You walk the path created by the lights. But first you must drink this potion. It will help you to see the Spirits. I will remain at the entrance."

"What will happen?"

"It is different for each who walks the path. The labyrinth's design is a sacred mathematical relationship to that which exists in Nature and in the spheres that rotate in the sky." She paused until Zabel nodded. "As you walk, you'll regain your natural harmony with the life force. It is time for you to rise to the next level of understanding. You have passed through another initiation. You killed a man. The forces will speak to you about that. Please begin. I assure you, your life path will become clear."

Zabel drank the herbs and stepped between the first two candles, feeling soft moss compress under her foot.

"When you reach the center you must meditate on what is troubling you. Take as much time as you need. I will be waiting for you."

The air was thick with the quiet of the ancient trees, the soft earth beckoning Zabel forward.

Just when she thought she knew the way to the centre, the path turned, making her way uncertain.

She sucked in her breath, tension increasing. Thoughts raced through her head. *Will I get this right? What if I can't find the centre?*

She stopped.

Then she took a deep breath and stepped again and again, until finally she could see an open space. The center.

But as she moved, the path took her in another direction once more.

She began to cry. With each step her crying intensified.

I won't reach the centre if I can't stay in control of where I'm going.

But then a feeling in her heart connected her to the soft earth, the Great Mother, yielding to every step. Like the vortex ceremony at her initiation, and the stone she had placed on Madame's belly, the Earth was absorbing her sorrow.

But the place she called "I", the place she must preserve or die, still insisted on control. Zabel continued to walk, wrestling with these thoughts. Then she was in the centre.

What is this place? It feels…full. Full of life, yet it is empty.

Zabel sat cross-legged, closed her eyes, and fell into a deep meditation. Her recurring dream in which her mother and uncle were killed came into her mind. She was walking in the alleys of the market. Baskets, earthen jars, beads, and cloth were displayed outside the shops to catch the eye of passers-by with their bright colors. At the end of the street a group of men played a game with cards and dice; all were deeply involved and animated. But suddenly, everyone disappeared except one man whose eyes matched the azure of his long robe and shone with an eerie light.

"I see you have come to me to find your fate," he said, taking a step forward.

Zabel backed away.

"Don't be afraid. It is the right of every individual to know. You can discover this the difficult way of trial and error or the easy way. Just throw the dice. Come over here and tell me your name." He held out his hand beckoning Zabel forward.

Is he suggesting that rolling the dice as I did in backgammon is the way to tell your fate? I have done that all my life and look where it has got me. I have killed a man.

The man waited for Zabel to finish her thoughts then he beckoned her forward again saying, "I have something you should observe. Come this way."

It was impossible to refuse. Zabel moved forward and found she was in the dream she had before her initiation, the sacred grove where she had witnessed the deer being slain. The slaughter happened again.

She stood there as helpless as she had always been.

When the villains left she again hugged the animal to her heart and wept uncontrollably.

The usual lament passed through her mind. *Why would they kill this noble creature, this sacred animal that does not kill for food?*

That was where the vision had always ended, but this time it continued.

With weapons reflecting the light of a full moon, the marauders returned to attack women celebrants in the grove. They raped and then killed them, dumping their bodies into the sacred spring.

But three women, one of whom was her grandmother, Jnana, jumped onto their horses. Like the Furies, the conscience of the natural world, they were determined to avenge this crime against the kinship that existed for all time between women and the Spirits of the Earth.

Wild with anger, they became a force of violence, screeching and yelling.

The startled men climbed frantically on their horses and fled with the woman following, their long hair streaming out behind them as they rode.

The men's attempts at escape were no match for the passion of the women who caught each one and stabbed them to death with their ceremonial knives until the ground was awash with blood.

Zabel thought of her own ceremonial knife. She had used it to cut the umbilical cord that separated her daughter from herself. Then, like these Furies, she had used the same knife as an instrument of death.

A warm mist formed around Zabel, and Jnana appeared.

"Jnana, is it truly you?" Tears of joy streamed down Zabel's face. "How is it you have come to me like this?"

"I have recently passed to the other side, to the stream of consciousness beyond the world of time and space."

"How can I see you, then?"

"Sometimes we are allowed to resume the energetic body we had on earth to correct a situation. It is the reason you can see me now."

"You have no idea how I've longed for you.

"My granddaughter, remember I told you that much of your initiation was left unfinished when you left Armenia? In the past the Furies were the Spirits of anger and revenge. Whenever a mother was insulted or murdered, when our blood kinship was flouted, we appeared. We are as old as the Earth herself, here to avenge any wrong done to the Great Mother or Her creatures. I was named after the Goddess of love and war. That was my destiny. But now each woman must find the courage inside herself to rectify these evils as she sees fit. You killed a man who threatened your life and that of your daughter and your friends. It is permitted."

"But I vowed to my mother's memory that I would never kill. I have broken my promise to her." Zabel held her hands to her face and wept, her body racked with the grief.

"War is an act of greed, to take by force what is not yours, what you have not worked to create. What we permit: to protect ourselves, is another matter. In order to save your child you found the strength to break your vow. You became more than just a daughter. You found the strength to be a mother. You experienced the full cycle of your feminine nature by travelling to the depths of despair and you have returned. Now you must go and teach Izabel the ways of the Great Mother."

The image faded as quickly as it appeared. Zabel was left alone again in the resounding silence. She had no idea how long she sat, meditating on what had just happened. *I was born. I birthed a child. I killed a man. One day I, too, will die. I am part of the cycle. I see now that killing that man with my own hands was my fate.*

The night was fading as she rose and walked from the labyrinth.

With the constant attention of Brigit and Madame, Zabel's strength soon returned in full. She asked for an audience with Eleanor to thank her but the queen was still secluded with her advisors preparing for her impending nuptials with Henry of Anjou.

The next day Zabel was in the great hall working on an embroidery when Eleanor, radiant from her successes, stood before her.

"I see you have made a fine recovery."

"I am beholden to you for your generosity," Zabel said, curtseying. "I owe my life to you. I have seen the dark side of my nature and I accept it as part of my wholeness."

"I believe in the strength of women. It is always there, we just need to discover it, or rediscover it."

"I see now I was afraid. No matter how many times my grandmother told me about the triple nature of the Great Mother, the virgin, the mother and the crone, I only wanted to see the creative, nourishing side, not the aspect that destroys. Ignoring Her true nature brought me much pain and suffering."

"Brigit and Madame Noirfor have told me what you did to save their lives. And how much you wanted to warn me of Abbot Roule and Lord Bertrand. Fortunately, those two are known to me. We suspected their plot to abduct me and Henry put an end to it."

Zabel was surprised. "They told me others of your vassals were planning the abduction. But, of course, why would they have confided their plan in me?"

"You've shown great courage; and I'm pleased to see you've found peace within yourself."

Zabel toyed with the stitches on the cloth. "I must ask one more favor of you, Queen Eleanor. My friends and I need a home. Is there anywhere in your realm we could become of service to you as loyal subjects."

"But my dear, you must stay with me, remain part of my court."

Zabel studied her hands. It was not what she wanted, but how could she say that without sounding ungrateful. "I think I would be more useful to you if I controlled a small fief. You could always count on me to support you as queen."

Eleanor paused. "Will you be prepared to marry a man of my choosing?"

Zabel's heart sank. That was the one thing she would not do. "I will be loyal to the death but I won't meet that condition." Zabel again looked at her hands. *I know what I want. This time I will not let Fortune tempt me to take something less.* She missed the small smile that crossed Eleanor's lips.

Eleanor said, "Henry has a cousin in Brittany, one of his outer provinces. This cousin teeters in his loyalty. It would help us to have a trusted supporter there." She pursed her lips and then licked them. "Brittany adheres to the ancient ways. It remains isolated from the political intrigues that infest the rest of our domains. I'm sure it will be to your liking. I will arrange it with Henry. And," she smiled, "you can marry whomever you choose."

Chapter 19

Zabel, Brigit, and Madame found themselves aboard a sailing ship. It rocked violently as it plied its way past sharp jagged rocks poking dangerously out of the sea. Finally they landed amidst breaking waves and wildly blowing spray on the coast of Brittany. As she stepped ashore, Zabel felt the rawness, the utter primitiveness of the place. She was not displeased.

Eleanor had arranged for a local farmer to take the women to the land ceded to Zabel. The squat little man, Stephen, his hair cut straight across his forehead, was accompanied by an old sheep dog with hanging jowls and shaggy fur, that came up and sniffed the women and then moved away, contentedly wagging his tail.

Only a short distance from the sea, they arrived at a small thatched cottage surrounded by hayfields and grazing cattle. The grain had been harvested, the remaining stubble being the only testament to its earlier fertility. A kitchen garden adjacent to the cottage had also been stripped of its produce, except for the flounced blue green kale that would grow all winter.

"There is a meadow just over that low hill filled with apple and pear trees. They were picked two months ago. Your share of the cider is stored in the barn," Stephen said.

"We don't want to take the produce of the previous man. Can we send the cider to him?" Zabel inquired.

"There's no need. Serfs did his work. We work our lands cooperatively. Because he didn't share in the work, he's not entitled to anything. We would like you to have his portion."

Zabel was moved by this sign of community good will. "Rest assured, we will work for our share."

Stephen ushered the women into the cottage. The stone hearth was set but no fire blazed. "Your neighbors will be here soon to welcome you. It is our custom to bring an ember from another hearth."

People began to arrive. A tall, dark-haired man, introduced as Taranis, carried a burning flame in a metal bowl. Women presented them with loaves of freshly baked bread. The men carried pots of stews and jugs of the newly fermented cider. The tiny cottage was soon filled with the sounds of jovial talk and laughter. Zabel sat at the table nursing Izabel, her heart glowing. *Perhaps this place will truly become my home, here in the heart of the ordinary.*

Early each morning Zabel rode along the beach as seagulls called overhead in their search for sustenance. As she watched each wave, crashing, dying, falling back to be one with the sea in endless repetition, she felt her spirit renewing itself. The great beauty of this lonely place fed her soul. *I hear you speaking, Great Mother. The constant flux of everything. When I am still, the edges of that which I think I am, blur and this vastness and I are one.*

She soon discovered that the sea, which surrounded Brittany on three sides, dominated life in the small dukedom. *It is as if the salty womb of the Great Mother protects it.* She found sheltered coves harboring shellfish, seabirds, and tiny fishing villages. Those she met assured her they owed their very lives to the sea. As she rode, she passed women collecting seaweed to enrich their garden soil. But she also learned that in less sheltered areas, frequent storms and gales had swept in from the sea for eons, denuding the land of all but the most tenacious lichens and course grasses. She vowed to hold on to this place with the same strength as these plants.

Zabel was happy to learn the locals celebrated the passage into spring by large bonfires on the hillocks. One brisk morning the three women walked through the forest deciding which of the many trees they would sacrifice for the ceremony.

"What we don't contribute to the communal fire will heat our cottage for the remainder of the season," Zabel said.

"It is a significant event to kill a tree, Brigit," Madame explained. "It nourishes other living beings in the forest just as a mother nourishes her child."

"It's what my mother always told me."

Zabel was grateful to Madame for assuming a motherly role with Brigit. The marriage her father had coveted would now never take place. To Brigit's credit she had never mentioned it, but Zabel thought the girl must have some regrets.

The women did much searching until they found a gnarled old oak, free of nests, with many of its branches broken off, and littering the forest floor.

"Felling this one will be too difficult for us," Zabel said. "I'll ride over to ask Taranis for assistance."

Fragmented mist, white and glimmering, pressed around the hills. By the time she reached Taranis' farmhouse she was soaked to the skin.

"You must warm yourself," Taranis said, directing Zabel to the ancient hearth where a fire wafted the spicy smell of wood smoke. Zabel shivered as she took a seat. Taranis pulled a colorful blanket from a wooden chest and covered her with it, turning her feet to the fire. Suddenly the room seemed small and intimate. He poured a mug of calvados that had been warming in a brass kettle and handed it to Zabel, then pulled up another chair and poured himself a mug.

"Now, you must tell me what has brought you out on such a damp day."

She took a sip of the apple brandy, its taste strong and sweet. She licked a thick drop from her lip. "We have selected a tree for the spring ritual and I've come to ask if you could fell it for us."

Zabel observed Taranis' strong and sinewy hands as he held the earthen mug. His coal black hair and aquamarine eyes spoke of his ancient link to this land. He was not descended from the red-haired intruders of Eleanor's race.

He smiled. "I would be happy to be of service to the women who have become our local midwives." *So news has spread of Brigit and Madame's gifts. We are being accepted.*

They sat for some time discussing the farm tasks that would soon be necessary throughout the region. He was easy to talk with, and Zabel felt herself becoming comfortable.

She remembered the spring ritual in Armenia,

shocked to realize that one yearly cycle had been completed since her father died and she was made queen. *So much has happened.* She recalled the passion with which she and Raymond had celebrated the coming of spring. She turned her face to the fire in the hope that Taranis did not see her blush.

"Your name. I've not heard it before. What does it mean?" she asked.

"It means thunder in the ancient tongue of this place. My people are all named after the Spirits that rule this land where our people have lived longer than any of us can remember."

Rain now beat heavily on the roof and they could hear thunder rumbling in the distance.

"As you've probably realized by now, it rains a good deal here this time of year. You should wait for the storm to pass before you head home."

"Thank you, Taranis. I will."

They sat silent, listening to the storm and the crackling of the fire. *This quiet stranger is intriguing. He's so unlike Siraj.* Images of the Persian flashed through her mind. She could hear his deep, heartfelt laughter, remember his powerful arms. But she sensed Taranis was strong in his own way.

"Would you like to play a game of chess or perhaps, backgammon?"

He cannot possibly know the significance of the suggestion he has just made. Zabel contemplated the choices. With her father she had always insisted on backgammon. Today, to honor him, she said, "chess."

Taranis dug deeper into the chest and lifted out a

board and a linen bag tied at the top with a stout string. He set out the pieces. Each had been intricately carved in oak, and glowed softly in the candlelight.

"How beautiful. Did you do the carving?"

"Yes. During the winter, when my wife was dying. I sat with her. It gave me something to do with my hands."

"To lose your wife is a terrible thing."

"Yes it was. We'd known each other since childhood. It was a fever. She wasn't strong enough to fight it." His pain was displayed openly on his face as he arranged the pieces on the board.

It is why he's so kind. He has suffered.

He held his fists out to her concealing one piece from each side and she chose. He would move first. He pushed a pawn forward. And she moved one opposite.

She looked up at him. "Taranis, do you think that backgammon is like life?"

"What do you mean?"

"When something happens in life, one is forced to make a choice, then discovers that they're forced to make another choice and soon people are doing things or are in places they couldn't have imagined? It is so different from chess, don't you think?"

Taranis moved his rook. "Are you asking me if I think that there is such a thing as chance? Or do I think events are a matter of Fate, determined by an outside agent?"

"Yes, those are both questions I would like answered."

He topped up both cups with more apple brandy. "Chess and backgammon look quite different at first glance, but both require that a player move in response to another's action. You move, I respond, then you move again, but you have to take into account what I did."

She took a sip of the calvados, savoring its warmth. "So these games *are* just like life?"

"Life is much more complicated. Instead of one opponent, there are thousands of agents acting on your decisions. Some you are aware of and try to take into consideration, while you are oblivious to others that will also impact you."

Zabel lost track of the game. She looked over at Taranis, trying to refocus her thoughts. "You seem to be able to plan your game strategy and explain complicated cosmological understanding all at once. Is this attempt to sidetrack your opponent part of your desire to win at all costs?"

A slow smile spread across his face. "I hadn't thought about that, but perhaps, if I do win, I'll use it in the future. Truthfully, I am interested in both playing and in explaining what I believe to be true. But I can limit myself to one at a time, if that is your wish."

She took his bishop. "That won't be necessary. I can do both." She suddenly felt energized by the competition. He held another pawn between his fingers, ready to place it. He moved, stretching his legs under the table.

Zabel sat analyzing what he had said, thinking of her own experiences, as the game continued. *Deciding to have Izabel was the result of lots of things happening at once. I wanted to choose the man who would father my child. Bishop Scarfos wanted the Franks to be our allies. Raymond wanted to impress his father by acquiring some land. Jnana wanted to imprint the teachings of the Great Mother on me so the understanding would not die out in our line of women. Siraj wanted to enjoy an intimacy with me.*

"When my father asked if I wanted to play chess or backgammon, I always picked backgammon."

"Why?"

"Because you roll the dice, chance has more of a hand it the outcome. Chess is ponderous. You must consider all the possible moves before you have moved one of your tokens. In backgammon there are fewer choices, with a much simpler strategy. I thought it was easier, but now, I think that perhaps I just preferred backgammon because it moved faster."

"Um."

Taranis removed her rook and she saw her mistake. She would have to rethink her entire strategy to make up for it.

He leaned his elbows on the table and studied the board closely. She became aware of his musky odor. *Another distraction. Zabel. Ignore him and concentrate.*

"But, I maintain both games are essentially the same," he said.

"I see that. Even if there is a chance event, you still have to decide what to do about it. Correct?"

Taranis said, "We have not yet answered the question of whether or not there's an outside agent leading us to a final result. That was part of your question, was it not? Is there fate or destiny? Or is the universe merely random?"

She tried to concentrate on her next move, when he

said "Checkmate."

She pushed herself away from the table. Her back ached from leaning over the board. She reached the tight muscle and rubbed absently, then stood and moved to the fire, letting its heat penetrate her back. "Is it random? Are we just bounced around like a ball in a polo match?"

"It's complicated. You understand that I'm simplifying to try to make my point. But I believe that we *think* we make a decision to do something. For instance, you rode over here today to ask for my help. Was that Dame Fortune at work or just randomness?"

I've come here because I was attracted to him that first night in my cottage. I could never have predicted his being there. "Many decisions and many events led me to Brittany. Each decision seemed perfectly logical, but what forced the decisions were often events outside my control. The results were sometimes surprising."

"But that is the very point I've been trying to suggest. What if there are so many forces at work, some that you are aware of and some that you are not. But given your nature and experience each time you decide something, perhaps there was really only one way you could decide. It seems like we have choice, but it this strange way, it *is* determined. But, in my way of reasoning, it is not determined by a god. It is just the way life works."

"As a young woman I studied philosophy. But I have not heard of an idea like yours. Do you mean that, although it appears we have many choices, given our natures and experience, there is only one decision to make? One logical thing to do, even if later, we think we have been foolish?"

"Exactly. You know, I have never spoken about this with anyone. It seemed too abstract to discuss with my neighbors. Most of them are unable to read. But, when I heard you had come from Queen Eleanor's court, I thought you would be educated." He drained the remaining brandy from his cup and offered her more before refilling his.

"You have studied also. Where?"

"My father sent me to the university in Paris. I am not sure what he had in mind for me; he died while I was away. But I realized I wanted to come back here to tend the land."

"I'm sure he would be proud of you."

He blushed and Zabel found it endearing.

"One more thought. The thing you said about feeling foolish after a decision turns out badly. It seems to me at each moment, we become a new person. We have added to our experience, gained wisdom. Perhaps we would choose differently at a different time. In any event, I believe you had no choice but to come here this afternoon. But I'm also sure a year ago, you would not have been able to predict it."

The storm abated and the sky became a sea of crimson and purple, the moon already out. As Taranis helped her saddle her horse she felt rejuvenated and clear like the air after the storm. She heard cows lowing from the hill behind Taranis' farmhouse, their bells ringing with the same lilting tone as his voice. A sense of peace flooded through her.

She took a path to the sea. On the edge of the cliffs she looked out at surprising calm. The water, the shore, the trees and grasses shone a translucent gray in an instant of time when all was still, before choices began again and the world spiraled into action. Movement, continuous movement. One thing affecting another continuously. *I see how it works. The beauty. The truth of what Taranis said.*

She gently urged her horse toward her farm.

A few days later, as the women hitched Brigit's horse to the wagon they heard the clatter of horse's hooves on the frozen ground. Taranis entered the yard and they headed into the woods for the felling. The night of the ritual was two days hence.

At the base of the chosen tree they sat, drinking apple cider until their cheeks warmed. Then Zabel said, "Brigit, will you call the Spirits of the Four Directions. We should begin our ritual."

After she did, Madame began to pound the skin of her tambourine. The women beat their feet into the ground in time with her. Taranis watched them for a while then placed his mug on the ground. "Wait," he said. He pulled a small stringed lute from his saddlebag and plucked the strings producing a soft high-pitched tone that created a meditative effect. As his fingers moved skillfully among the strings a sweet music filled the forest. The women danced around the tree, searching for the Spirit of the Great Mother within themselves as they moved. Soon they were one with the tree, one with Nature.

Then Taranis removed his outer cloak to reveal a fine cambric tunic that clung to his taut body. He struck the giant trunk with his ax, sending bits of bark flying, the muscles of his back rippling as he swung. Brigit took up her drum, and Taranis chopped harder and swifter to keep time with her. Exhilarated, Zabel took off her boots, feeling the energy of the Earth. "We honour you, oh giant oak, you who draw sustenance from the soil through your roots, you, whose branches interact with the wind, you whose changes augur the seasons. The mystery that is Life."

The great tree creaked as it began to lean. Only a few more blows and the ax would bring it to the ground. Taranis stopped to catch his breath, his face strained. Zabel could not tell if it was from the effort of the work or from the fact that it was he who was killing this tree, this Great Spirit of the forest. *But we must do this to be warm and to cook our food.*

Taranis motioned them to safety. With a final swing of the ax, the great ancestor fell. Then the ground trembled and dust from the forest floor rose, as with a final shuddering, the life force left it.

The night of the spring ritual was filled with the chirping of tree frogs in their mating ritual. Zabel and Taranis walked up the hill to the crackling fire they helped set earlier, the lit branches now sent large swirls of smoke skyward. Zabel felt the warmth of Taranis' arm around her as she leaned against him. She reached up and ran her finger along the fine lines on his face thinking of the spiral she had etched into the ground before she left Armenia, and of the spiral dance she had done during her initiation. Jnana had told her that life was a circle but with each rotation it became richer, fuller. She was no longer a queen, but she owned a piece of land she shared with two friends, and a community of neighbors. She had completed her initiation as she promised Jnana. And now, she had chosen a lover. *I will have a child with this man.*

It is easier to live in this land on the edge of civilization. Here, the voice of the Earth whispers its laws for those who care to listen with their hearts. I spend my days weaving, measuring time by the number of rows I complete. I have discovered that I must be sensitive to what is carded out and what is woven in. At night, if my eyes are not too tired, I write of my understanding in my journal. What I know should never be lost. We spiral upward, returning like the cycles of Nature but evolving to more profound understanding as we live through each cycle of seasons.

Through the open window I can see Brigit kneeling on a flat rock washing our clothes. By the dreamy look on her face, I know that she is thinking of the young man she met on the hillock. Perhaps she is with child. I can hear Madame mixing her herbs and fermentations.

Izabel, in her cradle, lies at my feet. She twitches, dreaming. I wonder, as my hand lingers on my belly, if there is a quickening in my womb.

ACKNOWLEDGMENTS

As Zabel remembers the Ancient Ways, I wish to acknowledge those who have perished at the hands of authorities who did not believe there could be another way.

An article in the Encyclopedia Britannica explains there were two queens named Zabel in Lesser Armenia. Their father was King Leo. One of the Zabels is forced to marry a crusader and then they are exiled to France. No explanation is given. The article said that was the end of her line. As queen of Lesser Armenia, the story may be over, but as a woman she had a whole life to lead, possibly with children. I decided to create that life for her as well as the reason for her being exiled.

I have spent my life trying to discover what will have me grow and flourish as a human being. Part of that understanding came by studying Art History; it was an attempt to know myself, the great admonition of the oracle at Delphi. How could I know myself if I didn't understand what cultural and historical influences had been foisted on me without my being aware? The understanding that Zabel and her grandmother have was my attempt to come to terms with formulating my own understanding of how the world could work with no one or no thing left out.

I am grateful to Eileen Stubbe for her most generous financial support. Her faith in the story offered incredible encouragement.

Foremost I want to thank my best friend, my husband, and the love of my life, Richard Weatherall, who understood from the beginning my need to search and create. He not only tolerated the long hours I spent with my nose in books and the computer, but whole-heartedly embraced it. Your faith in me, Rick, allowed me to push forward on the darkest days when I thought I should give up.

I thank my son, Jason Gray, for bringing to my attention the plight of medieval witches that became a major plot-point of this book. He had me see that Zabel saw the Great Mother and the Spirits in a way no longer open to us with our expanded consciousness.

I thank my book club friends and beta readers, Ellie Thorburn, Susan Russell, Eileen Stubbe, Sheila McEachern, Anne Stewart, Margaret Woldridge, Sylvia Leedham, Joni White, Barbara Wood, and the late Hettie Clews. For twenty-four years we have debated the worth and meaning of countless books of great literature. I learned so much from you.

I thank my editor, Veronica Knox, for her masterful suggestions and insights.

I am grateful to and appreciate Lynda Crawford who met with me weekly for many years. We read and dissected each other's works in progress. Thank you for your patience. Our small group expanded to include at various times, John Cowhig and most recently Marlyn Horsdal and Sharon Bronstein.

I thank my daughter, Samantha Gray for our years of discussions groping with the question of what it is to be a woman, to be feminine. Her way of being is rooted in her love of Nature.

With a smile I thank my granddaughters, Uma and Layla Veeravagu and Rick's granddaughter, Sophia Gordon. This book was written for them in the hope they will honour and remember the Great Mother, and the work it takes to keep Her safe.

I honor all those who wrote the countless historical, mythological, philosophical, and theological books I read in order to understand the period in which Zabel lived and thought. I'm especially grateful to Alison Weir's book, "Eleanor of Aquitaine" for its insights into the life and character of the great queen.

I thank Lorraine Gane, an early editor, who encouraged me as I sorted out what this book would be about, and Gillian Campbell who was also there in the beginning.

Finally I wish to remember and acknowledge my parents, Ann and Grant Thompson, who loved me and encouraged my love of learning. For their dedication.

About the Author...

Pearl Gray

A city woman moves to Salt Spring Island and deepens her relationship to the earth.

I moved to Salt Spring Island in 1991 after a business career in Vancouver and owned and operated Cottage Resort on St. Mary Lake. During that time I finished a degree in Art History from UBC, wrote *Salt Spring Island: A Place to be* and painted.

I sold the resort in 2004 and devoted myself to the craft of writing fiction.

www.pearlgray.ca